John "Doc"

Happily married for forty years and about to renew their wedding vows. Now they're itchin' for grandchildren—especially since they personally delivered *every* baby in Laramie, Texas!

Jackson

Texas tall and fit—the doctor every mother orders for a son-in-law.

Wade

Self-made millionaire oilman with the Midas touch in business—and in bed.

Shane

The "baby" of the family and the wildest of the four McCabe boys—"It'll be a cold day in Hades before I ever settle down!"

Travis

The oldest, the most serious McCabe son is a single cattle rancher about to become an instant father of three....

Dear Reader,

Welcome to another month of wonderful stories at Harlequin American Romance—where you'll find more of what you love to read. Every month we'll bring you a variety of plots from some of the genre's best-loved authors. Harlequin American Romance is all about the pursuit of love and family in the backyards, big cities and wide-open spaces of America!

This month you won't want to miss *A Cowboy's Woman*, the continuation of Cathy Gillen Thacker's series, THE McCABES OF TEXAS. This family of bachelors is in for some surprises when their parents take to matchmaking. And talented author Muriel Jensen brings us *Countdown to Baby*, the second book in the DELIVERY ROOM DADS series. In this three-author, three-book series you'll meet the McIntyre brothers of Bison City, Wyoming. They're in a race to see who'll have the New Year's first baby.

Also this month is Mollie Molay's *Daddy by Christmas*, a compelling story of blended families— just in time for the holidays. And Mindy Neff wraps up her TALL, DARK & IRRESISTIBLE duo with *The Playboy & the Mommy*.

Please drop us a note to tell us what you love about Harlequin American Romance and what you'd like to see in the future. Write to us c/o Harlequin Books, 300 East 42nd Street, 6th Floor, New York, NY 10017.

Happy reading!

Melissa Jeglinski
Associate Senior Editor

A Cowboy's Woman

CATHY GILLEN THACKER

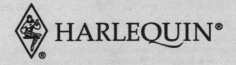

HARLEQUIN®

TORONTO • NEW YORK • LONDON
AMSTERDAM • PARIS • SYDNEY • HAMBURG
STOCKHOLM • ATHENS • TOKYO • MILAN • MADRID
PRAGUE • WARSAW • BUDAPEST • AUCKLAND

ISBN 0-373-16797-0

A COWBOY'S WOMAN

Copyright © 1999 by Cathy Gillen Thacker.

This edition published by arrangement with Harlequin Books S.A.

® and TM are trademarks of the publisher. Trademarks indicated with
® are registered in the United States Patent and Trademark Office, the
Canadian Trade Marks Office and in other countries.

Visit us at www.romance.net

Printed in U.S.A.

ABOUT THE AUTHOR

Cathy Gillen Thacker is a full-time wife/mother/
author who began typing stories for her own
amusement during "nap time" when her children
were toddlers. Twenty years and more than 50
published novels later, Cathy is almost as well-known
for her witty romantic comedies and warm, family
stories as she is for her ability to get grass stains and
red clay out of almost anything, her triple-layer
brownies and her knack for knowing what her three
grown and nearly grown children are up to almost
before they do! Her books have made numerous
appearances on bestseller lists and are now published
in 17 languages and 35 countries around the world.

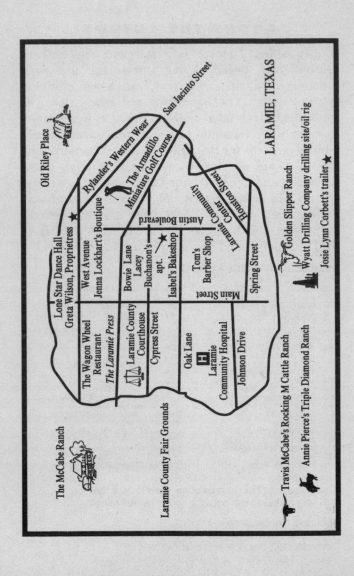

LARAMIE, TEXAS

Old Riley Place

Rylander's Western Wear

The Armadillo
Miniature Golf Course

San Jacinto Street

Lone Star Dance Hall
Greta Wilson, Proprietress

West Avenue
Jenna Lockhart's Boutique

Austin Boulevard

Laramie Community
Center

Houston Street

The Wagon Wheel
Restaurant
The Laramie Press

Bowie Lane
Lacey
Buchanon's
apt.
Isabel's Bakeshop

Tom's
Barber Shop

Main Street

Spring Street

Laramie County
Courthouse

Cypress Street

Oak Lane

Laramie
Community Hospital

Johnson Drive

The McCabe Ranch

Laramie County Fair Grounds

Travis McCabe's Rocking M Cattle Ranch

Annie Pierce's Triple Diamond Ranch

Golden Slipper Ranch

Wyatt Drilling Company drilling site/oil rig

Josie Lynn Corbett's trailer

Chapter One

It was just after ten Monday evening when Shane McCabe let himself into the ranch house on his brother Wade's Golden Slipper Ranch. Grinning at all he'd accomplished—and a day earlier than expected, too!—he kicked off his boots, leaving them where they lay. It didn't matter how messy the house was, since Wade and Josie were still on their honeymoon and not expected back for a couple of days, so he headed up the stairs, ripping off hot, sweaty clothes as he went. His socks landed on the bottom tread, his Western shirt ended up on the banister, his jeans and briefs decorated the upstairs hall.

Bypassing the guest room where he'd been bunking since returning to his hometown of Laramie, Texas, Shane headed for the bathroom and the glass-walled shower. He turned the brass knob as far left as it would go, adjusted the shower head to maximum massage and stepped beneath the spray. After a day spent inspecting every inch of the horse ranch he had his eye on, the hot steamy water was just what he needed. Luxuriating in the feel of the water pulsating against his skin, he washed himself from head to toe, rinsed off just as thoroughly and then stepped out of the shower.

Not bothering to dry off, he wrapped a towel around his waist. Exhaustion seeping into his every pore, he ran a comb through his just-shampooed hair, brushed his teeth, switched off the light and then headed down the darkened hall to his bed.

Before he'd left, a couple of days ago, he closed all the drapes in the house against the hot Texas sun. Doing so had left the guest room pitch-black, but Shane didn't need to turn on a light to find his way to the rumpled covers on the bed. He dropped his towel on the floor, flung the covers back and hopped in. He had just grabbed his pillow and flipped onto his side when he caught a whiff of a delicate floral scent and encountered a very warm, very silky, very feminine-feeling body.

Abruptly realizing he was not alone, Shane swore roundly. And heard a soft, startled gasp.

"What the—" The woman beside Shane scrambled to the other side of the double bed, knocking a book to the floor.

"Heck?" Shane filled in the blank as the feminine interloper switched on the bedside lamp, temporarily blinding them both.

"—are you doing here?" the woman beside him demanded.

Shane folded his arm behind his head and lay back against the pillows, all too aware he was buck naked beneath the sheet. Not that she was that much better off—given the brevity of her clinging lilac undershirt and matching bikini panties.

"I could ask the same of you," he drawled, and lifted a brow as the beauty beside him snatched the sheet up over her waist, hiding the rest of her curvaceous body from view.

"I asked you first, Shane McCabe!"

Shane peered at her. He'd encountered many a groupie in his years on the pro rodeo circuit, but he sure didn't remember her. And he was certain if he'd met this woman he would have remembered her. He tilted his head slightly to the side. "Have we met?"

The woman looked down her cute little nose at him. "Very funny."

"I'm serious," Shane persisted. "You do look... familiar."

Especially around her eyes, which were a very pretty light-blue and framed by thick golden lashes a shade darker than her wildly curling pale-blond hair.

"I'm Greta Wilson!"

"Nah—" Shane focused on her pretty face and luscious lips, delicate cheekbones carved above a stubborn chin. "I remember little Greta." She hadn't begun to have such luminous skin. Never mind self-assurance and grace. Shane swallowed. "She was—"

"A nerdy little kid, always running around in some sort of dancer's outfit?"

That was exactly what she'd been. Not this sexy beauty with full, ripe breasts, jutting nipples, slender waist and equally sensuous hips. Shane shifted slightly, trying to ease the growing pressure in his groin. "How come you're sleeping here, instead of at your folks' place?"

"Because I'm exhausted from trying to get my dance hall ready to open next weekend. And my mother's having the whole bridge club over tonight."

Shane winced and sent Greta Wilson a sympathetic glance, knowing full well what that was like. Twenty-four chattering, chuckling women in one house was too many, in his opinion. Worse, their marathon sessions often went on to well after midnight, or whenever the food and beverages ran out.

Greta released a beleaguered sigh and continued, "My mom found out from your mom that Wade and Josie were on their honeymoon, so she got permission for me to sack out here for the night, as well as the keys to the ranch house, from your mom, and voilà—here I am!"

"Just how long have you been asleep?" Shane asked curiously.

"About two hours," Greta grumbled, shoving a hand through the length of her hair.

Shane did his level best to keep his eyes away from her breasts and the way her nipples were jutting against the thin lilac fabric of her undershirt in the air-conditioned air. To little avail. His lower half was now rigid with desire. Which made getting out of the bed an impossible task. At least until that part of him settled down. Which left him with only one choice. Make conversation and wait for blood flow to return to normal.

"That's awful early to go to bed," he said, wishing he at least had some briefs within reach.

Greta rolled her eyes. "Like I said, I was exhausted."

Shane lifted a brow. She didn't look exhausted now. She looked all "het up," as the old-timers would have said, to have found herself unexpectedly in bed with him. But then, Shane was all het up, too.

"What are you doing here?" Greta demanded.

"With the exception of the past few days, when I was out looking at property all over central Texas," Shane replied, "I've been sleeping here, ever since I hit Laramie again. And furthermore, my mother knows that, too, because I called this morning and left a message on my parents' answering machine to let them know I'd be back at the Golden Slipper Ranch a day earlier than expected.''

Shane glanced at Greta, realization of what this was all about dawning. He blew out an exasperated breath. "Are you married?"

Not surprisingly, she looked as annoyed by the question as he was at the set-up. "No. Not that it's any of your business," Greta snapped. "Why? Are you?"

"No."

"So what does that have to do with anything?" Greta demanded, her blue eyes blazing.

"Everything." Shane sighed. "You and I have been the victims of a matchmaking scam."

Greta eyed him warily. She leaned against the headboard and brought her long, dancer's legs up to her chest. She wrapped her arms about her knees. "What are you talking about?"

Shane rolled onto his side. "My parents are celebrating their fortieth wedding anniversary by renewing their marriage vows next week."

"I know. My parents and I were invited to attend the ceremony and the reception afterward, at their ranch." As she frowned, a sexy little pleat appeared between her delicate golden eyebrows. It was all Shane could do not to smooth it away with his thumb. "But I don't see what that has to do with us."

Shane's eyes tracked the soft silky curls falling over her shoulders before returning to her face. "My mother has gotten it into her head that my brothers and I should all be married, too, as soon as humanly possible."

Greta rolled her eyes and shook her head grimly. "Sounds like my folks."

"They want you married off, too?" he asked, wondering why she wasn't. Women as sexy and sweet and appealing as Greta were usually taken off the market way before now. She had to be—what? He was thirty. She'd been two years behind him in school. That made her twenty-eight now, he guessed.

"They want it so badly I can't begin to tell you." Oblivious to his reverie, Greta continued talking about marriage.

She froze at the sound of several cars moving up the lane to the ranch house. Without getting out of bed, Greta leaned over to lift the edge of the drape and peer out the window. "I don't believe it," she murmured unhappily.

Shane was annoyed, too. He was enjoying this little tête-à-tête of theirs. He didn't want it interrupted. He didn't want anything happening that would force them to get out of this bed. "Who is it?"

Greta's slender fingers tightened on the edge of the drapes. "Both our mothers!"

It figured, Shane thought resentfully. Wasn't it enough that he'd been the only McCabe son to disappoint his parents almost from day one? Did they have to make things worse by interfering in his life with their match-making?

"Here to gloat, no doubt, at the 'success' of their romantically motivated manipulations," Shane muttered as the arc of car lights swept their window.

"And—oh, my heavens—it looks like the entire bridge club," Greta continued with a moan of dismay.

"No doubt about it," Shane said, his jaw set. "It's time I set my mother straight, once and for all."

Greta dropped the edge of the drape. "Lots a luck."

"You should read your mother the riot act, too," Shane advised.

Greta shook her head. "My mother hasn't listened to

anything I've said for the past twenty-eight years! There's nothing to indicate she's going to start now.''

Shane thought about the clothes he'd left tossed here and there. He knew what it would look like. Knew the conclusions his mother and her friends would likely make. ''Maybe she just needs a wake-up call.''

The front door opened. Feet tromped across the wooden floor. ''Yoo-hoo! Shane! Greta!''

Greta slid her legs over the edge of the bed. Shane looked at Greta, a plan already forming. He grabbed her wrist, preventing her from leaping from the bed. There was no time to spare if they wanted this to work. ''You with me or not?'' he demanded.

Greta hesitated, delicate color blooming in her cheeks as her bare feet touched the floor. ''I—''

''Play along with me on this, Greta,'' Shane tucked a hand around her thighs and gently guided her legs all the way back onto the bed, ''and I promise you—something like this will never happen to either of us again.''

GRETA RECOGNIZED the wicked gleam in Shane Mc-Cabe's silver-gray eyes. It meant trouble with a capital *T.* Just as did the warmth of his big, callused palm on her bare legs. Hadn't her childhood fantasy always been to be part of one of Shane's wild and crazy schemes? Wasn't it a lifelong dream of hers to have the reckless rodeo star in bed with her?

The footsteps of their mothers—and indeed their entire bridge club—were already moving up the stairs. Telling herself her days of being cautious were over, Greta met Shane's sexy grin with a reckless one of her own and said, ''Count me in.''

The next thing she knew she was on her back and Shane's muscular, six-foot-plus frame was draped over top of her. She barely had time to draw a quick breath, and then his lips were locked on hers in an overwhelmingly deep, sexy kiss that took her breath away. He caught her head between his hands, and she melted against him, completely caught up in the warm, minty taste of his mouth, the unhurried pressure of his lips and the liquid stroking of tongue. The hardness of his chest pressed against the softness of her breasts, then lower, the washboard flatness of his abs and tummy, and lower still he was even harder. Velvety smooth. Hot to the touch. And naked. Naked as could be. Her pulse increased at the realization, while inside of her desire swirled and caught flame. Tremors of arousal swept through her as she moved against him, every inch of her surging to life. Shock and surprise warred within her, and she knew, as their tongues continued to twine and parry and stroke that it was the most exciting, sensual embrace she'd ever experienced. Even if it was all for show.

"Shane McCabe!" Lilah McCabe's shocked voice resounded from the upstairs hallway.

"Greta Wilson!" Tillie Wilson's voice exclaimed in utter mortification. "For heaven's sake!"

To Greta's chagrin Shane took his sweet time about ending the steamy kiss, and ever so slowly unlocked their lips. For one brief second she thought—or was it hoped?—he'd been as affected as she by the electricity surging between them. Then, his silver-gray eyes glimmering with mischief, he chuckled and said to both Greta and the women in the doorway, "Whoops. Busted!"

As Shane propped himself on his elbows, his body still aligned vertically with hers, Greta curved her hands around the solidity of his shoulders and shot a glance at their mothers. Both mothers continued to sputter at the sight of Tillie's daughter and Lilah's son in bed together.

"You didn't tell us they were dating!" One of the bridge club members—Greta couldn't tell which one, exactly—accused both Tillie and Lilah.

Keeping one arm tucked beneath Greta's head, Shane rolled over onto his back. "We're not. But when we ended up in the same house for the night—" Shane gave Lilah McCabe a look that was steely with resolve "—we figured why not?"

At the sound of his casually uttered words, the entire bridge club, most of whom had now crowded into the bedroom along with Tillie and Lilah, gasped loudly.

Tillie Wilson stomped forward, all too ready to come to her only child's defense. "I'll tell you why not, Shane McCabe!" Greta's mother snatched up Greta's robe and tossed it to her.

Lilah extended a staying hand when it looked like Greta's mom was going to grab Shane by the ear and haul him out of bed. "I'll handle this, Tillie," Lilah said firmly. "Shane McCabe, I want you up and out of that bed right now."

At Lilah's order, it was all Greta could do not to groan out loud. "No, Lilah. You don't," she said firmly.

Lilah reached for the edge of the sheet closest to Shane. "The heck I don't!" she said, looking all the madder.

Desperate to stop her, Greta blurted out, "He's naked underneath!"

Shane should have blushed at her announcement. He didn't. "See where all this matchmaking has gotten us?"

The bridge club, having seen quite enough and obviously knowing how they would feel if their grown children had been caught in a similarly compromising situ-

ation, tripped all over each other as they beat a hasty
retreat. "We'll let you two handle this," said one.

They trooped down the stairs in dreadful silence. The
front door shut behind them. Car doors opened and
closed, engines sprang to life. Meanwhile, inside the
ranch house, steam was practically pouring out of Lilah
McCabe's ears. Greta's mom, Tillie, was fanning herself
weakly, looking as though she might get hit with an
attack of the vapors at any moment.

Lilah tossed aside her handbag as she stared down her
youngest son. "Do you know what you have done?"

Shane shrugged his broad shoulders. "Don't blame
me. I'm not the one who set the trap that had me stum-
bling fresh from the shower into my own bed, only to
find someone else already in it!"

Lilah flushed and, sweeping a hand through her sil-
very-blond bob, began to pace. "Your being here together like this was an accident," the petite sixty-two-
year-old woman with the bright-blue eyes swore. "I
didn't find your message on the machine until well after
we had started playing bridge. As soon as we realized
what had happened, we rushed right over to straighten
things out."

Shane's lips clamped together in a skeptical moue.
"And brought the whole bridge club with you to bear
witness?"

Tillie Wilson's thin rail-like figure was as tense as
could be. "We thought it might be cute to see the two
of you together," Tillie grumbled. She shook her head.
"Little did we know."

Greta remained silent while Shane studied his mother,
then Tillie, both of whom were now blushing fiercely.
"Why don't I believe you?" he asked finally.

"Okay, so we realized a few hours ago that there was

a mix-up," Tillie admitted, patting her light brown, bouffant hairdo.

"And we were hoping a little spark might have occurred to get the two of you interested in possibly dating each other," Lilah McCabe continued, shaking an admonishing finger at her son. "But you cannot blame us for this, Shane McCabe! We certainly didn't expect the two of you to burst into flames!"

WASN'T THAT THE UNDERSTATEMENT of the year? Greta thought. Their short but potent embrace was like spontaneous combustion and then some. She was still tingling. And all they'd done was share one hot, steamy kiss. She didn't want to think what it might be like to be in this bed with Shane when they weren't proving a point or *staging* lovemaking.

Lilah continued shaking her head at her youngest son. "I just do not understand how you could take advantage of Greta like this, Shane," she scolded him. "Your father and I taught you better."

"Oh, for Pete's sake, Ma. Nothing of any consequence happened. It was just a kiss. We were putting you on to pay you back. It was a little joke. That's all."

Maybe for him, Greta thought even more uncomfortably. For her it had been much more. For her it had been an awakening, a taste of how wonderful true physical passion could be.

Lilah began to pace, looking more like a worried mother than the capable nurse supervisor of Laramie Community Hospital. "Some joke! You have ruined Greta's reputation."

Greta felt Shane tense beside her.

Lilah continued, becoming more furious, "This won't hurt you, of course. There's nothing left of your reputation around here after your wild, misspent youth. And in any case, incidents like this tend to only enhance a man's reputation. But a woman's? Like it or not there is still a considerable double standard in this world.''

Tillie nodded and poked an accusing finger at Shane. ''Till now, our Greta's always had a stellar reputation!'' Tillie stomped closer to the bed and glared at Shane. ''At least until you came along. Now look what you've done!''

Looking truly taken aback, Shane turned to Greta. Clearly, the dual lecture had gotten him where it hurt. ''I'll make it right,'' he assured her bluntly, apology in his silver-gray eyes.

''How?'' Greta's mother interrupted. ''My word, with the bridge club here, it's going to be all over town by tomorrow morning!''

Lilah turned to Tillie. Shane's mother looked as exhausted and emotionally wrung out as Greta'd felt when she'd entered the Golden Slipper ranch house earlier in the evening. ''Come along, dear.'' Lilah McCabe patted Tillie Wilson's arm. ''I'll drive you home.'' To Greta Lilah said, ''I am so sorry for all of this.'' And to Shane, ''Your father and I want to see you at the ranch first thing tomorrow morning.''

Shane nodded grimly but did not argue.

Tillie turned to Greta. ''Perhaps you should come home with me now.''

Before Greta could answer, Shane put a staying hand on Greta. ''No. Greta and I have some things to work out. But you needn't worry, Mrs. Wilson. I'll be every inch the gentleman from here on out.''

Lilah McCabe seemed reassured by her wayward son's promise.

Tillie Wilson, however, was not. So Greta jumped in

and said soothingly, "It's all right, Mom. There are two bedrooms here. And Shane and I do need to talk. I'll see you and Dad first thing in the morning."

Lilah turned to Tillie in a consulting manner. "Maybe it'd be best if we all—six of us—met at our ranch before work. Say around 8:00 a.m.?"

Tillie nodded. "We'll be there."

THEIR MOTHERS LEFT IN UNISON, just as they'd come in.

Greta waited until the cars had driven away, then sighed. "Talk about a disaster!"

"Tell me about it," Shane grumbled. As he stalked, naked and unashamed, to the bureau, Greta saw what she'd only felt before.

Shane yanked open a dresser drawer and pulled out a pair of briefs. He stepped into them and tugged them up long, muscled legs covered with golden brown hair two shades darker than the halo of shaggy, sun-streaked hair on his head. "'Course, I didn't figure everyone in the entire darn bridge club would end up in the bedroom with us." He strode to the closet, pulled out a pair of faded jeans and yanked them on. "I assumed just one of our mothers, at most both, would witness that kiss."

As much as part of her would have liked to blame him for the entire misadventure, Greta knew she was just as responsible for the calamity. She'd wanted to kiss him for years. And the truth was she'd jumped at the opportunity to do so. She could hardly blame him for that. After all, she could have said no to his game plan from the get-go, and that would have been that, but she hadn't.

"You couldn't possibly have known how this would turn out," she said. "Neither of us could have."

Shane turned to face her. "We'll just have to fix it."

"How?" Greta asked. She swallowed hard, unable to

even bear thinking about what it was going to be like to face her father's wrath.

Shane ran a comb through his still-damp hair, restoring order to the rumpled mass. He slid the comb into the back pocket of his jeans and turned to face her calmly. "By getting married, of course."

Chapter Two

"Married," Greta repeated, absolutely sure she had not heard right.

Shane nodded. Grabbing a red-and-blue Western shirt from the closet, he continued to dress. "It's the right thing to do."

"Really," Greta said dryly, looking into Shane's handsome face. "And how do you figure that?" Long-considered the runt of the McCabe litter, at six-one, 180 pounds, Shane was the smallest as well as the youngest of the four sons of John and Lilah McCabe. He was also the scrappiest, as was reflected in the jagged, quarter-inch scar on his right cheekbone, a half-inch battle scar just left of center on his chin and an eighth-inch half-moon scar above his left eyebrow. He was also in need of a shave, and judging by the length of the stubble lining his jaw, had been for several days. Yet none of that detracted from his rugged appeal one bit.

"Because, as much as I hate to admit it, our moms were right."

Shane quickly closed the pearl snaps on his shirt and tucked it into his jeans. "If the word gets out tomorrow, and it will, that we were found in bed together on a whim, then your reputation will be trashed." Shane strode out into the hallway, zipping up, and came back with a leather belt sporting a championship buckle. He threaded it through the loops on his jeans and fastened the ends. "Whereas when it comes to grown-up, dignified behavior, mine is already about as bad as it can get. Although what happened between us here tonight—" Shane nodded his head at Greta as he rummaged through yet another bureau drawer and emerged with a pair of clean socks "—will probably be considered a new low."

"Except nothing happened," Greta said as Shane sat on the edge of the bed to pull on his socks.

"We know that," he agreed, before bounding back to his feet and heading for the closet. "No one else does."

Greta rolled her eyes and folded her arms in front of her. "Is this supposed to comfort me?"

"Yes." Shane pulled out a pair of alligator cowboy boots that were polished to a high gloss. "And you know why?" He sat again and tugged them on.

Greta flashed him a smile she couldn't begin to really feel, considering the mess they were in. "I'm breathless with anticipation, waiting to hear."

"Because our climbing into bed together on a whim is a promiscuous thing to do." Shane explained. Boots on, he pushed to his feet.

"But if we were to run off and get married tonight, what happened earlier would merely be seen as romantic, foolhardy and impulsive."

He was great at making unexpected moves, she thought, not so great at long-range planning. "Aren't you forgetting one thing?" Greta asked Shane, stepping closer. "We're not in love." Although, she added silently, given half a chance and a lot more kisses, she certainly could be.

Shane grinned as he took her hand in his. "That's the beauty of the plan."

"No one's going to want us to stay married if we're not in love," Shane continued, wondering how it was he had never noticed Greta before. Not in the way he was noticing her now.

Greta disengaged her hand from his and began to get dressed. "You think they'll try to convince us to reconsider and get it annulled?" she asked as she tugged a T-shirt over her head, then stepped into a denim skirt.

"Don't you?" Shane watched Greta tug a brush through her mane of hair. She sat on the edge of the bed, and put on a pair of white cotton crew socks, then tugged on a pair of bright blue Western boots that showed off her long, sexy dancer's legs to heart-stopping advantage. It was all Shane could do to keep from taking her in his arms and kissing her again. Just to see how it'd end without an audience.

Greta frowned. "My parents think there's only one reason to get married, and that's true love."

Till now Shane had agreed. "Same with mine." And yet, for reasons he chose not to examine too closely, the idea of pitching a tent with Greta and calling it home was very appealing.

Greta sighed. "Well, my parents always did have their hearts set on giving me a big, romantic wedding. My mother's been planning it for years, right down to the tiniest details, even when there's no groom in sight."

"So if we elope, it stands to reason they'd want you to back up and do it with someone else, and do it right." Although come to think of it, Shane realized, stunned, the idea of Greta as someone else's bride bothered him. Though why that should be he didn't know—all they had done was kiss and embark on one all-too-limited escapade together.

Greta bit her lip. She turned to him, her eyes searching his in a way that suddenly made him feel very protective of her. "What if our folks don't ask us to get it annulled?" she asked softly.

Shane brushed off her worries. There'd never been a father who truly welcomed him in his daughter's life yet. "Trust me," Shane told Greta, taking her arm and leading her down the front stairs. "They will."

"So when did you want to do this?" Greta asked.

Shane shrugged. He knew from experience the more you planned and delayed, the more an adventure lost steam. "How about right now?"

A LITTLE OVER AN HOUR LATER Shane and Greta stood beneath the glowing neon beer sign in the front window of J. P. Randall's Bait and Tackle Shop. Located some forty-five miles west of Laramie, Texas, the squat, flat-roofed building with the peeling white paint was out in the middle of nowhere. Just rundown enough to make it disreputable without being dangerous.

Greta sighed and shook her head to think that the two of them would actually get married here. "You take me to all the best places," she drawled.

Shane grinned and squeezed her arm before he returned to pounding on the front door of an establishment that was obviously closed for the night. "Don't I though?" he quipped.

"This does not look like a wedding chapel," Greta continued, trying hard not to notice just how cute Shane looked with his cowboy hat tipped back on his head that way.

"Sure it is," Shane replied affably and pointed to the

tattered yellow sign next to the door. The clock behind it indicated it was nearly one o'clock in the morning. "Says so right here. 'Bait, fresh and frozen, for sale,' he read. 'Tackle, all kinds. Groceries, beer, coolers and ice available.'"

"'Hunting knives sharpened. Spare tires repaired,'" Greta continued reading, picking up where he left off.

"'Marriage licenses issued. Ceremonies performed.'" Shane finished, still grinning, and went back to pounding on the door.

Seconds later the fluorescent lights inside flipped on. A stooped old man in pajama top, pants and suspenders came shuffling to the door. His glasses were sliding off the end of his nose, and what hair he had left was sticking up at odd angles all over his head. He had a rifle in his hand, but when he saw Shane he broke out in a wide grin. He put the rifle down, released the chain and unlocked the front door. "Shane McCabe! Now ain't you a sight for sore eyes."

"Howdy, J.P." Shane hugged the old man warmly.

J.P. returned the hug, slapped Shane on the back and looked over at Greta. He greeted her with a welcoming smile. "And who might this pretty thing be?"

"Greta Wilson," Shane made the introductions graciously.

"How do." J.P. extended a gnarled hand.

Greta shook it warmly. "Nice to meet you, too, J.P."

"So now," J.P. ushered them in straightaway. "What can I do for you? Going night fishin' on the lake? Need some bait?"

"Marriage license," Shane stated, not bothering to check either his mischievous grin or the twinkle in his eyes. He clamped a hand over Greta's shoulders and drew her close. "And a ceremony."

Greta's heart pounded even as her spirits rose. So this was what it felt like to be in one of Shane's devil-may-care adventures, she thought excitedly.

J.P. slid his glasses lower on his nose. He peered at Shane. "No one'd be coming after you with a shotgun, would they now, Shane?"

Shane chuckled and tugged Greta even closer. "Not as long as I get a ring on Greta's finger by morning."

Satisfied with their explanation such as it was, J.P. waved them to the back of the store. As they shuffled along, J.P. hooked his arm through Greta's. "You sure you want to get hitched to this young son of a gun? He's a wild one."

"Tell me about it," Greta concurred. And the truth was, she wasn't sure at all she was doing the right thing, even if it was kind of fun, carrying on like this. But at the same time she couldn't seem to resist his antics, either. And maybe that told her something, too.

J.P. chuckled. "But you'll have him, anyway, huh?"

"For the moment," Greta answered cautiously, warning herself not to wear her heart on her sleeve, no matter how much fun she was having. Besides, this wasn't a real marriage, they were just making a statement to their parents that what they chose to do with their private lives was their business, and theirs alone. They were adults, after all. And if this was the only reason to get their parents to stop interfering and simultaneously save Greta's "reputation" by making their foray into bed together a prelude to an elopement instead of merely a one-night stand, then so be it.

J.P. handed over the paperwork to fill out. "Did you bring the rings?"

Greta and Shane groaned in unison. Shane stroked his jaw. "Uh, no—"

"Not to worry, I got just the thing." J.P. reached beneath the counter and brought out a tray of plain silver and gold bands. "They're five dollars each," he said, and waited while they studied the "gold" and "silver" rings. "Now, how about a witness?" J.P. continued.

Shane spread his hands wide and offered a hapless shrug of his strong, broad shoulders. "Can't say we remembered that, either."

"Hang on. I'll get the missus. Normally, she don't cotton to bein' rolled outta bed at this hour, but seein' as how it's you, Shane, and your bride-to-be," J.P. winked, "I'm bettin' she won't mind. You two pick out your rings, there. I'll be right back." One suspender falling off his shoulder, J.P. shuffled off.

Shane turned to Greta. He traced the curve of her cheek with the pad of his thumb. "Getting cold feet?"

Greta pretended to be as cool as he was about all this bad-boy stuff. Tingles swept through her as he continued to gently stroke her face. "Why would you ask that?"

Shane's sensually carved lips curved upward slightly. "Because for a second there just now," he murmured softly, his eyes simultaneously searching and challenging hers, "you looked terrified."

Greta stepped back, away from the disturbingly sensual stroking of his thumb. She forced herself to hold his mesmerizing gaze. "I probably would be, if the marriage were real," she admitted, in the same soft tone. She looked down at the display case and began trying on various "gold" wedding bands for size, while Shane did the same. "But since it's not, and it'll probably be over with before we know it, there's no reason for me to be afraid, now, is there?"

"Exactly." Shane nodded his approval at her proudly.

Letting her know that maybe she was up to participating in one of his legendary escapades, after all.

No sooner had they selected the rings, than J.P.'s wife Belinda came in. She was wearing an old-fashioned cotton housedress that snapped up the front and ballet-style house slippers. Her hair was wrapped in pink sponge curlers, and she had a lacy, pink hair net over top. She hugged them both warmly, then looked at Shane and shook her head in affectionate rebuke. "I always knew it would happen this way, on some wild and crazy impulse. Unless—" Belinda paused and grasped Greta's forearm "—honey, you aren't pregnant, are you?"

"Heavens no!" Greta gasped, and continued impulsively before she could think, "We haven't even slept together!"

Belinda immediately nodded her approval. "Good thinking, honey. These days there are too many young'uns just giving it away. So of course the young fellas aren't gonna be in any hurry to marry."

At the unabashedly frank talk from someone she had just met, Greta felt herself blush to the roots of her hair.

J.P. winked at Shane. "Looks like you've got yourself a prize. You take good care of her, you hear?" J.P. cupped a hand over his mouth and whispered, "And for pity's sake, be gentle!"

Greta blushed all the more while Shane grinned and slapped a hand on J.P.'s bony shoulder. "Don't worry, J.P. I'm sure Greta'll do her best to keep me in check."

The guys exchanged a man-to-man look. Belinda continued to look at Greta so sympathetically that Greta knew if she blushed any harder her face would be on fire.

Bowing to the awkwardness of the moment, J.P. cleared his throat and pushed his glasses farther up on the bridge of his nose. He wiggled his shoulders, assumed a serious pose and folded his hands in front of him. "Maybe we'd better get on with it," he said.

Shane smothered a grin so impish it was all Greta could do not to elbow him in the side. "Good idea," Shane said.

"What kind of music do you want?" Belinda asked, as she held up two cassette tapes.

Shane shrugged and asked, "What do you got?"

"'Here Comes The Bride,' on organ. And Elvis singing 'Love Me Tender.'"

"'Love Me Tender,'" Shane and Greta said in unison, surprised but pleased to find they were immediately of one mind on that, too.

"Look, they're agreeing on everything already!" J.P. beamed. "Isn't that sweet?"

It was something all right, Greta thought.

"You need some flowers, too." Belinda hurried forward with a bouquet of multicolored silk flowers that had obviously seen many a wedding. "Of course I can only loan them to you," she apologized.

"That's perfectly all right. Thank you." Greta smiled, knowing if her mother could see her now she really would faint.

The mellow voice of Elvis surrounded the foursome. J.P. turned to Shane. "Shane, do you take this woman to be your lawful-wedded wife?"

Shane suddenly remembered his hat. He yanked it off and put it aside, then turned back to Greta with a grin as wide as all Texas. "You bet I do."

"And, Greta," J.P. continued, "do you take Shane to be your lawful-wedded husband?"

Remember, this isn't real, Greta scolded herself firmly, aware everyone was looking at her, waiting for her answer. She drew a deep breath and held Shane's eyes. "I do."

"All rightee! Shane, put the ring on Greta's finger. Greta, put the ring on Shane's." J.P. waited for them to comply. "I now pronounce you husband and wife. Shane, you may kiss your bride."

Under the circumstances, Greta didn't think Shane would do it, and of course not in any trumped-up, passionate sort of way. Which was, of course, probably why he did. One minute she was standing beside him, bouquet of silk flowers in hand, the next she was clasped in the warm, strong cradle of his arms and bent backward from the waist. For one long second his eyes met hers. She saw laughter. And lust. And something else much more disturbing. Need. And then his lips were lowering to hers. Her eyes were closing. The world narrowed to just the two of them. And then there was nothing but the feel of his warm, sure mouth on hers. Caressing. Evoking. Commanding. First taking what she would not give, then persuading, seducing. Greta sighed as the warm, silky pressure of his tongue gently traced the seam of her lips. Her lips parted, and her heart fluttered as he deepened the kiss even more, first sweetly, then erotically. She felt the sandpapery rub of his two-day-old shadow against her skin, inhaled the scent of man that was him, tasted the minty flavor on his tongue. Desire swept through her in undulating waves. And then, just as her knees began to give ever so slightly, just as her arms came up to wrap around his neck and she was about to surrender herself to him in earnest, he stopped. Just like that. With no warning at all. And withdrew. Having ended the kiss as unexpectedly as it began, he lifted his head, and gently guided her upright. Zeroing in on the ire in her eyes, he gave her a wickedly teasing look that hinted they needed to save something for their "honeymoon."

"So," Shane said. One arm still hooked around her waist, he reclaimed his Stetson and settled it back on his head; one arm still locked around her possessively, he looked at her with warm, silvery-gray eyes. "How does it feel to be Mrs. Shane McCabe?"

It felt surreal, Greta thought. Like she was in the middle of some highly comical, incredibly romantic and erotic dream.

"I think the besotted look on Greta's face is your answer to that, Shane," Belinda teased.

J.P. handed their marriage license and certificate to Shane.

"You'll be needing these. As well as—" J.P. went to the cooler and emerged with a bottle of nonalcoholic champagne, which he promptly handed over.

"And some chocolates." Belinda went to the back of the store. "Oh, dear, we're out."

"How about some nacho chips, then?" Shane said.

J.P.'s wife beamed. "You always did like those, didn't you?"

J.P. handed them over, then reached beneath the counter for a small pink-and-blue gift bag. "And we give all our newlyweds one of these, too." J.P. winked as Shane and Greta took that, too. "Now you're all set."

GRETA WAS STILL EMBARRASSED ten minutes later. "I can't believe J.P. and his wife actually gave us..."

"Honeymoon supplies?" Shane said for her as he steered the truck down the lonely two-lane Texas highway.

Greta blushed as she thought of the scented and flavored lotions, soaps, condoms and lubricants that had been contained in their gift bag. Plus a road map, a deck of cards with a bride and groom on them and a pamphlet issued by the state on the essential components and responsibility required of marriage, with all the phone numbers of the local and state social service agencies. "To put it delicately, yes."

"Think of it this way." Shane reached over and patted her bare knee. "Now you won't get pregnant."

Greta gaped at him. "Like that was going to happen, anyway!"

Shane shrugged and concentrated on driving. "You never know," he said, slanting her a mischievous glance. "We are married."

Okay, Greta thought. *That does it. It's time we get a few things straight.* She set the bag of honeymoon essentials on the floor, next to the non-alcoholic champagne and nacho chips. "Pull over!"

Shane did a double take. "Now?"

"Right now!"

Wordlessly he did as directed, pulling onto the berm. As soon as he'd put his truck in park and switched on the hazard lights, Greta slammed out of the cab. Shane cut the engine but left the interior lights on and came after her. She leaned against the tailgate, arms crossed impatiently in front of her. Taking his time about closing the distance between them, Shane tipped his hat back with one poke of his finger and swaggered toward her. "You want to do it here?"

Greta refused to be amused. "I don't want to do it at all!"

"Sure about that now?" Shane teased as he gently guided her aside and lowered the tailgate. "After all, we are legally married."

Not sure why she'd married him after all—even as

part of a Shane McCabe escapade—Greta began to pace. "Fortunately for us we're not staying married."

Shane sighed and didn't bother to mask his disappointment as he returned to the front of the truck, reached into the cab and emerged with the bottle of nonalcoholic champagne and bag of nacho chips. Given the fact they were going to stay put until they got a few things ironed out, he clearly intended to make himself quite comfortable.

"Got a point there," he said, holding the bag of chips between his teeth while he twisted off the metal cap on the nonalcoholic champagne. It opened up with only a hint of bubbles. He set the cap aside, removed the bag from his teeth and took a long swig of the chilled liquid. Wiping his mouth on his forearm, he offered the bottle to her.

Greta took the bottle from him and sipped a little. It tasted like flat, flavorless soda pop. But it was cold and wet and eased the dryness in her throat and mouth, so she took several more gulps before she said, "No more talk about sex!"

"How about making love then?" Shane asked as he tore open the bag of nacho chips. "Can we talk about that?" He hoisted himself up and sat on the tailgate of the truck.

Greta refused his offer of chips and handed over the champagne. "No-o-o-o," she said, drawing out the syllable unequivocally. Damn but this bad boy had earned every bit of his reputation.

"Okay." Shane munched on a few more chips as the hazard lights on his truck flashed rhythmically. "But just so you know—" he paused to eye her up and down "—if you change your mind it's okay with me."

"I won't," Greta said flatly. Deciding they'd dallied long enough, she headed back for the passenger side.

"Suit yourself." Shane stood up and followed her. "But just in case?" He slid inside the cab, picked up the gift bag J.P. and his wife had given them and settled it between his spread thighs. "I'll take charge of the honeymoon essentials and have them at the ready anyway."

WHEN THEY ARRIVED back at the Golden Slipper Ranch, Greta and Shane split up. He took the master bedroom; she went to the guest room. They had four hours to sleep, and both tried their best to get some shut-eye. But as their respective alarms went off around seven, they met up in the only bathroom—she in her robe, he in nothing but his briefs. Greta could easily see that he hadn't fared much better than she had. Worse, all she really wanted to do at that point was tumble back into bed—with him. "You need to shave."

Shane narrowed his eyes at her. "What?"

Greta stabbed her finger at his chest, trying not to notice what a beautifully sculpted body he had. From his broad shoulders and handsome chest to his narrow waist and lean hips, there wasn't an inch of him that wasn't fit and toned and covered with suntanned skin and swirls of golden-brown hair. "You can't go to meet our parents to tell them we've just gotten married looking as if you and your razor parted company three days ago."

Shane ran his hand across the stubble on his jaw, tracing the sexy growth above his upper lip with the pad of his index finger. Amusement glimmered in his sleepy silver-gray eyes. "How do you know how long it's been since I've shaved?"

With effort Greta kept her gaze from drifting past his

waist. "Lucky guess." Noting he hadn't moved yet, Greta reached for his razor and shaving cream on the sink and planted one in each hand. "Get moving, cowboy," she ordered, taking charge.

Shane drew a long, slow breath and to her dismay stayed exactly as he was. "Just cause we're married does not give you the right to give orders."

If playing the part of the nag would help keep the roving cowboy-turned-instant-husband at arm's length, so much the better, Greta thought. Meanwhile, she had an escapade to finish if she wanted this lesson to be a success for her parents. "Then consider it a suggestion." Greta started to skirt past him in the narrow aisle between the sink and glass-doored shower and tub, only to have him move back directly into her path.

Seemingly oblivious to the fact she couldn't get past him, either front or back, Shane squirted a golf-ball-size lump of shaving cream into his palm. With the fingers of his other hand, he began spreading it over his face with slow, sensual strokes. "What about you?" He gave her the once-over, then turned and waggled his eyebrows at her in the mirror. "Have you shaved? Wouldn't do for you to meet up with your new in-laws if you're needing a comb and rake to tame the hair on your legs."

Not about to let him intimidate her with his accidental bumping, Greta stubbornly stood her ground. He knew she'd shaved her legs—he'd playfully squeezed her bare knee during the drive home from their elopement. "You know I did, dear."

"Let me see?" Shane leaned down and before she could do more than gasp her outrage dragged a fingerful of shaving cream from her knee up her thigh. "That's right." He blew off the tip of his finger the way one would blow off the end of a smoking gun. His smile was slow and ready. "You sure have."

Trying not to think about the way her leg was tingling from his touch or the fact she still couldn't get out of the tiny bathroom without first climbing over him—a feat she was sure he'd just love and waste no time in taking great advantage of—Greta folded her arms in front of her. "You're a laugh a minute, you know that?" she said sarcastically.

"And you, Greta darlin', are completely humorless this morning." Eyes darkening to a pewter-gray, Shane turned back to the mirror and began shaving the underside of his jaw with long, clean strokes. "What happened?" His eyes were abruptly serious as they met hers in the mirror. "Get up on the wrong side of the bed?"

Beneath the teasing words was a matter-of-fact prompting for an explanation.

Greta knew he deserved an answer if they wanted to have a prayer of pulling this off. And now that she had invested so much in it, she did. She wouldn't be able to bear it if this escapade of theirs ended up with her parents thinking she needed more help than ever living her life.

Greta frowned. "I woke up thinking clearly, that's all."

Shane continued shaving. "And...?"

"And I'm not so sure this was a good idea." It was going to take an enormous amount of finesse and teamwork to pull it off. Thus far Shane had proved to be a cowboy who called his own shots and kept very much to his own solo trails.

Finished with the underside of his jaw, Shane rinsed his blade and started on the side of his face. "Just wait till you see our parents' faces,'' he told her, confidence exuding from his every pore.

Greta mentally pictured just that and felt her mood plummet even farther. "Exactly what I'm afraid of. They're going to be mortified when we tell them what we've done."

Shane shrugged, his expression grim. "So much the better, wouldn't you say," he queried in a low, surprisingly serious voice, "after the prank they played on us last night that landed us in the same bed?"

Greta thought about what it had been like to lie beneath a very naked, very virile Shane. It didn't matter how they had gotten there. Or why they had started to kiss the way they had. As long as she lived she would never forget his sexy kisses or the way his body felt pressed against hers. As long as she lived she would wish they had been able to take it all the way to fruition. But that wasn't the case now, nor would it ever be. Because she didn't make love with someone casually. Nor would she ever. For her making love was a commitment; not necessarily so for Shane. Hence, it was unlikely, despite their steamy start, they'd ever go all the way. And like it or not, she was going to have to live with that disappointment the rest of her life. "You're right," Greta replied with a sigh. "That was low of our mothers."

"Exactly." Finished shaving, Shane wiped his face and playfully tapped the end of her nose. "Now you get a move on, too, Greta, darlin'. Our chariot of fate awaits."

WHEN GRETA AND SHANE ARRIVED, all four parents were already inside John and Lilah McCabe's sprawling stone-and-cedar ranch house, waiting. Shane wasted no time in getting down to brass tacks. To Greta's chagrin, he said hello and told everyone about their elopement the previous evening in the same breath. Not surprisingly, his announcement caused the expected chaos.

"You did what?" Bart Wilson demanded, every inch of his five-eleven bearlike frame tensed and poised for battle. Dressed in a sport coat, starched shirt and tie, he was ready for work at his insurance agency in Laramie. He was also flushed beet-red from his neck to the roots of his white-blond hair.

"Got married," Shane repeated patiently but politely, while Lilah and Tillie both hung on to their husbands, tightly gripping their forearms. *"M-a-r-r-i-e-d."* He spelled it out.

John McCabe gave Shane a sharp look and shoved a hand through dark-brown hair threaded liberally with gray. "There's no need to spell, Shane." John McCabe fixed his son with a penetrating gaze. "We know what you mean."

Lilah threw up her hands as she regarded her youngest son. "Honestly, Shane! Of all the—! I just can't believe you'd go off and do something so foolhardy!"

"That goes double for us!" Tillie Wilson cried, equally upset, her face almost as pink as her summer-weight sweater set. "Greta, for heaven's sake, what were the two of you thinking?"

Shane stepped in to wrap a protective arm about Greta's shoulders. "It's the only way I could figure to save Greta's reputation." Shane gave his mother a telling look. "Of course, had I known Greta was staying at Wade's place last night, in advance of arriving there, if someone had just bothered to leave me a note on the front door or call me on my cell phone, I never would've accidentally crawled into bed with her, never mind been naked at the time.''

Tillie fanned herself wildly, again looking as though she was going to faint. Bart eased her into a chair.

John McCabe closed the distance between himself and his son. ''Are you being smart with us, son?'' he demanded, and it appeared he wasn't above taking Shane to the woodshed then and there.

''No, sir, I am not.'' Shane held his ground in the face of his father's wrath and continued to look completely ticked off. ''I'm merely stating what everyone in Mom and Tillie's bridge club already knows. What the whole town of Laramie—if not the entire state of Texas—will be privy to before breakfast is over. Unsavory as it may be, we have to deal with the facts as they happened. Now, if it will make you all feel better—'' Shane paused to look all four parents in the eye, one by one ''—our hasty marriage has not been consummated just yet.''

''Thank heaven for small miracles,'' Tillie and Lilah McCabe murmured in unison, exchanging commiserating glances and clasping hands.

''But,'' Shane continued, ''as soon as Greta makes up her mind to invite me back into her bed, that can be remedied.''

Greta flushed bright-red.

It was Bart Wilson's turn to step forward. Blond brows raised, he gave his only child a stern look. ''What have you got to say for yourself, young lady?''

Maybe it was his tone, the fact he was treating her like some wayward teenager instead of a twenty-eight-year-old woman who'd just put together her own business, but it rankled Greta.

''Did Shane push you into this?'' Lilah McCabe demanded. Her hand shook as she freshened everyone's coffee.

"No one talks Greta in to or out of anything," Tillie Wilson stated emphatically, before thoughtfully biting her lower lip. "But it could very well have something to do with that rascal Beauregard Chamberlain."

Shane blinked in amazement. Clearly he wasn't following. "What's that movie star got to do with Greta?" he demanded.

All four parents sighed and shook their heads. "Honey, where have you been?" Lilah said.

"Greta has been dating that blackguard for two whole years!" Tillie said. "He's taken her to every awards show there is—Golden Globes, Academy Awards, People's Choice. You name it. If Beauregard Chamberlain has been there in the past two years, so has Greta!"

Lilah nodded. "They've been on TV together at least two or three dozen times. In magazines and tabloids. Tillie even gave me a videotape of all the TV clips."

Tillie turned back to Greta. "Honey, I know I told you to give that bounder a wake-up call when it came to marriage, but not this!"

"Mom, I told you!" Extricating herself from Shane's lightly possessive arm, Greta took a seat on one end of the sofa and explained, "Beau is not the marrying kind—not anymore—not since his divorce."

Bart looked at Greta in stunned amazement, trying to make sense of what his daughter had said. "So this elopement of yours is a rebound thing then?"

"No!" Greta cried, leaning forward and wringing her hands together in frustration. "Beau and I are just friends! I've told you guys that a hundred times, at the very least!"

Shane frowned but was silent as he sat down on the arm of the sofa, next to Greta.

"That's not what the tabloids and all the magazines say," Tillie argued. "They say you're one of the hottest couples going, and the reason you've left Los Angeles is because Beau wouldn't marry you."

Greta planted her palms on either side of her head, as if she were losing her mind. "But that's not what I say," Greta repeated, even less patiently.

"What do you say?" Shane asked, ever so casually, his eyes never leaving hers.

"I say I better try and call Beau and let him know what's happened before he finds out some other way," Greta muttered as she leaped off the sofa and rushed into the hall.

Unfortunately he wasn't in. The best she could do was leave a message for Beau to call her. All too aware everyone was waiting for her, and that thus far nothing had gone as they'd planned, she hung up and returned to the group gathered in the McCabe living room. "I forgot how early it is out there," she said, "barely the crack of dawn."

"Forget the different time zones!" her father fumed. "Did you or did you not pull this this stunt just to get Beauregard Chamberlain's attention?" he demanded.

Greta sighed, wondering what it would take to show her parents that she was an adult, fully capable of living her own life without their constant commentary and interference. "No, Dad. Beau had nothing to do with what went on last night." Greta looked at her father, then her mother, then Shane's parents, before finishing heavily, "What went on last night—what is going on here this morning—only has to do with Shane and with me."

SHANE WISHED he could believe that. Maybe if past experience hadn't taught him to question when a woman claimed she and the man she constantly spent time with were just friends, he would have believed it. But as it was, he was suddenly full of doubts. As was everyone else in the room.

"You didn't answer my question," Lilah said gently. "Did Shane push you into this?"

"No. Shane did not coerce me into anything."

Although, Shane thought, *I might have* tempted *her.*

"Then why," Bart roared, incensed, "would you go off and do such a reckless, foolhardy thing, instead of turning to me and your mama to make everything better and get you out of this mess?"

How about the fact she's a grown woman, perfectly capable of running her own life and obviously has been for some time, Shane thought.

"Because I don't need you and Mama to make everything better, Daddy," Greta told her father hotly, with so much gumption it was all Shane could do not to stand up and cheer her on. "I can do that for myself!"

"Not like this—" Bart pointed to the marriage license and certificate they'd brought with them for proof "—you can't!"

John McCabe held up a hand, commanding everyone to silence. He looked at Lilah, Bart and Tillie. "Maybe Shane has a point here," John said quietly.

At last! Shane thought. *Someone is finally listening.*

The other adults turned to John, gaping in astonishment.

John continued with typical McCabe self-assurance, "A hasty marriage isn't what any of us would have wanted for Greta and Shane—"

You're right about that too, Dad, Shane thought, as

the other three parents in the room murmured their assent.

"But now that they've gone and done it," John McCabe continued firmly, "I think we ought to let them stick with it. And try and make this marriage of theirs work."

Chapter Three

"That's the last time I let you play John Wayne," Greta fumed as she and Shane smiled and waved and drove away, several minutes later.

"What do you mean?" Shane asked, slanting her an astonished glance. "I thought it went very well."

Greta blinked at the happiness glittering in his eyes. "Are you completely loco or did you just fall down at the rodeo too many times?" She turned toward him as much as her seat belt would allow. "They've decided they like the fact we ran off and eloped. At J. P. Randall's Bait and Tackle shop, no less!"

His large hands circling the wheel, Shane shrugged off her concern. "Ah, they're just pulling our chains, trying to make us cry uncle first." He predicted with a wicked smile.

Greta drew a bolstering breath. "Well, it's working!"

"Maybe for you," Shane drawled, continuing to radiate a distinctly male satisfaction. "Not for me."

Greta shook her head and tugged her fingers through her hair, pushing the heavy length of it off her face. "Meaning?" she prodded mercilessly.

Shane's jaw set. "They haven't learned their lesson yet about interfering in our lives. If they had, they wouldn't still be calling us onto the carpet and telling us what to do!''

Much as Greta didn't want to admit it, Shane had a point about that. They were a little too old to be getting lectures from their parents on the state of their love lives. Any mistakes they made these days were theirs to make and pay for, no one else's. And that was a rule she'd still like to drive home to them. ''So what are you suggesting we do now?'' Greta asked impatiently as they bumped along the gravel road leading to the highway back to town.

Shane squinted against the rising morning sun and reached up to pull a pair of aviator-style sunglasses from the visor. He opened them with one hand and slid them on, managing in that one instant to look sexier and more emotionally unapproachable than ever. ''I'm suggesting,'' he said slowly as he turned to give her an enigmatic look, ''that we play along until they cry uncle and promise never to interfere in our lives again.''

''How long do you think that'll take?''

''Trust me.'' Jaw set, he stared at the road straight ahead. ''If we play our cards right, they'll be begging us to get an annulment by the end of the week.''

Wonderful, Greta thought. ''And in the meantime?'' she asked dryly, amazed at Shane's ability to keep his cool in the face of so much familial angst. But then, he'd grown up that way, always getting himself in and out of one scrape after another. Whereas she rarely, if ever, did anything to upset her parents in the slightest, even if it meant forgetting all about what *she* wanted and concentrating only on what *they* wanted for her.

''Until then, we keep to our plan and prove together in many subtle and not-so-subtle ways that we are about as mismatched a couple as they come. After a while our families will stop wanting us to be a cute couple. They'll be relieved when we split. And not at all inclined to match either of us with anyone again, which will in turn leave us free to pursue our own lives exactly as we please—without comment from our folks—exactly as we should've been doing for years now,'' he finished stubbornly.

Was his convoluted logic beginning to make sense? Greta wondered uneasily. Or had she simply gone loco, too? With a great deal of effort Greta forced her mind back to even more important matters they had yet to touch on. ''Normally, Shane, that would be fine,'' she told him. ''Unfortunately I have a reputation to maintain.''

Shane slanted her a bad-boy smile that was enough to make her stomach drop. ''That's what I thought we were workin' on, Greta, darlin','' he teased in a soft, sexy voice that had her tingling all over.

And it was then Greta knew she couldn't even think about ever kissing him again. Because if she did, there was no telling what would happen.

''A *professional* reputation,'' Greta said. ''You may not have heard, but I've just bought a business. My dinner and dance hall—''

''The Lone Star Dance Hall, right?''

''Right.'' Greta nodded, then continued. ''It's opening on Saturday night.''

Shane shrugged his broad shoulders, unconcerned. ''And I close on my new horse ranch later this afternoon if all the paperwork is in order by then and I suspect it will be.''

Her new ''husband'' wasn't the first person not to take her seriously but by golly he was sure going to be the last. Greta's lips set stubbornly. "I don't want to lose any bookings because of this."

"You need publicity to open a place like that, don't you?"

"Of course." She twisted the wedding band on her left hand, hating the cheap insubstantial feel of it even as she relished the memory of their wildly exciting escapade the night before.

"And publicity is expensive?" Shane persisted in that excessively smooth, practical tone that always preceded one of his misadventures.

Greta regarded Shane cautiously, aware it would be all too easy to get hopelessly caught up in whatever Shane was planning next. To her own detriment, of course. Determined not to let him get her into any scrape she couldn't handle, Greta calmly answered his question about publicity. "Some types are...like radio and newspaper advertising." She'd done a limited amount already, but unfortunately her budget had fallen far short of what she would have liked to do.

"Think of all the free publicity our elopement will get you," Shane continued enthusiastically as he reached over and gave her bare knee a warm, companionable squeeze. "Everyone's going to be talking about it. And everyone's gonna want to get a gander at the two of us."

Greta plucked his warm, callused hand—which was causing far too many tingles just sitting there—from her skin and set it on his own. "You think they'd show up at Greta's just to see us?"

"Oh, yeah." Shane braked as they approached the turn-off from the main highway to a less-traveled ranch road. "Come opening night," Shane predicted boldly,

"I think it's gonna take a fire marshal to keep the crowds away."

Greta wasn't so sure about that. She did know if they were in for a penny, they were in for a pound. Like it or not, it was simply too late to back out now, she thought, as she passed the drilling platform the Wyatt Oil company had erected. Greta sighed as Shane by-passed several large fields, filled with yellow grass and wildflowers, and a large grove of scrub oak and cedar, before turning his pickup into the lane leading to his brother's Golden Slipper Ranch. Greta frowned contemplatively. "It would seem we have a lot of work to do."

Shane nodded his agreement as he circled around the barn and parked beside her car. "We better get started."

"SHANE MCCABE, what are you doing back so soon?" Lilah asked several hours later when she caught him standing in front of the cabinet that held their collection of videotapes. "And where's Greta?"

Shane bit back an oath of frustration. He'd assumed his mother would be at the hospital now, where she was busy turning over the reins to Meg Lockhart, the Laramie Community Hospital's newest nursing supervisor.

Or, at the very least, planning the repeat of her wedding vows to his dad or their retirement or second honeymoon. Something! Instead she was here at the ranch, catching him red-handed. Masking his discomfort, he continued studying the vast collection of tapes in front of him, most of which were not clearly marked.

"She's working," he said finally.

"Today?" Lilah McCabe pulled on her favorite white cardigan over her blue nurse's uniform and made no effort to hide her surprise. "When you just got married last night?"

Shane deliberately kept his gaze from his mother's gentle countenance. He shrugged. "Her Lone Star Dinner and Dance Hall opens on Saturday night. She has a lot to do to get ready for it."

A beat of silence followed. "Then, shouldn't you be there helping her?" Lilah persisted as she paused to put on her name tag and badge.

Shane knew a golden opportunity to prove himself unworthy of his new bride when he saw it. And since that was the plan, he did his best to look dumfounded. "It never occurred to me."

Lilah's brows knit together in a disapproving frown. Shane felt a lecture about how to treat a lady coming on. He circumvented it with a change of subject. "Greta wanted to see the videotape of her and Beauregard Chamberlain."

Lilah gave him a look that let Shane know he hadn't fooled his mother for one single second. About that or anything else. "Greta wants to see it or you do?" Lilah asked dryly.

When he was up to something, his mom had always been able to read him like a book.

Right now Shane did not want his thoughts—or feelings—read. "We both would," he said simply, figuring it didn't do any good to deny his curiosity. Lilah would see right through it, anyway. "She was gonna tell me all about him—them—whatever." At least she would when he asked.

"Hmm." Lilah plucked the requested tape off the shelf and handed it over to him.

"Don't let me keep you," Shane said politely, hoping to hurry his mother along.

"I don't have to be anywhere just yet," Lilah replied, just as smoothly.

Knowing he didn't have all day, as he had other things to do, too, and that if he wanted to watch the tape he'd have to watch it here since Wade did not have a VCR at his place, Shane switched on the VCR and popped the tape in.

"Should I make some popcorn?" Lilah asked sarcastically.

Shane wasted no time calling his mother's bluff. "Actually, Ma, that'd be great," Shane quipped as his lips formed his most devil-may-care smile. "Some lemonade, too, if you wouldn't mind." Seeing as how he and Greta hadn't stopped to eat breakfast, he was a little hungry in any case.

Lilah rolled her eyes. "I'll fix you a sandwich," she said in a knowing tone of voice. Before Shane could comment, she was gone.

Relieved, Shane hit the play button on the remote. To his frustration the videotape had barely started to roll when Shane's older brother, Travis—a successful cattle rancher who should never have been there at that time of a day, either—strode in, dressed as always in the plainest blue chambray shirt a person could find and work-worn jeans.

"What are you doing here?" Shane grumbled as the TV screen showed Greta on Beauregard Chamberlain's arm at the Golden Globes two years ago. They were walking up the carpet, photographers and film crews on either side of them. Fans screamed in the background. Greta looked incredibly beautiful in a low-cut, beaded gold dress that showed off her dancer's figure to stunning advantage. Her long blond hair floated over her shoulders and down her back in long, sexy waves. She looked stunning and completely at ease in a way she never had back in high school when he'd known her.

Travis frowned and slapped his dusty hat against his thigh. "I'm here to ask Mom's advice on some flowers for a friend."

"What friend?"

"Annie Pierce. She and her three boys just moved back to Laramie. She's taking over the ranch her dad left her. I figured I should do something to welcome her."

Maybe. But flowers? That didn't sound like the Travis he knew. "You sweet on her?" Shane cut right to the chase.

Travis gave Shane a quelling look. "I'm just being neighborly, that's all."

Unable to resist—it was rare his serious older brother gave him anything to tease him about—Shane drawled, "Funny, I don't recall you sending any of your other neighbors flowers."

Travis frowned and slapped his Stetson back on his head, tugging it down low over his eyes. "That's cause they're all men and it'd look a little funny."

"I'll say!"

Travis shot a look at the TV screen, which was now showing Greta with Beauregard Chamberlain at the Academy Awards the previous spring. "So it's true," Travis murmured, immediately seeing all, as most older brothers could. He reached over and tapped the cheap dime-store wedding ring on Shane's left hand. "The two of you did elope last night."

"How'd you hear?" Shane demanded, incensed that Travis had all the details so quickly.

"Jackson," Travis replied. Shane's other brother. "How'd he hear?" Shane demanded, as Greta and Beau appeared onscreen again looking equally as glamorous.

"From Dad, at the hospital." Travis sat on the cushioned arm of the sturdy, brown leather sofa that had seen all four of the McCabe sons through their adolescence, into adulthood.

Lilah came in, carrying a tray with a brisket sandwich layered thick with beef and barbecue sauce, an apple, and a glass of icy lemonade. "A sandwich at this hour?" Travis asked, studying the contents of the tray.

"Shane needed to get rid of me for a few minutes," Lilah explained. She inclined her head at the TV screen, where the tape of Greta and Beau was playing. "Pretty, isn't she?" Lilah said dryly.

Gorgeous, Shane thought with more than a tad of wistfulness. Unfortunately so was her date. Shane frowned as he bit into the thick, delicious sandwich his mother had prepared for him. For several minutes, they all watched in silence. "How many of these things did Greta go to?" Shane asked finally.

"Jealous?" Lilah suggested.

"Fine. Don't tell me." Shane chugged his lemonade and, ignoring the napkin next to his plate, wiped his mouth with the back of his hand.

Unable to stop mothering him, even for a moment, Lilah reached over to pointedly hand him his napkin. "Shane..." Her low tone carried both a warning to behave himself and a plea for peace between him and his folks. An impossible combination under the circumstances.

His temper soared at the ever-increasing scrutiny of both his mother and his oldest brother. "I'm interested. And why not? It's the kind of thing I should probably know since I'm now married to her." Actually, he amended silently, it was the kind of thing he should have known before he married her.

"But for how long?" Lilah asked gently.

Travis shook his head as yet another image of Beau and Greta came on the screen. "Give it up, kid. You're never gonna compete with that." Travis stabbed his finger at the screen.

The hell he couldn't, Shane fumed. There wasn't a competition on this earth he couldn't win if he set his mind to it. After ten-plus years on the professional rodeo circuit, he was rich and famous, too. Maybe not that famous. Or that rich. But he doubted Greta responded to Beau's kisses the way she had responded to his. He'd seen the look in her eyes when their kisses ended, all soft and yearning and completely vulnerable. He'd felt the way she melted against him. He'd seen the way she looked at him when she thought he didn't notice. He'd felt her desire...and let it ignite his own. She couldn't have felt that for Beau, or she never would have been there with *him*. No matter what her parents had alleged that morning about Greta using Shane to teach her movie-star boyfriend a lesson.

"Ten-to-one," Travis continued with a confidence that really grated, "Beauregard Chamberlain is here to rescue our Miss Greta from her impulsive elopement with you before week's end."

Grabbing what was left of his sandwich, Shane ignored the warning. "You're just jealous because you don't have a love life," he retorted grimly.

Besides, risk was something Shane thrived on. He didn't understand—or sanction—ever turning away from it. Because without great risk, there could be no great happiness.

Having temporarily silenced his older brother, Shane turned back to the TV. *Like it or not, Travis is right,* Shane admitted reluctantly to himself. *I might lose Greta before all is said and done,* Shane thought as he continued to study his arch rival on the videotape. It was, after all, a logical conclusion to their hasty involvement with each other. But he damn well would not lose her to him!

"HOW DO YOU KEEP a ring from turning your finger green?" Greta asked her friend Dani Lockhart shortly after noon. Roommates since their college days, first in Dallas and later Los Angeles, the two were as close as family. In fact, in many ways Dani was the sibling Greta had never had.

Dani stepped around the empty packing boxes that cluttered the dance hall. Fresh from L.A., the auburn-haired film critic was wearing a white linen pantsuit, pale green silk shell and delicate Italian sandals. She had a soft leather carry-all thrown casually over one shoulder, and sunglasses perched on her head. "Looks like I hit town just in time." Dani's gray-green eyes sparkled merrily as she neared while at the other end of the hall an electrician and an engineer continued installing the new sound system. "When I heard about you and Shane McCabe this morning, I couldn't believe it."

Greta motioned Dani away from the pounding and drilling. "How did you hear?" Greta went back to sorting out the old Texas license plates, cactus plants, Texas flags, southwestern art, branding irons and other assorted Texas memorabilia that would decorate the walls of her new establishment.

"My sister, Meg." Dani paused to finger framed photos of several recent chili cook-offs. "She had an appointment with your dad at his insurance office this morning. Apparently he's still stunned."

Greta shook her head in silent aggravation. Although she'd only been at work a few hours, she'd already fielded half a dozen phone calls on the subject—to the point she'd had to turn on her answering machine. She could only imagine that, as well known as he was, Shane was having the same experience. At this rate, by sundown there would be no one left in Laramie County who didn't know.

"Although I must say," Dani continued brightly, as Greta climbed the step ladder to reach the foot-wide shelf installed eighteen inches beneath the ceiling around the entire perimeter of the room, "it was smart of you to dump that arrogant lump head, Beauregard Chamberlain."

Greta motioned to the cactus plant in the terra cotta planter. "Hand that up to me, would you please?" As Dani complied, Greta continued, "And that lump head, as you put it, used to be a very good friend of both of ours. You even introduced me to him, remember?"

"What can I say?" Dani lamented with a frown, watching as Greta placed the cactus plant next to a wrought-iron weather vane. "Women tend to get wiser with age. I only wish I'd been wiser a lot sooner."

"You and Beau really ought to call a truce and make up," Greta counseled, knowing there had never been too more hotheaded people on earth.

"I take it that means you haven't dumped him, after all?" Dani asked, clearly disappointed.

Greta pointed to the big book of Texas history with the photo of the Alamo on the front. She smiled as Dani handed it up and at that moment the front door of the dance hall opened and shot in an arc of morning sunshine. "Not as a friend, no, I haven't."

"Well, you should." Dani scowled as Greta situated the book to the left of the weather vane and straightened once again to view her handiwork.

"Can't say I disagree with that," Shane drawled, his

eyes twinkling as he strode up to join them. Standing next to the ladder, he curved a lightly possessive hand around the back of Greta's knee and looked up at her. "Now that you're a married woman."

All too aware his face was nearly at eye level with the hem of her dress, and that all he had to do was look up to see a lot more than she wanted him to see, Greta swiftly climbed down the ladder, with him gallantly assisting her. Once her feet were firmly on the floor, she swung around to face him.

Unsure whether it was excitement or annoyance speeding up her heartbeat, she asked, "Shane, what are you doing here?" She thought they'd agreed to spend the day apart, each of them doing their own thing.

Yet she couldn't deny she was just the tiniest bit glad to see him nevertheless.

Shane nodded at Dani politely then handed Greta a videotape.

Although they'd all been in different grades, the four of them had gone to high school together. Shane had run in a very fast, popular crowd. Dani and Greta had both been on the dance team and the debate team. Greta had made a profession out of dancing. Dani had used her oratory and writing skills to become a much-quoted film critic who worked for the *Dallas Morning News*. Both of them had been somewhat nerdy in high school, only to find themselves blossoming after they left Laramie and hobnobbing with many a celebrity as adults. It was odd, Greta thought, how life worked out sometimes.

"My mom sent this," Shane told Greta with a quietly assessing look. "She thought you might like to see it."

Greta's spirits plummeted as she saw her mother's handwriting on the label. Trying her best to hide her aggravation, she handed it right back to Shane. "I already have. Dozens of times. My parents insist on screening it every time I come home,'' she told him bluntly.

Some emotion she couldn't quite identify flickered in Shane's silver-gray eyes. ''They like Beauregard Chamberlain that much, huh?''

Greta didn't know why, but suddenly she felt as if she were in the midst of some sort of test. A test she was destined to fail. ''No, as a matter of fact, they don't like him at all,'' she returned quietly, puzzling over his strangely subdued mood. ''Although how they formed that opinion, I don't know,'' Greta continued, attempting to insert some levity into the conversation, ''since they've never actually met him.''

Dani selected a miniature oil derrick, moved the ladder slightly to the left and then climbed up to try her hand at arranging the Texas memorabilia.

Shane took Greta's elbow and guided her well out of Dani's way. ''How come you didn't bring him home to meet the folks if it was so serious between the two of you?''

Greta watched Dani a moment, then turned back to Shane. He sounded jealous. To the point he was about to become bossy. She folded her arms in front of her mutinously. ''I never said it was serious between Beau and me.''

''Is that what you call him—Beau?'' Shane demanded. When what he really wanted to ask her, Greta guessed, was if what her parents had asserted that morning—about her marrying Shane to give Beau a wake-up call—was true.

''Yes,'' Greta replied carefully, not about to make it easy for Shane to butt into her personal business, any more than she was going to let her parents, even if he was her "husband" temporarily. "And so do the rest of his friends," she stated unequivocally.

"Ohh sparks!" Dani said as, her mission complete, she climbed back down the stepladder to join them.

Shane and Greta turned to Dani in unison, their aggravation obvious. "Don't you have a movie to watch or review?" Shane asked impatiently.

"Actually, no." Dani grinned at him brightly, reminding Greta there wasn't a man on earth Dani didn't want to provoke in the worst way, and that went triple for Dani's former friend Beauregard Chamberlain.

"Then maybe you'd like to run off and watch this." Shane waved the aforementioned videotape under Dani's nose.

Dani didn't move a muscle. "I've seen it."

At that Shane lifted a skeptical brow, and Greta felt her embarrassment over her parents nonstop bragging about her increase. "It's true, Shane," Dani continued knowingly. "Half the families in town have copies of Greta's Hollywood Moments, courtesy of Greta's folks."

Greta sighed. "Tillie and Bart do go overboard when it comes to me, don't they?"

Dani rolled her eyes in sympathy. "And then some, kiddo. Listen—" Dani paused to glance at her Cartier watch. "I just came over to make sure we're still on for lunch tomorrow."

Greta nodded. "Absolutely."

Dani looked at Shane, then back at Greta. "Honeymoon won't get in the way?" She grinned.

"Not a bit," Greta said, refusing to shoot so much as a glance at Shane.

"Hmm." Dani studied them both. "I hope you two know what you're doing," Dani murmured finally.

So do I, Greta thought, even more urgently.

"Anyway, congrats," Dani leaned forward to hug first Greta and then—somewhat less enthusiastically—Shane. "I don't know what's gotten into you two crazy love-birds—" Dani grinned at them both and shook her head "—but I hope it lasts."

The question was, Greta wondered, did she?

SENSING THE TWO GALS WANTED a moment alone, Shane looked around as Greta walked Dani out. He remembered what the place had been. Once a garment factory that had turned out curtains, the large brick building had been closed for years, since much of that industry had gone overseas.

It had stood empty until Greta had bought it late last spring. Since then, much of the existing interior had been ripped out, the cement floor overlaid with a varnished oak dance floor. The high-beamed ceiling had been exposed, the interior walls painted white. Four raised dining areas, walled off by a rustic split-cedar railing, surrounded a central dance floor. The kitchen was at the rear of the building. To the left of that stood a raised play booth for a DJ or host, complete with state-of-the-art sound system, now currently being installed.

Shane looked around. "Where's the bar?"

"We're not having one. Nor are we serving alcohol," Greta told him.

Shane quirked a brow. All of the dance halls he'd seen had revolved around the liquor they sold. "I wanted a place where people could bring their kids. Have dinner. And dance and have fun. When we really get up and running, I'll have dance lessons here every afternoon for every age group. Luncheon parties. Maybe even wedding receptions. But for now, we'll just be open seven nights a week, from five-thirty till ten Sunday through Thursday, and till midnight Friday and Saturday.''

''Sounds nice.''

''Thanks.'' Greta beamed.

''Place looks nice, too.'' Shane said, impressed and not afraid to show it. ''You've done a heck of a lot with it.''

Greta nodded. As a delivery truck pulled up at the service entrance, she went to the door, braced it open and motioned the delivery man in. ''We've got a ways to go before Saturday night,'' she told Shane.

He watched her sign for a shipment of plantation shutters for the interior windows. ''Nervous about the grand opening?''

Greta smiled and tucked a strand of hair behind her ear. ''A little.''

It was all Shane could do to resist taking her in his arms. A surprise, since by nature he wasn't exactly a warm and fuzzy kind of guy. ''You'll do fine,'' he said firmly.

Greta's pale-blue eyes lit up. ''How do you know?'' Greta asked, drawing herself up to her full height.

''Just a feeling.'' Shane continued to hold her gaze.

The moment drew out. ''Hard to believe we're both back in Laramie, isn't it?'' Greta murmured, after a moment.

Shane nodded, feeling just as momentarily spellbound as she looked. ''But it's time. For me, anyway.''

Greta stepped back to let the deliveryman bring the first of the dozen or so, long, rectangular boxes inside. ''You won't miss the rodeo?''

Shane shook his head. About that he had no regret. ''I got tired of a life lived solely on the road, going from one competition to the next. It was time to call it a day.''

Greta smiled as she showed the deliveryman where she wanted the boxes stacked. "I felt the same way about dancing. As much as I loved it, I got tired of never knowing where or when my next job was going to be. It was time to build more of a future for myself and—" her luscious breasts rose and fell as she let out a wistful sigh "—I really wanted to come back to Laramie, which is why I'm braving the constant interference of my parents."

Shane tore his glance from her tempting curves, returned it to her face. Damn, but she was pretty, he thought, even when she'd bitten off all her lipstick, was covered with some sort of dust and had a pencil stuck in her hair.

He wondered if she knew how well her snug-fitting T-shirt and vest defined her breasts, or how great she looked in a short skirt and cowgirl boots. He wondered if she knew he got a hard-on just looking at her long, sexy legs.

Probably not, given the innocent glimmer in her gaze.

Aware they were supposed to be talking about their parents—and that the deliveryman was headed for them, his dolly packed with another load of boxes, Shane said, "Your folks seem to want a hand in your life as much as mine do. Hopefully, though," Shane paused significantly, "that will change."

Greta rolled her eyes. "One can hope." She looked at Shane. "Anything else?"

Shane nodded and tipped his hat back with one lazy poke of his index finger. "I wanted to tell you I'm headed out to my ranch." He reached into his pocket and gave her a sheet with a hand-drawn map and directions. "I'm buying the old Riley place. Do you know it?"

Greta nodded. "It's not too far from your brother Travis's ranch, is it?"

"No, it's not." Although, after all of Travis's smart remarks that morning—many of which had been right on target—Shane was beginning to rethink that decision, too. "I'm meeting someone from the bank, and we're having a final inspection and appraisal of the place," he continued telling Greta. "If all's in order, the attorneys will meet us out there with the paperwork, and the closing will be held at four this afternoon. I figured—us being married and all—that I better show you around. Gotta keep up appearances you know, at least for a few days, and people would think it odd if you hadn't even seen the place."

Greta chuckled. "People probably think our whole relationship is odd."

Shane laughed softly, too. "You're probably right about that."

Greta took the pencil from her hair and pensively rubbed the eraser end of it across her lower lip, drawing his gaze once again to the pouty pink softness.

Pressure started in the front of his jeans.

"But you don't mind, do you?" Greta said.

Shane shrugged. Willing the flow of blood to dissipate—immediately—he rolled forward on the balls of his feet. And involuntarily became aware just how well someone as tall as Greta fit against his frame. "I stopped caring what people thought about me a long time ago." Shane glanced away briefly, pushing the image of their two bodies, intimately intertwined, from his mind. "Anyway, I thought maybe we could have dinner someplace in town before we went back to Wade's ranch for the night." The more public they were in this relationship of theirs, the better.

As the pounding and drilling started up again, Greta leaned closer. "How much longer are he and Josie going to be gone?" She cupped her hand around her mouth and directed her voice to his ear.

Shane told himself he was unaffected by the warmth of her breath flowing over his skin. He cupped his hand around his mouth, leaned down and spoke directly in her ear, too. "They weren't real specific when they left for their honeymoon, but Wade did promise they'd be back in plenty of time to see my folks renew their marriage vows next week. So meantime we've got the Golden Slipper Ranch to ourselves." And though there were two bedrooms there, Shane couldn't help but hope he and Greta might end up sharing a single bed for an entire night, perhaps even seeing just how potent the chemistry between them was, before the week—and their sham marriage—was through.

Deciding enough was enough, Greta put her hand on his forearm and directed him just outside the Lone Star Dance Hall. The day was sunny and warm, the temperature inching up into the nineties, with nary a hint of breeze at the moment. The sky overhead was a brilliant Texas blue and dotted with fluffy white cumulus clouds.

Her hair sparkling white-gold in the sunlight, Greta regarded him curiously, as light traffic moved by on the Laramie city streets. "You don't want to move our stuff over to your own ranch?" she asked.

Shane wasn't ready to get into that just yet. Better she just see the ranch than he try to explain. He took his sunglasses from his shirt pocket and slid them on. "No," he answered her question succinctly. "I don't." *And when you see my place, you'll know why.* He touched the silky skin of her bare arm lightly. "Anyway,

I'll meet you out at my ranch say about six this evening?''

Greta nodded, obviously curious as to what he wasn't telling her, but cooperative nevertheless. She regarded him determinedly. "You can count on it," she said.

GRETA SLAVED AWAY the rest of the day, her thoughts never far from Shane. There were moments when she could swear he was every bit as attracted to her as she was to him. And moments when she was just as sure she was only a means to an end.

Not that it mattered.

Their marriage wasn't real.

Nor was it ever likely to be.

In fact, when this was all over they probably wouldn't be able to so much as look at each other again without setting all the tongues in Laramie to wagging.

And that was a shame.

Part of her wanted to see how her teenage crush on him would weather a foray into adulthood, if only for a little while....

And the other part knew it was too dangerous a proposition to even contemplate. She knew she couldn't risk mixing up her feelings with her fantasies, or her wishes with hard cold reality. No, it was best to remember this was all a ruse, she told herself sternly. A way to get their parents to sit up and pay attention. And nothing more.

At five-thirty, when the sound engineer and electrician finally left for the day, she closed up the dance hall and headed out to Shane's ranch. As she neared the roadside mailbox marking the entrance to his property, she saw four vehicles turning out of the lane, one right after another. She guessed them to be the previous owners—the two Riley brothers, if memory served correct, two attorneys—one to represent each party, and someone else from the bank. She turned into the lane and drove past pastures grown weedy with neglect. Realizing Shane had his work cut out for him if he wanted to make this rundown ranch something he could be proud of, she continued along the half mile or so to the somewhat dilapidated ranch house and even seedier looking stables. There were two cars in front of the ranch house. Wondering who was still inside with Shane, Greta emerged from the car and dashed up the steps, breezed through the sweltering heat into the open screen door.

Seeing who was with Shane, Greta came to a dead stop.

Shane turned to Greta. "You remember Bonnie Sue Baxter, don't you?"

Chapter Four

It would have been impossible to forget the girl who'd been the most popular girl in school the whole time Greta had been growing up, the girl Shane had dated his last two years of high school, and—if the reports she'd heard were true—for four more after that. Head cheerleader, valedictorian of her class, homecoming queen to Shane's homecoming king; University of Texas, Stanford Law School graduate; Bonnie Sue Baxter had won and enjoyed it all. And still did, judging from the pricey ecru silk sheath she was wearing.

Bonnie Sue turned with a dazzling smile and zeroed in on Greta's paint and dust-smeared denim attire. "Oh!" *I get it,* Bonnie Sue's smile said. "Your cleaning woman is here!"

"Bonnie Sue," Shane's moderately pitched voice carried a warning, "Greta is my wife."

Bonnie Sue looked at Greta down the bridge of her perfect, slender nose. "Surely you jest, Shane," she said drolly, not a hint of her former Texas drawl remaining in her perfectly modulated high-priced-attorney tones.

She already knows, Greta thought, not sure whether she was jealous or just annoyed. *That's why she drove all the way out here.*

Bonnie Sue touched a hand to her chin-length ash brown hair. "I thought you were never going to marry." She looked at Shane steadily. *"Not ever."*

Shane shrugged. His expression was set, his tone uncaring. "Things change."

Unable to resist, Greta culled up what local gossip she knew and said, "Come to think of it, I thought *you* were married, Bonnie Sue. To a lawyer out in San Francisco?" Someone very rich and successful.

Bonnie Sue's eyes turned icy as she pivoted back to Greta. "We're divorced."

Damn. "That I hadn't heard." Greta smiled politely.

Bonnie Sue took a deep breath and turned, putting herself directly between Shane and Greta. "So, Shane," Bonnie Sue began, her back to Greta, "about dinner..."

"Sorry, Bonnie Sue. I already have a date with my wife. Some other time." Shane wrapped an arm around Bonnie Sue's waist and practically pushed her to the door.

Bonnie Sue dug in her heels when she reached the portal. She stepped across the threshhold, then, still standing in the open doorway, turned to face Shane. An even tenser silence ticked out between them. "You call me when you come to your senses, Shane." Bonnie Sue slipped on a pair of movie-star sunglasses. Head held high, nose in the air, she regally made her way to her car.

Shane continued staring after her, visibly upset.

Greta wasn't feeling too calm herself. It had been bad enough competing with Bonnie Sue in high school. She didn't want to do it now. Bonnie Sue was probably just visiting, Greta hoped.

She looked over at Shane, who was busy putting a stack of legal papers in a portable file case. It was easy to see he didn't want to talk about whatever it was that had just gone on. "Sorry. I seem to have interrupted something," Greta murmured when Bonnie Sue had gunned the motor on her Mercedes and driven off.

"Nothing that didn't need interrupting," Shane muttered.

Greta promised herself she would not act jealous or inquire as to the purported reason for the haughty Bonnie Sue's visit. For starters, since Shane wasn't her real husband, just a pretend one for a week or so, it was none of her business. "So did you finish your closing?" she asked, smiling.

Shane nodded, looking happy as could be about that, anyway. "Property's mine, lock, stock and barrel." He reached out and gave the bandanna holding her hastily assembled ponytail in place a playful tug. "Want me to show you around?"

She nodded. "Please." Greta tried not to think what a kid-sister kind of gesture that had been. Or how just being around Bonnie Sue Baxter again had brought back all the uncertainty she'd felt—all the yearning to be part of the popular crowd—when she was in high school. Those days were past. As one day her sham marriage to Shane would be, too. All she had was the present, and that she intended to enjoy.

"I KNOW IT'S NOT MUCH to look at now," Shane said, as he walked her quickly through the rustic, two-story, fieldstone-and-cedar ranch house with the aging roof. The interior was coated with at least twenty years of grime. All the wood floors needed a good scouring and maybe some refinishing after that; the walls needed fresh paper and paint. The appliances in the kitchen were ancient, and the two tiny bathrooms—one up and a half down—were about as appealing as a gas station rest room.

And yet, Greta thought, she saw what he did.

"But it's big," Shane continued.

"And roomy," Greta agreed. In fact, once it was fixed up it was the perfect place to raise a family. She turned to Shane with a smile. "It's going to be great when you get it finished." He grinned at her enthusiasm. Impulsively Greta tucked her arm in his and looked up at him. Maybe allowing Shane to eventually fill the role of her big brother wouldn't be so bad. It was better than having him forget all about her again, anyway. "Want to show me the stables, too?" she asked cheerfully.

"Sure." Shane covered her hand with his and brought her arm in close to his body. They stepped into the shimmering Texas heat and walked across the yard, the back of his arm brushing against hers. Deciding this was a little too cozy, Greta let go of his arm as they stepped into the shadowy interior of the stables. "What kind of horses are you going to have here?"

"Cutting horses. I'm going to breed and train them myself."

Greta remembered how well Shane had ridden a bronc, even back in high school, one hand held high above his head, the other sure and steady on the reins, his body one with the wildly bucking horse. He'd been so athletic, so physically attuned, even then. She could only imagine how good he'd be at it now, after the years of championship rodeo wins under his belt.

Unfortunately the interior of the stables was in as bad shape as the rest of the property.

"Looks like you've got your work cut out for you here, too," Greta said, being careful to hold her breath as much as possible.

Hands braced loosely on his waist, Shane swaggered up and down the length of the barn. "Fine with me." His boots echoed on the cement aisle. "I like the idea of more or less building a place from the bottom up. Anyway—" Shane paused, dug in his pocket, and pulled out two sets of keys "—I figured that as long as we're supposed to be making a go of it, you better have keys to this place, too." He closed the distance between them and pressed one set of keys into the palm of her hand, curling her fingers around them.

Greta looked down at them, stunned. "Are you sure?"

Shane nodded and let go of her hand. "You should keep them however long we're together—it'll help convince our folks we're serious."

Greta struggled not to show how let down she'd really felt. For a moment there she'd foolishly thought his gesture had really meant something. She should have known, like everything else, that it was just another detail of his latest escapade. If there was one thing Shane was good at, it was playing pranks.

Shane ran a hand along the underside of his jaw, which—despite the fact he'd shaved that very morning—was already starting to sport a healthy golden-brown stubble. "I was thinking, maybe we should stop by the hardware store before it closes and pick up some paint samples and wallpaper books, too. You know, to make it really look good."

"Sure," Greta said, feeling her shoulders tense.

"Maybe you could even help me pick out some stuff for the interior of the house," Shane continued enthusiastically. "I'm no good at that, anyway, and I sure as heck don't want my mother doing it for me."

How about Bonnie Sue Baxter then? I bet she'd volunteer for the job in a nanosecond, Greta thought, then immediately chastised herself for her jealousy, which she had no business feeling. "I understand totally," Greta said, struggling for outward calm.

"Then you'll do it?" He searched her eyes.

She nodded, telling herself she could do this without getting emotionally involved. After all, it wasn't as if she was going to be living there forever or something. She was just helping out a friend.

"No problem."

Shane breathed a sigh of relief and swept off his hat. "Thanks."

Silence fell between them as Shane shoved a hand through the rumpled, sun-streaked layers of his hair. Aware he was watching her closely, his own expression inscrutable, she tucked her hands in the pockets of her denim skirt. Telling herself firmly she was not going to think about kissing him again, she took a deep, bolstering breath. Then, considering the unwashed state of the stables, was immediately sorry. Wrinkling her nose up at the decidedly funky smell, she hurried outside and gulped in several breaths of fresh air.

Shane followed, chuckling, the horsey smell of the interior of the stables clearly no problem for him. "Don't worry, kid." He patted her consolingly on the shoulder while she struggled to catch her breath. "That's first on my list of things to start mucking out."

"Good!" Greta said in relief, even as she resented having been called a kid.

She watched as Shane resettled his hat on his head and tugged the brim low over his eyes. "You said you wanted to have dinner somewhere?" *Anything to get them out of here.*

Shane brightened at the reminder and angled his head

at his pickup truck and her car sitting side by side in the drive. "And I know just the place."

"Just the place" turned out to be the Wagon Wheel Restaurant & Grill, the most popular restaurant in Laramie. They'd almost reached the front door of the large, homey establishment when Greta's glance landed on the newspaper stand beside it. "If you don't mind, I'd like to get a newspaper and check to see if my ad ran okay today," Greta said. She wanted the biggest crowd possible at the opening Saturday night. She'd even arranged a ribbon-cutting ceremony with the mayor of Laramie.

Shane backtracked to stand beside her while she searched the bottom of her handbag for two quarters. "No problem."

Greta found what she needed and approached the machine. To her surprise there was nothing behind the glass front. "That's odd." She frowned, perplexed. "There aren't any."

"Sold out? By 7:00 p.m.?" Shance glanced at his watch. "That *is* odd. Usually they have plenty of papers." He touched Greta's arm lightly. "Let me try the stand up the street."

"You don't have to do that," Greta said.

"Now, honey," Shane chucked her under the chin. With barely a glance at the sidewalk behind her, he leaned forward and kissed her on the lips. He drew back slowly and rubbed the moisture from her lips with the pad of his thumb. "What kind of hubby would I be if I let your wishes go unfulfilled?"

Lips tingling, Greta could only stare up at him speechlessly. *Now what had gotten into him?* Before she could ask, Shane had turned and headed for the newspaper stand up the block.

Greta was still watching him and admiring how well he filled out a pair of jeans, when Bonnie Sue Baxter came up to stand beside her. She had an extra-large iced coffee in her hand. "My, you really do have him at your beck and call, don't you?" Bonnie Sue Baxter goaded, animosity radiating from her low voice. She took a long sip of her drink. "I don't ever remember him being that anxious to please me."

To her satisfaction, Greta couldn't say she had, either. Although she also knew the kiss Shane had just given her had probably been more for Bonnie Sue's benefit than for her own.

She wondered what had broken the two of them up. Would Shane tell her? Would it be pathetic of her to ask? Heaven knew she didn't want to come off like Bonnie Sue.

"You must be very pleased with yourself," Bonnie Sue continued, angrily glaring at Greta.

As a gangly kid Greta had never been able to stand up for herself with the girls in the popular crowd when they teased her. As an adult it was a different story. Greta propped her hands on her hips. It was past time she put Bonnie Sue in her place. "What did I do to tick you off?" Greta demanded, perfectly willing to have a showdown with her, then and there, if that's what it took to clear the air.

"For starters?" Bonnie Sue arched one perfectly plucked eyebrow. She drained the rest of her icy drink, then pitched the cup in the trash. "Try showing up in his bed last night. Arranging an audience. Playing the helpless victim. Claiming your reputation was ruined. Twisting his arm to get him to marry you!"

Put that way it did sound calculating. Worse, Greta

couldn't exactly say she was sorry about any of it, especially the eloping and kissing part.

"I think you've got it all wrong, Bonnie Sue," Shane said, as he came up to join them. He looked at Greta, baffled, and spread his hands wide. "No newspapers there, either," he reported.

"I wonder what's going on," Greta said, in reference to the absent newspapers.

"Oh, don't tell me you're going to play innocent there, too," Bonnie Sue Baxter fumed.

For a self-assured attorney, Bonnie Sue sure was acting awfully paranoid, Greta thought. Guess it just went to show how crazy even old love could make you. And Bonnie Sue was still in love with Shane. That was getting more and more clear. "Now I really don't know what you're talking about," Greta said dryly.

"Make that two," Shane drawled.

Bonnie Sue marched back to her car and returned with an evening paper. She slapped it at Shane. "How's that for fulfilling a high school crush?" she demanded.

Shane and Greta looked down at the front page of the *Laramie Press*. Their pictures were plastered side by side beneath the headline:

Local Lovebirds Elope!

National champion rodeo star Shane McCabe surprised everyone when he eloped with local dinner and dance hall proprietor and former high school classmate, Greta Wilson. Greta was last seen on the arm of movie star Beauregard Chamberlain while Shane McCabe has reportedly not dated anyone seriously since his breakup with another former classmate, San Francisco attorney Bonnie Sue Baxter.

Parents of the happy couple are planning a joint wedding reception at John and Lilah McCabe's ranch Friday evening. John and Lilah McCabe, and Bart and Tillie Wilson, want everyone to know the entire community is invited to the celebration.

Shane looked at Greta. Greta looked at Shane. "Did you know about this?" he demanded.

"No," Greta said, equally nonplussed. "Did you?"

Shane shook his head. "I guess we do now, though."

Bonnie Sue leveled an accusing finger at Greta. "I always knew you had a giant-size crush on Shane, Greta Wilson, but this is too much!" she declared hotly.

Shane looked at Greta. Despite herself, she was blushing fiercely. "You really had a crush on me?" he said.

"All through high school!" Bonnie Sue Baxter fumed.

Refusing to deny or confirm it—there was a limit, Greta thought, as to just how much humiliation any one woman could stand in one day—Greta snatched the paper from Shane and stared down at the pictures of them. She was wearing her Dallas Cowboys cheerleader outfit. Shane was in full cowboy regalia, accepting a rodeo award. You didn't get more Texas than that. Or more embarrassing.

Greta tucked the paper under her arm. "I'm going to call my mother!" She marched off.

Shane left Bonnie Sue Baxter where she stood and dashed after her. "I'll call mine, too."

"No need for that!" Bart and Tillie said, as they walked up to join them. They were swiftly followed by John and Lilah McCabe.

It's just one big ol' reunion after another, Greta thought.

"I see you heard about the party," Tillie said happily.

"We were going in to have dinner and plan it right now," Lilah said, motioning at the Wagon Wheel Restaurant.

"Perhaps you and Shane could join us?" John McCabe said, looking steadily at his son.

Bart nodded sternly at Greta. "I think it would be wise."

"IT'S WHAT WE GET," Greta moaned to Shane several hours later, when they'd finally returned to the Golden Slipper Ranch, "for moving back to such a small town."

Shane paused to unlock the front door, then held the door for her. "You don't like being on the front page of the newspaper?"

"As your new bride in what we both know is a sham marriage?" Greta brushed past him and stepped into the darkened interior of the front hall. "I hardly think so."

Shane switched on the lights, then headed straight for the kitchen. He took two beers from the refrigerator, twisted off the caps, handed one to her and kept the other for himself. "I really wish our parents hadn't joined together to throw us this big reception."

Greta sipped the icy golden brew. It was just what she needed after the tense but polite dinner with their parents. "Did you get the feeling they were secretly challenging us?"

"To break down and confess all?" Shane grabbed her hand and led her into the living room. He waited for her to take a seat on the sofa, then dropped down beside her and stretched his long legs out in front of him. "Yep. I did."

Greta lay her head on the back of the sofa and sighed. "So did I."

Shane slanted her an intrigued glance. "But you didn't do it," he said softly, pleased.

Greta took another sip straight from the bottle and held his eyes. "Neither did you."

"Why not?"

Because I don't want it to be over. Greta shrugged. "Call me stubborn," she said lightly.

"Guess so," Shane allowed.

The seconds ticked by. Suddenly all Greta could think about was kissing him again. And this time not for show.

Shane swallowed, tensed, took another swig of beer, looked away. "I don't know about you, but I'm exhausted."

Greta tried not to be hurt by his abrupt change of mood. Or the switch from intimacy to tension. "Me, too," she said softly.

Shane stood and began to pace the room restlessly. "Want to call it a night?" he asked.

Greta nodded. It was safer that way.

"I'll give you first shot at the bathroom," Shane continued.

"Thanks."

Greta showered, changed into a cotton nightshirt and told herself to be thankful there would evidently be no more kissing or talking or laughing that night.

She'd just belted her robe on when there was a commotion—Shane's voice and what sounded like a helicopter landing!—outside. "Now what?" Greta groaned, almost afraid to look. Hastily wrapping her damp hair in a towel, she emerged from the bathroom, strode down the hall to the head of the stairs. She was just in time to see Wade McCabe and his new bride, Josie, loaded down with suitcases, coming in the front door.

SHANE DIDN'T KNOW whether he was happy or sad to see his brother. The good thing was that he and Greta were no longer alone. The bad thing was that he and Greta were no longer alone. He strode forward to help them with their bags, setting them down just left of the front door. Straightening, Shane gave Josie and Wade a proper welcome home.

"I didn't think you'd be back," Shane said, hugging them both.

Wade grinned and slapped Shane on the back. "I didn't think you'd be married when we got back."

Shane did his best to suppress his chagrin. "You heard?"

"Who hasn't?" Josie said, kissing his cheek. "It's on the national news."

"What!" Shane exclaimed as Greta came down the stairs to greet them, too.

Wade shrugged and offered Greta a warm, brotherly hug. "You can't be that surprised. I mean, Greta dumped one of the hottest movie stars in the country for you, Shane. Of course that's news."

"Not to mention the fact that Shane is something of a celebrity in his own right," Josie added, as she strode forward to hug Greta, too. "Which makes it quite a love triangle."

"Make that quadrangle," Greta muttered. She was obviously thinking of Bonnie Sue Baxter.

"Yeah, we heard Bonnie Sue's back, too," Wade said as he wrapped both his arms around Josie's waist and tugged her against him. "Apparently she told half the town—before she even hit Laramie yesterday—that she'd made a mistake, giving you the heave-ho, and she'd decided to give you another chance. To say she now has egg on her face—'' Wade stopped and shook his head. *You're in for it now, buddy,* his look said.

And knowing Bonnie Sue, Shane thought, Wade was probably right.

Immediately Greta turned to Shane. ''Did you know about this?''

Shane tensed, not sure how much he should tell Greta about what Bonnie Sue had said to him earlier. Or his own feelings on the matter. Besides, Greta was acting kind of jealous. And he liked that. For reasons that had nothing to do with the playacting going on between them.

''Maybe we should let them discuss this on their own,'' Wade said.

''I'm ready for bed, in any case,'' Josie teased as she turned to Wade and kissed him thoroughly.

Wade swung Josie up in his arms and headed for the stairs. ''See you guys in the morning.''

There was no doubt what they had on their minds. Given that, Shane called after Wade and Josie. ''Your hospitality has been great, but maybe we should leave, give you newlyweds some privacy.''

Unfortunately for them, Wade was not about to be so inhospitable as to kick his baby brother and his new wife out on the street. ''Hey, it's no problem. Really,'' Wade reassured them.

Sensing their hesitation, Wade continued in the same warm, brotherly tone, ''We're both married.'' It was easy to see in Wade's view, a little passion was nothing to be ashamed about. And if the situation were a bit more normal, Shane would have agreed.

''Josie and I'll take the master bedroom. You and Greta take the guest room. It'll work out fine. Unless—'' Wade paused, Josie still cradled lovingly in his arms, and studied their stricken, uneasy expressions, "—there really is something fishy going on here, as Mom and Dad suspect?"

"THAT," GRETA TOLD SHANE breathlessly, seconds later as he shut their bedroom door with his foot, traversed the room gracefully and set her down, ever so gently, in the rumpled covers on the double bed, "was going overboard." Even if it had gotten a lot of laughs!

"What?" Shane dropped down onto the bed and stretched out beside her, a picture of lazy male assurance.

"You know what!" Greta retorted hotly. "Grabbing me behind the knees, lifting me off my feet, throwing me over your shoulder like a duffel bag and carrying me up the stairs."

Shane's eyes twinkled mischievously. "We are on our honeymoon," he teased.

Determined not to let him wiggle out of this so easily, Greta grabbed the front of his shirt and kept him from exiting the bed. "Sure you weren't just competing with your older brother and his bride?" she demanded, because she didn't want to think what had happened between the two of them had anything remotely to do with Shane's two middle brothers' recent, hasty, but oh-so-romantic marriages to the women of their dreams.

Shane's eyes darkened with an emotion Greta couldn't quite identify. He cupped her face between his hands. "Maybe I carried you differently from the way Wade carried Josie just to put my own individual stamp on things. But as for the rest—what I do, I do for me." That said, he extricated her hands from the front of his shirt. He brought one of her hands to his lips and kissed the back of it. Greta was still tingling long after he released her, straightened and strode across the room to the door. He stuck his head out and peered into the hall. "Bathroom's free," he reported. "I'm going to hit the shower."

Before Greta could say anything else, he slipped out the door, shutting it behind him.

Greta sighed and shut her eyes. Was she really going to be forced to share this cozy double bed with Shane tonight? It appeared so. Not that she feared Shane would not respect whatever boundaries she set. No, she knew that despite his wild nature and unbridled thirst for adventure, he was a gentleman at heart. One "No way, cowboy!" from her, and that would be the end of it.

The question was, did she really want to say no?

Because Bonnie Sue Baxter had been right. Growing up, Greta—like most every other girl at Laramie High School—had suffered one heck of a schoolgirl crush on Shane McCabe. More than his sexy, come-hither cowboy looks, she'd been in love with his daredevil nature, how, even then he'd lived his life to the max, no matter what anyone else had thought or wanted for him. Always the first to stand up against unfair authority of any kind, he took on their childhood bullies as fearlessly as he climbed on the back of the wild broncs in the junior rodeo. Quick with jokes that never failed to get a laugh, incessantly flirting, always playing pranks, pulling stunts and thinking up escapades, he had a bad-boy rep unparalleled in their small town. And yet, everyone knew there beat a heart as good as gold beneath all the grandstanding.

She'd shaken her head at him. She'd admired him. She'd lusted after him with all her heart and soul. And hoped, in many ways, to grow up one day to be just like him.

And now, here she was, she thought dreamily, married to the man she had measured everyone else against.

Shane breezed back in, a damp towel draped around his waist, his tall, toned body glistening, his hair wet and scented with shampoo. Greta's heart began to pound as she vaulted to a sitting position and thought about what had gone on between them the night before, under almost precisely the same circumstances. With her body already tingling in anticipation, another kiss was not something she could afford. Nor could she guarantee things would end with a simple kiss. "Shane McCabe, you tell me," she demanded, "that you have something on beneath that towel."

Grinning wickedly, Shane reached over and switched off the light. The covers lifted, and he slipped beneath the sheets. "Sorry, but—" she felt rather than saw him roll over onto his back "—this is how I sleep."

Greta's eyes gradually adjusted to the darkness. "In the buff?"

"You could, too." Shane chuckled softly as he burrowed down into the mattress. "I wouldn't mind."

"I just bet you wouldn't," Greta huffed, bristling at the unbridled lust—not love—in his voice. Honestly, she didn't know why she had ever thought—for one wild and crazy second—his bad-boy antics were attractive!

Greta pounded her pillow and rolled onto her side, facing away from him—as far as she could go without falling off the edge of the bed. "Mad at me, aren't you?" Shane asked.

"What do you think?" Greta grumbled back as she struggled to get comfortable once again.

Shane stretched lazily, taking up even more of the bed, his brawny hair-roughened leg coming into contact with hers from the tip of her toes to the curve of her hips. "I think if you don't calm down, it's going to be a long night," he said.

That did it! Greta threw back the covers on her side, bounded out of the bed and whipped around to turn on the bedside light once again. She stood over him, hands on her hips, hating the fact he looked so damn sexy. "What happens if I insist you put on a pair of pajamas?"

Shane shaded his eyes with a hand turned palm-out. "Don't own any."

Refusing to give up, Greta insisted, "Jeans then."

He taunted her with an impudent smile and predicted, "You'd lose."

Greta fixed him with a withering stare. "Boxers."

Shane shrugged and kept his eyes firmly on hers. "Don't own any of those, either."

"Briefs?"

"You're getting warm." Shane winked. "But if I wore briefs—" Shane angled a thumb at his chest "—*I* wouldn't be able to sleep."

Greta shook her head in indignation. "Then that would be your problem, wouldn't it?"

"Considering how small this bed is," Shane said, his heated glance roving over her from head to toe before settling back on her face, "it would be *our* problem."

Greta rolled her eyes and gave up. Deciding she had wasted enough time arguing with him when she should be sleeping, she left the bedside lamp on and stomped back over to her side of the bed. "Fine," she snapped, waggling a censuring finger at him. "Just keep your…your—"

"Toes?" Shane queried with an innocence that set her teeth on edge.

"—on your side."

Shane saluted her mockingly. "Will do."

"And Shane?"

"Hmm?" Gallantly he held back the covers for her and tried not to think how sexy she looked in the thigh-length cotton nightshirt.

She ripped the covers out of his hand and covered herself to her chin. "I'm paying you back for this. I swear it."

AN HOUR LATER, a still-fuming Greta had finally drifted off to sleep. Shane had switched off the bedside lamp again and was still wide awake. He knew Greta thought he'd come to bed the way he had because he was hoping she'd let him take advantage of the situation and her. When the truth was he hadn't worn briefs because it wasn't his habit to wear anything to bed. And that being the case, he hadn't thought to take any clean ones into the bathroom with him. By the time he'd remembered, he'd already been standing under the spray, scrubbing himself from head to toe. His situation set, he'd been curious about what her reaction would be if he again came to bed in the buff.

Now he knew.

She'd been furious. As well as aroused.

He could've remedied the situation in an instant, of course, by putting something—anything—on, but he hadn't. Maybe because he knew, given the lusty state his body was in, that it was just as well she was mad at him. The last thing they needed was to consummate this temporary marriage of theirs. When it was plain to see that, deep down, she was as sweet and innocent as he was cynical. When it was easy to see that his new bride was not the kind of woman who would take lovemaking lightly.

And if she weren't mad at him, they might lie here

whispering in the dark. One thing could lead to another. Before they knew it, they might be sharing another kiss. And then maybe another, and perhaps a touch or two, and who the heck knew what would happen after that?

No, Shane decided firmly. The two of them had an agenda here. To teach their parents a lesson about meddling in their love lives. Meantime they did not need to be mistaking lust for love or a blossoming friendship for the kind of lifelong compatibility lasting marriages were based on. She needed to stay on her side of the bed—which she was—and he needed to stay on his. That was the best way—the only way—to handle this.

Chapter Five

Shane wasn't sure what time he fell asleep, but he woke at dawn with an enormous feeling of well-being. He was lying on his back in the center of the cozy double bed. Greta was curled up beside him. One of her long, silky thighs lay across his, and she had her head on his chest, her arm draped around his waist, her palm flattened on his lower abdomen. It was obvious by the deep, slow meter of her breathing and the rhythmic rise and fall of her soft, curvaceous breasts that she was sound asleep. Just as it became very clear, very quickly, that his body was most definitely not. In fact, as she cuddled closer, rubbing the silk of her hair and face against his skin, and her fingers inched even lower, his body was wide awake and raring to go.

The pulse of his yearning picking up as steadily as his heartbeat; he wanted nothing more than to turn her onto her back, lower his lips to hers and make her his. Right here. Right now. But he couldn't do that, and because he couldn't, he decided he had to get up and get going before she awoke and realized how aroused he was. Ever so carefully Shane eased his arm from beneath her head. Before he could scoot over, Greta started sleepily. She opened her eyes. Focusing on him, she smiled drowsily, dropped her head back to his chest and cuddled even closer.

Shane's lower half jumped alertly. Before he could stop it, his arousal brushed the edge of her hand. Greta sighed and snuggled closer still, her palm closing over the most heated part of him. This time he couldn't help it. He did let out a low, tortured groan.

Greta's eyes opened again. She looked at him curiously, struggling to understand—as she woke—where she was and what she was doing. She blinked, clearly not understanding what her head was doing on his chest. "How did I—we—" she murmured slowly. Focusing on his pained expression, realizing what she now cradled gently in her hand, she gasped in mortification and promptly released him.

Too late, Shane thought with no small trace of irony. He was aching like a teenager. The hint of a smile tugged at the corners of his lips as he looked her up and down. "I don't know about you, but that sure as shootin' woke me up," he drawled as Greta vaulted to a sitting position and scrambled to the far edge of the bed.

Face flaming, she pressed a hand to her breasts. "Mercy!" she exclaimed.

Unable to help himself from touching her again, Shane shifted a strand of hair away from her face. "I wish you'd had some," Shane drawled, wondering how he was ever going to get his body to relax enough to be able to get out of this bed. One thing was certain, he wasn't going anywhere right away.

"I was dreaming!" Greta explained as she shoved a hand through her wildly tousled blond curls.

Looking at the state of her nipples—which were pearled beneath the soft, clinging cotton of her nightshirt—it was easy to see what she'd been dreaming about. "Trust me." His lower half still throbbing, Shane continued, "What you were doing to me, was no dream."

"Don't blame me!" Greta's lower lip shot out petulantly, and she turned her glance away. "It wouldn't have happened if you'd worn some type of clothing to bed."

"Oh, I don't know about that." Shane clasped her shoulders, crowding her and forcing her to face him. "Cuddly thing that you are, you probably would've found a way to snuggle up. And let me tell you, nothing I had on would have stopped this—" he indicated his erection beneath the sheets "—if your hand was curled around me like that."

Color flooding her cheeks, Greta pushed his hands away, got up and grabbed her robe. She slipped it on and belted it with trembling fingers. "We can't sleep here again tonight," she declared.

Shane knew he was going to be aching all day and then some. "I agree." Aware he'd never wanted a woman the way he wanted Greta now, he looked at her steadily. "Tonight, we're sleeping at my ranch."

GRETA DIDN'T CLARIFY their future living-and-sleeping arrangements with Shane then, because she didn't want to take a chance on waking Wade and Josie, who, after being up half the night "honeymooning," were still sound asleep. So she left the bedroom and tiptoed to the bathroom, where she quickly pulled herself together and got ready to go to work. By the time she was dressed and had packed up her small bag of belongings, Shane was downstairs, waiting and pacing.

He grabbed her bag for her, and wordlessly they left the house.

Shane tossed her bag into the back but stopped her, a hand on her shoulder, before she could get in her car. "We need to talk."

Did they? Was there anything he could say that would erase the memory of the way he'd felt, all hot and velvety, in her hand? Was there anything that could erase the melting feeling of need deep inside her? He took her into the warm, strong cradle of his arms. "We'll have breakfast in town," Shane continued, as if the matter were already decided.

Greta shook her head as her hands came up to splay across his chest. "I haven't got time for that. I've got a ton of deliveries coming, and they're putting up the window coverings this morning." She put up a hand before he could say anything else. "It'll have to be later." When she'd had more time to compose herself and figure out how to handle this. "Say this evening."

He leaned forward, gave her an all-too-brief, all-too-casual kiss on the lips, then stepped back and looked at her in a way that made her heart skip a beat. "You're not always going to get your own way with me, you know," he said.

Trembling at the proprietary promise she saw in his gray eyes, Greta pushed away from him. "But I will this morning." She jumped in her car, shouted a breezy, "See you!" started the engine and drove away. She had the whole day to figure out how to somehow take charge of this situation. Meanwhile, she had a business to run.

Thirty minutes later Greta entered the dance hall. Five minutes after that her father popped in with a stack of insurance papers to sign. "I thought we were going to do this at four o'clock," Greta said as she kissed Bart hello and ushered him inside, then set about making a pot of coffee in the commercial kitchen. While it brewed, she led her father back to the closest dining area.

Bart held her chair for her, then sat down at the table opposite her. "We were, but I saw your car when I was driving past and figured I'd go ahead and bring them by, get them out of the way." Briefly they discussed the coverage Greta had asked her father's insurance company to provide. Agreeing all was in order, Greta signed everywhere she was supposed to sign and wrote a check to cover the first six months.

Bakery box in hand, Shane walked in the front door. He grinned at his new father-in-law and carried the aromatic goodies over to the table. "You're just in time. I've got two kinds of muffins and three kinds of donuts."

"Works for me."

It was all Greta could do not to scowl at Shane. He was not supposed to be kissing up to her father or trying to win his approval—just the opposite! "If you keep this up, they'll never want us to get an annulment," she whispered to Shane as the two of them went back to the kitchen to gather up some plates, napkins and coffee cups.

"Oh, don't get your knickers in a knot," Shane said right back, leaning over her so he could speak seductively in her ear. "It's just breakfast."

Greta blew out an aggravated breath. "I told you I didn't have time!" she hissed.

Shane braced his arms on either side of her and leaned in even closer. "And I told you we had to talk!"

Bart stuck his head around the corner. "Need any help?" he asked jovially, studying them shrewdly all the while.

Greta forced a smile as Shane wrapped a possessive

arm about her shoulders. "No, Dad, we're fine." Determined to maintain as much physical distance between them as possible, Greta squeezed Shane's hand, then stepped out of reach and went back to pouring the coffee.

Shane looked back at Bart. "I was just telling Greta I've got to go to San Angelo to take a look at a horse I'm thinking of buying and to purchase a pressure washer for the stables, and as long as I'm there, I thought I'd buy some furniture for the ranch house."

Greta understood why he wanted to combine the three activities. There were no furniture stores in Laramie. He could order a big-ticket item like a pressure cleaner from the local hardware store, but he'd have to wait to have it shipped. In San Angelo, he could buy a pressure cleaner, even some furniture, and possibly take both home with him the same day.

Shane looked at Greta steadily as she handed him a steaming mug. "I thought you might like to go with me and pick out the bare essentials."

Meaning what? Greta wondered. A bed? She arched a brow, not sure whether she was surprised or pleased by his persistence, just knowing she was surprised. "Today?"

Shane leaned negligently against the long, stainless steel counter and shrugged his broad shoulders affably. Like her, he was keeping up an oh-so-casual demeanor. "We've gotta have somewhere to sleep tonight—unless you want to camp out on the floor."

Greta didn't even want to think about sleeping with him again. Last night and this morning had been disturbing enough, throwing her senses into a turmoil she'd be weeks, maybe even months, recovering from.

"I could have you back here around lunchtime. Maybe a little later," Shane promised.

"Trust me on this. You won't be happy with what he gets unless you have a say in it, honey," Bart said as Greta handed him his coffee.

That would have been true if she actually planned on living there for more than a week or so, but since she didn't, Greta didn't really feel she had any right to say anything about what kind of furniture Shane wanted. Greta stirred cream and sugar into her coffee. "I'm sure whatever Shane picks out will be fine."

"You don't want to go with me, then?" Shane asked, studying the coffeemaker with more than necessary care.

Greta shook her head. To her dismay both men looked disappointed.

"Well, I better get a move on then," Shane drained the rest of his coffee in one gulp and set his mug back on the counter.

"Aren't you going to stay and have some breakfast?" Greta asked, thinking of the array of baked goods he'd brought.

Shane shook his head. "I'll grab something on the road. See you tonight."

Greta struggled between guilt and relief. She continued to eye him coolly. "What time?"

Shane shrugged, remote now. "I don't know. Late afternoon, maybe suppertime."

Shane said goodbye to Bart, gave Greta a husbandly kiss on the cheek and hugged her, then headed out the door.

"You should have gone with him, honey," Bart said as soon as Shane had left.

Greta knew she'd hurt Shane, brushing him off that way. Even if she was only doing what she was supposed to do—which was prove to everyone once and for all that she and Shane were not suited for each other. Tearing her eyes from Shane's handsome shoulders and sexy stride, Greta turned back to Bart. "Dad—"

"He's trying to make a home for the two of you. He deserves your help."

He deserved something all right, for putting me on the spot like that. "And I'll do what I can," Greta promised. Short of actually being a wife. Or sleeping in the same bed with him again. Or having hot, wild, sex with him. Or falling head over heels in love with him.

Bart regarded her with fatherly concern. "Look, honey, I wouldn't have advised you to enter into this hasty marriage, but now that you have, you owe it to Shane to be the best wife you can possibly be."

"YOUR FATHER TOLD ME what happened," Tillie said a scant half hour later.

Greta directed the two men carrying the plantation shutters into the dance hall to stack them beneath the windows where they were going to be put up. Another two workers were busy installing the hardware that would hold the window coverings in place. Greta waved her mother away from all the activity and put her hands over her ears to shut out the sound of the electric drills and screwdrivers. "Mom, really, this isn't a good time."

"Then when would be?" Tillie followed Greta into the dance hall kitchen, which was in an equal state of chaotic disarray, with boxes stacked everywhere. " I hate to say it, Greta, but maybe you should delay opening your dinner and dance hall for another few weeks, until you've got your home set up."

Greta slit open a box and began unwrapping stainless steel baking pans and piling them on the counter. "According to Lilah the ranch house is as filthy as can be and has absolutely no furniture,'' Tillie continued.

Finished, Greta folded up the empty box and put it in a stack for recycling. ''Shane's fixing that, Mom. He's buying some furniture this morning.''

Tillie followed Greta to the next box and continued to stand over her. ''What about cleaning the place?''

Greta shuddered at the memory of those bathrooms that had not been cleaned in a very very long time. ''I'll get to it when I can, Mom.'' *And until then,* a little voice said, *what are you going to do about taking a shower?* ''Maybe we can check into a hotel or something.''

''Greta, for heaven's sake!''

Greta lifted out sauté pans and began stacking them on the counter. ''Well, what do you expect?'' she asked impatiently.

Agitated, Tillie began lending a hand, too. ''Do you want to hang on to this man or not?''

Greta reached for a third box. This one contained glassware. ''What kind of question is that to ask?'' she demanded.

''A valid one.'' Silence fell between Greta and her mother as the tension of years past reasserted itself.

''I talked to Bonnie Sue Baxter last night. Let me tell you, she has not given up on getting him back,'' Tillie reported as she emptied and collapsed the third box.

Greta picked up wads of packing paper and carried it over to the box designated for that. ''What they had was over a long time ago,'' Greta said stubbornly.

''But will it stay over,'' Tillie returned, ''with you acting like anything but a wife?''

Leave it to her mother to make her feel no matter what she'd done, it wasn't enough. Exasperated, Greta deposited the packing paper and ran her hands through her hair. "Mom, I'm doing the best I can—"

"I know, honey, it's just sometimes you're not competitive enough."

And Shane was too competitive, Greta thought, recalling how Shane had hauled her up the stairs, honeymoon-style chez Shane, just to keep up with Wade.

"But you know what they say—" Tillie patted Greta's shoulder comfortingly "—opposites attract."

Or, in her and Shane's case, lit each other up like fuses on sticks of dynamite, Greta thought to herself as she stormed back to tackle another box of cooking utensils.

"So maybe your marriage to Shane will work out after all," Tillie continued helpfully.

This was a vote of confidence? A delivery truck pulled up at the rear of the building. Greta propped the door open and tried not to show her relief at the interruption. "Listen, thanks for stopping by, Mom. I appreciate the concern."

"You think about what I said, honey."

"I will," Greta promised, more to get her mother out the door than anything else.

"A man's ranch should be his castle," Tillie continued.

And if Greta couldn't—wouldn't—provide that, wasn't that even more reason for them to get an annulment at the end of the week? Greta grinned as she waved the deliveryman in. Unwittingly her mother had just given her—and Shane—the beginning of a way out.

GRETA WAS BUSY emptying one of two big commercial dishwashers when the back door opened. As a flood of late-afternoon sunlight spilled into the room, she turned and saw Beau Chamberlain stride in. He whipped off his movie-star sunglasses and gave her his trademark grin. "Aren't you a sight for sore eyes!"

"Beau!" Greta hopped down from the step stool she'd been standing on.

"How are you, kiddo?" Beau closed the distance between them and wrapped Greta in a big bear hug.

Greta welcomed the rugged ex-Texan with the black hair and the bedroom eyes like the big brother she'd always wanted but had never had until he'd come into her life several years before. "Come to see me or the dance hall?" she teased.

"How about a little of both," Beau quipped. He looked around appreciatively at the long stainless steel prep counters, commercial stoves and ovens, and walk-in refrigerator-freezer—none of which had been installed the last time he'd visited, several weeks prior. "Hey, it's really shaping up." He admired the whitewashed walls and terra-cotta floor. "Though you look a little worse for wear." Beau plucked a piece of clear tape out of her hair.

Greta wrinkled her nose and swatted his hand away. She'd been unpacking brand-new dishes, systematically running them through the dishwashers so they could be used and then putting them away, since early morning. "It's been a long day." Forty-eight boxes worth, to be exact, but it had needed to be done, and the sooner the better.

"A long couple of days from what I hear," Beau said.

Although it looked as if Beau was a man who had everything, Greta knew he was still reeling from an ugly, bitter divorce and a complete absence of privacy in his personal life. Hence, if anyone would understand what was going on with her, it would be him.

"You heard, hmm?" Aware she still had four boxes of dishes left to unpack and run through the dishwasher, Greta went back to stacking clean dishes on the open wood shelves above the counters.

"That I'd lost the love of my life? My publicist has been getting calls nonstop. There's more interest in your elopement than my new movie."

"How's that coming, by the way?" She knew he'd been in Mexico.

"I'm still scouting locations." Never one to stand around idle for long, Beau pitched in to help. "Hopefully we'll find something soon."

"Good luck," Greta said sincerely. Finished, they went back to the boxes that were left.

"So you want to tell me about the fella that gave you such a charming ring?" Beau asked as Greta sliced through the packing tape.

"No." Greta opened the flaps.

"Not even so my publicist can announce the terms of your marriage far and wide?" Beau teased as they began removing dozens of stoneware coffee cups and stacking them right in the dishwasher.

"Oh, Beau. It's such a mess." Briefly Greta explained how and why her marriage to Shane had come about.

Beau whistled. "And I thought my life was complicated." Silence fell as he folded up and carted off the box they'd emptied, and brought over another. The two looked at each other. "Tell me all this excitement isn't going to interfere with the deal you and I have going," Beau said.

Greta made a face. As much as she hated to let Beau down. "It already is," she admitted reluctantly. Then explained, "I've got people advising me how to make this marriage succeed every time I turn around."

"And you don't want it to succeed," Beau guessed.

Having filled the dishwasher to capacity, Greta put in some soap, shut and locked the door and switched it on. "I want a way out." *Before I get sucked into the fantasy of it all and start believing I can really have Shane in my life as my husband.*

"Your exit plan is no good?"

Greta sighed. She leaned against the counter, folding her arms in front of her. "Shane and I thought there'd be more resistance. That our folks would be clamoring for us to get the marriage annulled."

"And they're not."

Greta shook her head slowly. "With the exception of Shane's ex-girlfriend, no."

Beau's eyes sparkled, reminding Greta there was nothing he liked better than a good yarn. "This *is* getting complicated."

"Tell me about it." Greta sighed.

Beau stroked his jaw thoughtfully. "You still want me here Saturday night?"

"Yes. Absolutely." He was so much a part of it it was only right he be there. "Of course," Greta cautioned, "I'm not telling anyone you'll be here."

"I understand," Beau said grimly. "We don't want this turning into a Beauregard Chamberlain Fan Club event."

Greta rolled her eyes, knowing how crazy women could be when they saw Beau in person. "Exactly."

Dependable as always, practical down to his soles, Beau opened his arms, and Greta went into them for a much-needed, brotherly hug. "Well, you let me know," Beau said softly, patting her on the shoulder, "anything you need, hon, anything at all—"

"Greta will get from me," Shane said.

GRETA AND BEAU TURNED IN unison to see Shane standing in the doorway. He looked hot, dusty and tired. And more than a little provoked to see his "wife" in her former "boyfriend's" arms. "Shane," she said. Self-consciously, Greta struggled to extricate herself from Beau's arms. "You're back!"

"So it would seem." Without warning, Shane grabbed Greta, pulled her into his arms, and gave her one humdinger of a kiss hello. It didn't last long, but it had her tingling from her head to her toes. The romantic aura was muted, however, by the knowledge the gesture was all for show.

Head spinning, she watched him draw back, and she asked, "Did you get the pressure cleaner for the stables?"

"As well as a bed."

Greta flushed, aware she'd just sounded—unsettlingly—like a wife.

Beau strode forward, as curious about Shane as Shane was about him. He introduced himself casually and extended a hand. "You must be Greta's new husband," Beau said as they shook.

Shane nodded and asked with a graciousness that was strictly man to man. "What brings you to town?"

Beau looked at Greta. "Two reasons. I heard about the marriage, and I wanted to see how this place was shaping up for the grand opening Saturday night."

Feeling increasingly uncomfortable almost as if she were caught between the two men—which was ridiculous, since neither of them had any claim on her at all—Greta looked around briefly. "As you can see it's coming along great."

Beau grinned at their surroundings appreciatively, his

personal stake in her business apparent. "Yeah, I'd have to say so, too."

Shane studied his competition with an experienced eye. "You in town for long?"

Beau shook his head. "Unfortunately, no. I've got an appointment to scout out a location for a film later this evening." He glanced at his watch. "In fact, I better get a move on if I don't want to be late."

Abruptly Shane looked as if he couldn't wait to be rid of Beau and alone with Greta. "Well, don't let us keep you," Shane drawled, lacing a possessive arm around Greta's waist.

Beau looked at the way Shane was holding her close, and Greta knew exactly what Beau was thinking—that she had her hands full when it came to Shane McCabe. And Beau was right! From his nocturnal attire to his unexpected kisses, Shane had a way of perpetually throwing her off balance.

Beau nodded at Shane. "Nice meeting you." Then turned to Greta. "You call me if you need me. I'm here for you anytime." His words were laced with meaning.

"I know," Greta replied softly.

Beau slid his movie-star sunglasses back on and exited the building.

The moment he departed Shane let go of Greta as suddenly as if she had burned him, which in turn confirmed the fact that his possessiveness had been all for show. She did her best to conceal her hurt. The ruse they'd concocted had been for their parents, not for Beau, and darn it all, Shane knew it!

"That was really rude, Shane!" Greta sputtered. He couldn't have made Beau feel less welcome had he tried.

"And you're surprised?" Shane lifted a coolly discerning brow.

"Yes, as a matter of fact I am," Greta stormed right back. "I've known you to be a lot of things but rude isn't one of them!" It would have been nice if Shane and Beau could have been friends.

"Listen to me, Greta." Shane grabbed her by the shoulders and hauled her so close their bodies collided. "I've been cuckolded once! It damn well isn't going to happen again."

Chapter Six

Shane regretted the words the instant they were out, but it was too late to take them back.

Her pretty eyes alight with curiosity, Greta demanded, "Are you talking about Bonnie Sue?"

"Yes." Shane snapped as he released Greta and stepped back. Sympathy was not what he wanted from her. Pivoting on his heel, he headed for the main room. Greta followed him out of the kitchen, her footsteps echoing across the polished wood dance floor.

Glad to see all the workmen had left for the day—he didn't need any more witnesses to the slip of his tongue—Shane headed for the DJ booth and the newly installed sound system. He punched the button to turn it on. Immediately the room was filled with a rhythmic beat—the country blend of acoustic, electric and steel guitars and the sweet sounds of Trisha Yearwood singing "I Don't Fall in Love So Easy." The melancholy lyrics and foot-tapping melody matched his mood perfectly.

Shane vaulted down the steps, took Greta by the waist, and propelled her onto the center of the dance floor. He began a Texas two-step, hoping she'd forget all about what he'd just said. Which was, as it turned out, about as likely as a coat on a bull.

"I never heard anything about that!" she continued doggedly, kicking up her heels.

Unable to help admiring the graceful way she moved, the way she managed to hold her own in his arms, while at the same time letting him lead, Shane muttered bitterly, "That's because I never told anyone." It had been humiliating to discover that despite all the girls and rodeo groupies chasing him over the years, the one woman he'd pledged his heart to back then, had—in the end— not found him man enough to hold her.

"Not even your family?" Greta asked gently, as the first song faded and another slower one followed.

"No." Because the song demanded it, Shane pulled her close, so she was tightly alligned with him from breast to thigh.

"Why not?"

Shane buried his face in the fragrant softness of her hair and breathed deeply. "Because I didn't want to hear the inevitable I told you so's."

Obviously enjoying their dancing as much as he was, Greta let her head fall to his shoulder. "They saw something like this coming?"

Shane shrugged. "Although everyone liked Bonnie Sue well enough, my family never thought Bonnie Sue and I were right for each other in the long run." It had galled him to learn after nearly six years of dating her, of being faithful despite the many separations the two of them had endured, that his family had been right all along in their estimation of the situation.

Greta stopped dancing and looked up at him. "What happened?"

Suddenly Shane needed to unburden himself to someone. Taking her by the hand, he led her up the stairs to the sound booth. They sat down in the two comfortable swivel chairs behind the console. The music providing a comfortable backdrop, he turned the volume down slightly and began adjusting the ratio of bass to treble. "Bonnie Sue had this guy friend at UT. They were both prelaw and met as undergrads. She and Clint used to study together all the time. They were always talking law. When I was off on the rodeo circuit, he escorted her to sorority parties. She said he was like a brother to her, and I bought it hook, line and sinker."

"But then all that changed."

Shane nodded and swung his chair around so they were suddenly sitting knee to knee. "Her senior year. I showed up at UT to visit her unexpectedly." Shane took her hands in his and held them lightly, his thumbs absently stroking the silky insides of her wrists. "She was living in an apartment at that time. I had a key. When no one answered, I walked in, and caught them in bed together."

Greta's slender fingers tightened on his. "Oh, Shane." There was a wealth of understanding in those two words.

"She swore it didn't mean anything—that she was in love with me. Not him. She'd just been so lonely, with me gone for weeks at a time on the circuit," Shane swallowed hard, the humiliation and betrayal he'd felt then coming back at him full bore.

Loneliness was one thing. Infidelity another. "So you broke up. And she went off to Stanford Law School with him."

Shane nodded and turned back to the stacks of CDs on the DJ desk. "They married when they graduated." He'd been invited—but there was no way in hell he'd wanted to attend.

"And now they're getting a divorce because Clint cheated on her."

Shane went very still. This he hadn't heard. He glanced at Greta. "Is that why?"

Greta nodded, her pale-blue eyes serious. "According to Bonnie Sue's mother and the Laramie grapevine, yes."

The satisfaction he should have felt—that Bonnie Sue had finally gotten every bit as good as she had dished out to him—didn't come. Maybe because there was no happiness to be had from anyone else's misery. Aware Greta was still watching him carefully, Shane took out the Trisha Yearwood CD and popped in one by the Texas Tornados. "What comes around goes around, I guess," Shane said, as the sounds of "Little Bit Is Better than Nada" filled the room.

Looking restless herself, Greta got up and bounded down the stairs, her short denim skirt hugging her hips and thighs. She headed for the front door, made sure it was locked and bolted, then went to the newly installed plantation shutters and began shutting them one by one. "Do you still care for her?"

"No." Shane watched as the dance hall became darker and darker. "She killed what I felt for her when she was unfaithful to me." There was no way he was ever getting involved with anyone duplicitous again. He never wanted to be hoodwinked again—in any way, shape or form. He wanted a woman who was 100 percent honest and forthright with him about everything she wanted and did and felt. No more going behind his back.

More restless than ever, Shane stood. He caught up with Greta just as she closed the last shutter. "Would you have married her if you hadn't caught her in bed with Clint?"

Shane winced at the directness of the question. "Probably," he admitted reluctantly, embarrassed at what a chump he had been. "But it would have been a mistake." He caught her by the waist and brought her close. "Time has shown us that. But none of this has anything to do with what's still going on between you and Beau." She was holding something back; he knew it. There was more connection there than friendship. Beau's intense interest in Greta's business had proven it. "You want to tell me what's going on between the two of you?" Shane demanded.

"No." Greta made a face as she splayed her hands across his chest. "But I guess, since we're married, that I should...Beau is my silent partner," Greta said with a reluctant sigh as she propelled herself all the way out of Shane's arms. Getting into the cheerful beat of the music, Greta propped her hands on her waist and did a few heel-toe moves all by herself. "He put up almost all the funding for this place. If he hadn't offered me a loan, there's no way I could have bought this dance hall and had the money to set up the business on my own."

Shane fell into step beside her, and began line dancing, too. "Couldn't you have gone to a bank or gotten a small business loan?" He slid one hand behind her shoulders as was custom, hers slid around his waist.

"I suppose," Greta acknowledged, swaying to the beat and bending sexily at the knee, "but there was no need. Beau's got tons of money from his past few pictures. He's always looking for investments for tax reasons. And he wanted to help me."

A jealousy Shane had no right feeling knotted in his gut as the two of them made their way rhythmically around the dance floor. "And what does he expect in return?" Shane asked casually.

"Fifty percent of the profits." Greta stopped dead in her tracks, and disengaged herself from him. She tilted her face up to his and regarded him with an insolent, mocking look. "What did you think he would expect?"

Her sarcasm stung, but he refused to be less than honest. "I don't know." Shane paused, figuring now was as good a time as any to get into this. "What is this guy to you?" he demanded casually.

"Exactly what I've told you and everyone else—not that anyone listens to me," Greta lamented in obvious frustration. "A friend."

"Now," Shane qualified, hating the suspiciousness he felt, but unable to help it.

Greta fixed him with a withering stare. "No," she corrected icily. Turning her back on him, she marched into the dance hall kitchen and began closing up there, too. "Not just now, Shane. Always."

Silence fell between them as Greta began to rinse out the coffeemaker she had used earlier in the day.

Greta filled it with soap, then turned back to him. "You don't buy it." It was more a statement than a question.

Shane shrugged, aware she had never looked more beautiful than she did at that moment, in the fitted, short-sleeved denim blouse, skirt, boots. Her hair was twisted into a thick unruly rope and clipped on the back of her head. Wildly curling white blond tendrils escaped to frame her face. "I saw the videotape of you and Mr. Movie Star," Shane continued. Now he was sorry he had.

Greta arched a brow. "You must have been curious," she taunted lightly.

That wasn't the half of it. But unwilling to divulge how envious he'd been of all the dates Chamberlain had obviously had with Greta, Shane spread his hands carelessly on either side of him. "My mother insisted."

"So you humored her." Greta wasn't buying *that* for a moment.

Excitement building inside him, Shane struggled to examine his own emotions. "I was going to have to see it sometime. I figured I might as well get it over with."

Finished with the coffeepot, Greta set it on the counter to dry and then turned to face him. "What'd you think?"

"That you look every bit as gorgeous in evening clothes as you do in jeans and boots."

Greta finished drying her hands and tossed the dish towel aside. "I'm serious."

Okay, the hell with what was right. "I wondered if you had ever been lovers."

Color flamed in her cheeks. "No."

But had Beau wanted to be? Shane wondered.

"Not that it's any of your business," Greta finished haughtily.

Shane swallowed and cautioned himself not to move too fast. "We're married, and he's still hanging around. I'd say that makes it my business."

For once Greta didn't quibble with the validity of their union. "I told you why he was here." She brushed past him.

And Clint had always been there to *study* with Bonnie Sue.

Greta shook her head and leaned against the long stainless steel counter. "You don't believe me, do you?"

Shane stepped in front of her and held his ground. "He seems like a healthy, full-blooded American male." Shane let his glance rove slowly over Greta from head to toe, taking in her long, sexy legs, slender waist and generous breasts. "I can't see any reason why he wouldn't want to make love to you."

Her blue eyes were hot with temper, her breasts rising

and falling with every breath. "How about I didn't want to make love to him?"

"So he did hit on you," Shane ascertained grimly. Not sure why he minded so much. Just knowing he did.

Exasperation hissed through her teeth. She kept her gaze level with his. "We kissed the first time we went out together."

"And…?"

"And nothing!" She tilted her head back so their lips met in perfect alignment. "We promptly discovered that our relationship was more brother-sister than anything else."

Shane folded his arms in front of him. It would be so easy to get lost in her. In this thing they called a marriage. "Your parents don't seem to think that's the case."

Bracing her hands on either side of her, Greta hopped up on the counter, sat with her knees together, her legs hanging over the side. "That's not my fault. I told them. They just didn't believe me."

"Neither did the rest of the movie-going public." He watched as she self-consciously tugged the hem of her skirt closer to her knees. Stepping closer, he braced a hand on either side of her. And remembered all he had seen on the videotape. Beau Chamberlain, wrapping his arm around Greta's waist and shoulders, countless times. He moved in even closer. "Face it, if you and Beau really didn't have anything going between you—ever—then the two of you put on one heck of a show."

Greta sighed, her bent knees brushing his waist. "That's because he wanted it to look like we were dating, whenever we went to those premieres and award shows together."

"Why?"

Greta lifted her shoulders in a shrug. "Because it was the only way to get the fan magazines and tabloids off his back." She looked at him then continued softly, "After Beau's divorce, they were determined to pair him with someone. When he wouldn't cooperate by actually dating anyone, they started taking photos of whoever happened to be standing next to him—even if the woman happened to be a complete stranger!—and pawning those women off as his date. He got tired of it. And he felt sorry for the women it was happening to. So he said, 'Look, pretend to be my girlfriend at these things…we can go and have a good time…' And I said, 'Okay.'"

Shane wanted to know what had been in her heart and mind, too. "Because you enjoyed pretending to be his date?" he asked softly.

"No." Greta raked her teeth across her lower lip. "Because I was his friend. And I understood his conundrum. And if you want to know the truth," she stated, even more honestly, "after the years spent on the fringes in high school, I enjoyed being part of the 'popular' crowd. It was *fun* being the center of attention."

That Shane knew about. There was nothing he liked better than being the center of attention himself. "Well, just see the 'fun' stops as long as you're married to me," he grumbled right back

Greta planted her hands on her hips and clearly would have moved off the counter if he had stepped aside to let her. "Is that why you kissed me like that?" she demanded, looking thoroughly ticked off.

"When?" Shane asked, not sure which of their deliciously sexy kisses she was alluding.

"When you came in and found me with Beau."

Oh. That. "I kissed you because it's the normal thing

to do when you come in and greet your wife after a day spent apart.''

"Not that way, you don't.'' She pushed at him with her knees, signaling she wanted to get down.

"What way?'' Enjoying the feel of her, so warm and fiesty and close, Shane kept his hands planted firmly on either side of her and refused to budge. Having no success using her strong sexy legs as leverage, Greta plucked at his hands. Again he held fast.

"As if you were saying to him, 'This is my woman, buddy, now keep your mitts off'''

Shane grinned, amused. "Is that how you think I kissed you?'' he asked. He liked the way she looked, cheeks pink, blue eyes full of temper, soft bare lips on the verge of pouting.

"Isn't it?'' Greta shot back emotionally. Evidently giving up on prying his hands from the counter, she moved her hands to press against his shoulders.

"No,'' Shane said, leaning his weight into her palms even as he planted his hands between her knees, pushed them apart and stepped in between them. Grabbing her by the hips, he tugged her toward him so swiftly she barely had time to gasp her indignation before her legs were wrapped around him and she was straddling his waist. Tunneling a hand through her upswept hair, he tilted her head back and lifted her lips to his. *"This,''* he told her emphatically as he slowly, deliberately lowered his mouth, "is how I kiss you when I want to put my stamp of possession on you.''

GRETA SAW THE KISS COMING. Felt it. Wanted it. Yearned for it. And then his lips were on hers, possessing her in a way she had only dreamed about, making her heart pound, her spirits soar and her senses swim.

She moaned, whether in protest or surrender she could not say, as he kissed her, plundered her, consumed her with his mouth. Lips, teeth, tongue—he used them all to maximum advantage, conjuring up heat and speed and a dreamlike feeling of well-being unlike anything she had ever known. Needing, wanting, with a groan of pleasure and an ocean of desire, she tangled her fingers in his hair and pulled him closer yet. Overwhelmed by the hot, salty taste of him, she ran her hands over his cheekbones, kissed the voluptuously soft corners of his mouth, delved deep.

The tantalizing traces of his aftershave mingled with the clean fragrance of soap and the masculine scents of sweat and sun. He was hard, relentless, irresistible in his pursuit of her. She felt his hands move from her hips to her thighs, pushing her skirt higher still. And then his work-roughened hands were bypassing the barrier of lace to the soft, silky skin beneath. She arched as he touched her, the fabric of his jeans rubbing deliciously against her inner thighs. And then his hands were moving higher still, slipping past the lowest vestiges of her tummy to her waist, to the snaps on her blouse. Seconds later, the denim was open to her navel. Cool air rushed over her fevered skin. And still he kissed her, his lips warm and sure. Strength flowing through him to her, he brushed the straps aside. His hands palmed her breasts, molding and caressing.

SHANE HADN'T MEANT to do more than kiss Greta, but as her breasts swelled warmly and her nipples pearled against his palms, he knew there was no turning back. One way or another he was going to make love to her. Neither of them would rest until he did. Maybe it wouldn't be here. Maybe it wouldn't be now, he thought as their kiss turned even more sensual. But it would happen and it would happen soon. And when it did, it would have nothing at all to do with the ''deal'' they'd made.

Until then, he realized reluctantly, slowly bringing the erotic kiss to a halt, there were choices to be made. He doubted seriously that making love here was something Greta would choose.

Slowly he lifted his head.

Slowly their eyes met.

Greta blinked, clearly as stunned by the unbridled passion they'd felt as he was. A turn of events that made him feel damn good. Greta grabbed the edges of her blouse and fit them together. ''What do you think you're doing?'' she demanded irritably, pushing him away.

''Besides showing you what a this-is-my-woman kind of kiss is all about?'' Shane asked, knowing they'd discovered something special here…something that went far beyond the charade they'd cooked up to teach their parents a lesson about meddling.

''Besides that,'' Greta echoed breathlessly as she quickly tugged her blouse and bra into place.

Lower half throbbing, Shane watched her do up the snaps he'd just undone. ''Well then, I guess I'd have to say we were practicing for our wedding reception,'' he said.

GRETA ROLLED HER EYES as she smoothed her skirt down over her thighs. ''First of all, I hope we will have broken up before that occurs,'' she told him sternly, doing her best to appear as unaffected by their passion as he apparently was.

Shane guffawed. ''Not likely, given all that's at stake.''

''Wait a minute,'' Greta interrupted, putting up a hand

as she led the way back into the dance hall. She headed up the half dozen or so steps to the DJ's booth, taking them two at a time. "I thought we were only going to stay married a week or so."

His actions a lazy counterpoint to hers, Shane was, nevertheless, right behind her. "That was the original plan." His low voice was self-assured and faintly baiting.

Greta lifted her chin and angled her head back to see his face. She didn't like the sound of this. Aware her heart was pounding, she searched his face for any clue of what he was up to now. "But…?" she prodded lightly.

Shane reached over to turn off the sound system. "But I've been thinking about your business and mine, he said calmly, as the dance hall fell silent once again. He swaggered closer, his steps long and lazy. In tight-fitting jeans, boots and one of his custom-made Western shirts worn open at the throat, he looked rugged and every bit as at ease in the business world as he was in a rodeo arena. "Our professional reputations might do better if we appeared a little more stable than reckless," he pointed out practically.

"*Now* you consider that!" she flung at him furiously, wishing she'd never agreed to join in this crazy escapade of his. Just being close to him, never mind thinking of what they'd started—and both declined to finish—in the dance hall kitchen, made her heart skip a beat. Greta chided herself for the hopelessly romantic reaction. She knew better than to let her romantic fantasies and wishes cloud her thinking, especially when it came to dealing with men who had designs on her. Which Shane now clearly did! Never mind they'd be consummating a marriage they didn't intend to keep. He was going to try to bed her soon; she'd bet her bottom dollar on it!

"Hey." Shane flattened both hands on his chest. "We did what we had to do to save your reputation."

Greta turned away from Shane, trying not to think how incredibly alive he made her feel whenever she was around him. "True," she murmured, conceding his point. Small towns like Laramie were murder when it came to gossip and everyone knowing everyone else's business.

Shane came around to sit on a table in front of her. "Anyway, I don't think we should rush out of our marriage quite as quickly as we rushed into it. It might be better for us all around if it at least looked like we gave it the good old Texas try before the infatuation ended and we crashed and burned."

Greta picked up the play lists the DJ she had hired had given her. She had to make her selections and mark them all before opening night. "And how long do you think that will take?" She stuffed them in her briefcase, along with copies of the insurance papers her father had asked her to sign that morning.

"A couple weeks, at least."

Greta's eyes widened at the thought of staying married to Shane and continuing this charade for that long. "Shane!"

He regarded her steadily. "From a business point of view, you have to admit it makes sense. And bottom line, isn't business what it's all about?" Shane asked softly, rubbing a hand across his jaw. "For both of us?"

Greta threw up her hands and reluctantly gave in. Grabbing her briefcase, keys and handbag, she skipped back down the stairs before he could kiss her again. "All right. I'll agree to stay married a little longer than we originally thought we'd have to,'' she told him over her shoulder, already heading for the back door. ''But as far as the rest of it goes, as far as the reception our parents are throwing, we're not going to kiss at that…not like we just did!'' Because then their parents would jump to all sorts of conclusions—namely that the two of them were falling head over heels in love with each other. And they'd never give up on the ill-fated union.

''I agree,'' Shane said gravely, following her out the service entrance, then waiting while she locked up. He braced a shoulder on the wall. ''That was much too sexy a kiss for a wedding reception,'' he teased with a wink. ''Kisses like that belong on the honeymoon.''

Greta pivoted away from him and headed for her car. Unable to believe how wantonly she had just behaved, she said sternly, ''Will you stop teasing me and get serious?'' She was beginning to see why women fell for bad boys! They got a woman into trouble before she knew it, but it was so much fun being with one, that afterward she almost didn't mind.

''Okay.'' Shane waited for her to unlock her car door, open up all the doors and let the hot air out. ''Seriously—?''

''Seriously,'' Greta confirmed.

''Let's get out of here and go back to the ranch before we're tempted to do it all over again.''

GRETA HAD THOUGHT he was joking, Shane realized, as he got in his pickup and she got in her sports car and he followed her home to the ranch he'd just purchased for himself. But he hadn't been. He'd never wanted to possess a woman the way he wanted to possess her. And it hadn't—as he'd led her to believe—just started now. If he were totally honest, he'd have to admit that he'd been keenly aware of her the whole time they'd been growing up, but especially in high school. Except she'd been such a sweet kid then, two years younger and so vulnerable. Unlike him, she'd been so earnest in her desire to please. And like him, she'd been under so much pressure to achieve from her folks. Back then, she hadn't possessed nearly the poise and self-assurance she had now. Back then, the only time she had been able to shake off her almost painful self-consciousness and really come alive was when she was dancing with the school's dance line at football and basketball games. Back then, he hadn't dared come within a ten-foot pole of her for fear that he would somehow damage her life by succumbing to temptation and behaving more like a guy on a quest than the big brother she had so obviously needed.

So he'd done the right thing, the gentlemanly thing, and walked away from her without a backward glance. And what had happened in the meantime? She'd grown up. Blossomed. Seen nearly as much of the country as he had, following the whims of her career as a dancer. And she'd become so close to Beauregard Chamberlain that he'd not only become the big brother figure Shane now wished he had been for her, but was secretly bankrolling her new dinner and dance club.

Seeing her in Beau's arms had been like getting a knife in the gut. More telling yet, he didn't want Greta turning to Beau for anything. He wanted Greta turning to him. But how likely was that to happen? Shane wondered as Travis's words came back to haunt him. *Give it up, little brother. You can't compete with that.* And much as Shane was loath to admit it, Travis had been right. At least to a point. Shane couldn't give Greta the access to unlimited millions the way Beau could. Heck, he couldn't even give her a nice place to live.

He would like to fix up the ranch house, but what he knew about decorating could fit on the head of a pin. Greta obviously had a clue about such things. He had only to look at what she'd done with the dance hall to know that. He could ask his mother to help him out on that score, of course, or Jackson's new wife, Lacey, or even Wade's. But if he did that, then they'd wonder why his own wife wasn't tending to such things. They'd wonder why she hadn't just jumped in and started making the ranch house a home, or at least, had plans to do so in the future as soon as she had time. But, Shane thought, sighing, that wasn't likely to happen, either, so it was a good thing he'd seen to the absolute essentials while he was out buying horses.

"I FORGOT TO ASK," Greta said, as she got out of her car and he got out of his pickup, and the two of them stood in front of the ranch house they were now calling home. "How did the rest of your shopping expedition go earlier today? How was the horse you looked at, and were you able to find any furniture?"

"The horses were great. I bought two mares. They're going to be delivered first thing day after tomorrow." Which left him only one day to get the stables in shape. "The bed is about to be delivered this evening—"

"The bed?" Greta interrupted plaintively, not looking at all happy about that. "As in one bed?"

"Don't go off half-cocked on me." Shane unloaded the box containing the pressure cleaner from the bed of his pickup truck. He lifted it down and carried it over to the porch, then returned to get what he'd need to assemble it later that evening. "It's a king-size."

"I would have preferred twin beds, one for each of us," Greta said stiffly, as Shane hopped up onto the bed, strode over to the cargo box located behind the passenger compartment. "Or better yet, two big beds—one for your room, one for the master," she continued as he knelt in front of it, unlocked it, and lifted out his toolbox.

"That might've been possible if the place weren't such a filthy mess inside," Shane said, escorting her up the steps to the front door. He dropped his grip on her long enough to unlock the door. His eyes still on her face, he pushed the door open, pocketed his keys, and led the way inside. "But we're going to have a hard enough time as it is cleaning up the big front bedroom before the bed arrives." He stopped so abruptly she crashed into him, her soft breasts ramming against his back. "What in the—did you do all this?" He swung around to face her.

Greta flushed, obviously embarrassed at the reaction her actions had provoked. "I called the same professional cleaning company that helped me with the dance hall."

"It still needs new wallpaper and paint, but—" Shane shook his head in awe as he walked in. "The windows are actually sparkling." He couldn't help but grin as he shook his head and marveled openly. "And the floors—who would have thought they could gleam like that?" He turned to her, pleased beyond words that she'd thought to do that for them. "What do I owe you?"

"Nothing." Greta waved his concern away. "Consider us even. After all, you footed the bill for our wedding. You're letting me stay here for the next few weeks until we call a halt to our hasty marriage and get things sorted." Greta sighed. "Hopefully, by then the club will be such a success that I'll have the time and cash flow to find a place of my own so I don't have to move back in with my folks—which was nothing more than a stopgap measure, anyway. I never would have done it if I hadn't had so much to do to try and get the club up and running.''

"I'm with you there." Shane sighed in heartfelt commiseration. He grabbed her wrist and tugged her along from room to room with him. "I know what it's like to be moving back to your old stomping ground and trying to set up a business all at once," he said compassionately as they toured the entire downstairs. "Not to mention the fact that you and I are too old to be living at home with our folks. It was bad enough for me just crashing with my brothers for a few days."

He took her hand and led her into the kitchen, which, though still hopelessly outdated, had been cleaned from top to bottom. Ditto the upstairs bedrooms and two bathrooms.

When they had come to the end of the impromptu inspection of their surroundings, Shane wrapped his arm around her shoulders companionably, loving the way she felt against him, all soft and warm and womanly. "Thanks." He touched her face with the callused roughness of his hand, cupping her chin in his palm, scoring his thumb across the softness of her lower lip, wishing all the while he could kiss her again. And this time *not* have to stop. His voice dropped another intimate notch as he told her. "You don't know how I was dreading coming back here tonight and having to muck out the house." He swallowed hard around the sudden lump in his throat. "This means a lot. I'm not used to having anyone anticipate my needs."

Greta tensed. He was taking this so personally. It made her feel even more guilty. All she'd done was pick up the phone and dial. Not because she'd thought of it on her own, but because her parents had sort of guilted her into it. But Greta bet Bonnie Sue would have thought to do this and so much more.

The rumble of a truck sounded in the drive leading up to the house. Shane looked out the window, then gave her shoulders another squeeze. "There's our bed now," Shane said. "I'll go down and let them in."

Twenty minutes later their bed was all set up. While Greta still struggled with her feelings, Shane signed for it and walked the delivery men out. "If you give me the sheets, I'll put them on the bed," Greta said. All she wanted was a nice hot shower, something to eat. Then she'd tumble into bed and sleep into morning. Surely this one was big enough they could each take half and not touch each other all night long!

Shane made a face as if he were in pain, then glanced at his watch. "Oh, man."

"Is there a problem?" Greta asked, not sure what he was getting at. Just knowing whatever it was, it was bad news.

Shane rubbed his jaw sheepishly. "You could say that, yeah."

Chapter Seven

"Where were you and Shane last night?" Tillie asked early the next morning while Greta supervised the hanging of the new sign above the entrance.

"A little more to the right, I think," Greta told the painter and the electrician who were working together to do this for her. As they complied, she turned back to her mother. "What do you mean?"

"Your father and I tried to call you all evening and again early this morning out at Shane's ranch, and there was no answer." Tillie smoothed the edges of her lemon-yellow sweater set.

Greta continued to study the big white sign with the red lettering and the single navy-blue star. For days now she'd been unsure if what she'd chosen was right:

> Lone Star Dance Hall,
> Greta Wilson, proprietress
> Families welcome
> Dinner specials served daily

But now as she looked at it she knew it would strike just the right chord with potential customers. The Lone Star Dance Hall was going to be a place where people could come and bring their entire families, take dance lessons, and just have fun. Dancing—the sheer joy of it—had helped her forget her worries and given her hours of pleasure during her lifetime. And now, she realized with immense satisfaction, she would finally be able to offer the same opportunity to everyone else, young and old, in the area.

Aware Tillie was still waiting impatiently for an explanation of Greta and Shane's whereabouts the night before, Greta told her mother absently, "We were at a motel."

"Shane didn't buy a bed for you, after all?" Tillie turned as the food service truck stopped in front of the entrance and the uniformed driver jumped down from the cab, clipboard in hand.

"No. He bought one." Greta smiled and waved the deliveryman over. "He just didn't think to buy any sheets or towels or pillows, and by the time we realized it, it was too late. All the stores in town had already closed for the day, and we were too tired to drive forty-five minutes to the nearest shopping mall and back, so we just said to heck with it and went to a motel." They'd also—at her insistence—taken a room with two double beds. Shane had slept in his. Greta had slept in hers. It had been a relief not to have to worry about being curled up beside him again. Yet sleeping apart had left her feeling oddly bereft, too, as though she was missing out on the fulfillment of what had once been—and still was— her ultimate fantasy.

Tillie sighed and shook her head. Greta paused long enough to scan the paperwork and verify this was indeed the order she had put in, then directed the truck around to the service entrance.

As she and her mother headed that way, too, Greta

felt her mother's continued disapproval. "Honey, this is no way to start off a marriage," Tillie continued worriedly, wringing her hands.

Greta agreed. Fortunately, this wasn't a real marriage. And she'd do well to remember that. It was already far too easy to imagine them continuing their marriage indefinitely. Far too easy to imagine herself really becoming his woman, when he hadn't offered to make her that at all.

"Where is Shane?" Tillie persisted as Greta unlocked the service doors and propped them open.

"He's cleaning the stables from top to bottom this morning with the pressure washer he bought yesterday. And then he's going to spend the afternoon getting hay and feed in for the two horses that are being delivered tomorrow."

As Greta showed the deliveryman where to unload the stack of boxes on his dolly, Tillie persisted doggedly, "How long will all that take?"

Greta shrugged and opened the first box to make sure the contents inside matched the invoice taped to the outside. Doing her best to keep her exasperation with her mother under control, she said, "He said he'll be back late this evening."

"Then it's a perfect time to get your home life in order."

Greta stopped counting bags of flour and sugar and gave her mother a look that let Tillie know Greta didn't appreciate the meddling. "Mom, please—"

"I bet you didn't cook for him last night, either, did you?" Tillie persisted, almost beside herself with the scope of her worries.

Greta checked off the first box, then moved to the second. Here they went again, with her supercompetitive parents wanting her to be the very best at absolutely everything she did, and being frustrated and disappointed in her when the realities of her capabilities didn't measure up to their dreams for her. "We haven't had time to get any dishes or groceries. So, no," Greta said calmly, "I didn't."

"What about tonight?" Tillie demanded as Greta made a similar count of coffee and tea.

"I guess we'll eat out if he gets back in time to have dinner with me." Finding all was in order, Greta checked off another box. She looked up at her mother and knew that, like it or not, just as Shane had assured her it would, their plan was working. She and Shane were proving they were all wrong for each other and for marriage...with practically no effort at all. So why didn't she feel better about that? Greta wondered, disappointed, too. She swallowed hard around the sudden lump in her throat, pushed aside the feeling of failure in her heart. "Mom. Relax. I know what I'm doing," Greta said, telling herself all the while this really was for the best. Even if she couldn't quite make her heart believe it. *I'm proving what a terrible wife I'll make so that no one, least of all me, will be surprised in a few weeks when we call it quits.*

"WHAT'S THE EMERGENCY?" Shane demanded eight hours later as he and Greta arrived back at the ranch almost simultaneously and parked down by the stables.

Greta regarded her "husband" incredulously as they vaulted out of their vehicles and came face-to-face. "I was hoping you'd tell me!" She'd been sure from the brief, frantic message she'd received that Shane was hurt, in terrible trouble or worse. Yet here he was, looking a bit dusty and tired after a long, hard day but all in one ruggedly masculine piece nevertheless.

Shane looked her over from head to toe, too, his gaze lingering briefly on the swell of her breasts, before his gaze returned to her face. Looking every inch as confused and aggravated as she felt, he said, "Wait a minute. Your mother called me on the car phone—"

"And yours called me at the dance hall!" Greta said, just as animated.

Shane shoved his hat back with one poke of his index finger, swore heartily. Spinning around on his heel, he began unloading bales of straw from the back of his truck, and carrying them into the stables, where he dumped them unceremoniously in the first two stalls. "Let me guess. My mom said there was an emergency at the ranch involving me and to get out here right away."

"How did you know?" Greta asked, amazed. Figuring she might as well help him out, as long as she was there, Greta carried a few bales, too, and set them down where Shane directed.

Shane whipped a Swiss Army knife from his jeans, swiftly cut the ropes, and spread the straw around with a pitchfork. "Because your mother told me there was an emergency involving you," he said grimly.

"Not only that," Greta quipped, unable to tear her eyes from the swell of powerful muscles beneath his damp, clinging shirt, "but like complete idiots we fell for it."

Looking as exasperated with both their mothers as she felt, Shane swore again. They studied each other, then turned their glances to the ranch house. "Dare we—?" Greta asked after a moment.

Shane grimaced. "Given what our two mamas are capable of, I'm almost afraid to go in," Shane said. In fact, Greta noted, given the trick that had been played on them, he seemed to have half a mind to just get back in his pickup truck and drive away. That wasn't an option for her. Curiosity alone was killing her. Besides, she had learned a long time ago there was no use putting off the inevitable when it came to Tillie. Waiting to discover anything would just make it worse. "Well, there are no cars around here, no sign of life, so I hardly think it's a surprise party for us," Greta said. She curled her hand around his bicep and half guided and half pushed Shane toward the ranch house. This predicament they were in was his fault, too. No way was she dealing with any of the fallout from their escapade by herself.

"Thank heavens for small favors," Shane grumbled as they crossed the yard and mounted the steps leading up to the front porch. No sooner had they stepped inside, than they were assailed by the delicious aroma of home cooking. Greta looked around with mingled feelings of pleasure and surprise. In their absense, a miracle had been wrought. White panel curtains had been hung on all the windows. Two comfy armchairs Greta recognized from her parents' attic had been set up before the fireplace. A table and chairs had been added to the kitchen. A bouquet of flowers and candles sat on the table. Dinner was warming in the oven.

Shane plucked the note off the center of the table and read it out loud: "Just a few things to make you more at home while you settle in. Jackson and Lacey are throwing a small, family welcome home party for Wade and Josie tonight at their place around eight. Greta's parents will be joining us. We hope you'll join us, too. Love, Lilah and Tillie."

Greta peeked in the cabinets, all of which had been

stocked with hand-me-down dinnerware, glasses and utensils. A set of pots and pans hung on the rack above the stove. The pantry was stocked with the basics. Same with the refrigerator.

"My, they have been busy," she said, not sure whether to be pleased at their mothers' thoughtfulness or aggravated by the continued interference in their lives. In any case, their mothers' mutual kindness was going to make it even harder to undo this when their time was up. Just being in such a cozy atmosphere with Shane gave rise to all sorts of female fantasies.

She turned back to Shane and studied his stunned expression. She was beginning to wish they had never decided to elope, never mind move in here together. He looked similarly beset with a mixture of aggravation and regrets. "You didn't expect this?"

Shane walked over to the sink, rolled his sleeves up to the elbow and began washing his hands. "Did you?"

"No," Greta said dryly, joining him at the sink, "but if I'd thought about it, I should have." Her shoulder nudged his as they reached for the soap at the same time. "My parents are always hovering over me, trying to help me live my life. It's one of the reasons I moved away from Laramie in the first place."

"Well, this is a first for me," Shane muttered unhappily, drying his hands. He grabbed a pot holder off the counter, removed the casserole of sour cream and chicken enchiladas warming in the oven and set it in the center of the table. Finding she was famished, too, Greta got out the tossed salad, bottle of ranch dressing and iced tea from the fridge.

"With the exception of this matchmaking business with you, I'm usually the son to whom my folks pay the least attention. Comes with being the baby of the family,

I guess. Given the freedom their lack of scrutiny allowed me, it's not something I can say I minded all that much,'' Shane confided mischievously as he pulled up a chair and dished a generous amount of bubbling casserole on both their plates. "I wouldn't have managed to have nearly as many...ah...adventures...growing up, if they'd been paying closer attention.''

"I can't even imagine what that would be like.'' Greta sighed wistfully as she dishes up salad for them both. "Being an only child, I've had just the opposite experience. My parents have been overinvolved in my life— physically, intellectually and emotionally—every step of the way.'' Greta liberally dosed her salad with dressing and sprinkled some croutons on top. "To the point that their lack of confidence in me, their wanting me to succeed so badly they feel they have to help, has just driven me nuts.''

Shane dug into his enchiladas with gusto while Greta started on her salad. "You think that's what all this is about?'' he asked, intrigued.

Greta nodded. She wished her parents would pay more attention to what she was achieving in her business life than what she had failed to achieve in her personal life. "My mother's been on my case about me paying more attention to getting my new business off the ground than playing Martha Stewart to my cowboy husband. And now your mother obviously feels that way, too.''

"Oh, I wouldn't say all this was necessarily directed at you.'' Shane reached across the table, took her hand and squeezed it briefly. "My mother blames me for encouraging you to elope with me and depriving you of the big wedding every girl dreams of. And then, to make matters even worse, bringing you home to a house that doesn't even have a lick of furniture, linen or dishes, and expecting you to somehow set up a home for us. I'm sure she sees that as gross negligence on my part. Of course," Shane said, sighing unhappily, his gray eyes darkening, "given the way they've always felt about me as the perpetual black sheep, it makes sense that they wouldn't expect me to be able to handle being married to you, either."

Greta took comfort in the fact that Shane hadn't always lived up to the considerable expectations of his parents, either. It helped to know they understood firsthand what the other was going through. "Isn't that what we want them to think, though?" Greta persisted, wanting to do whatever she could to cheer him up and put a positive spin on their increasingly sticky situation. "That we're completely inept at this—so inept and not ready for it, indeed, that we've got no choice but to end the marriage?"

Shane grinned at the reminder as he sipped his tea. "You're right." His gloom faded abruptly and his eyes sparkled with mischief.

"Uh-oh. What are you thinking, Shane?" Greta asked, knowing by his slow, thoughtful smile that he was up to something again.

Shane helped himself to more of the delicious enchilada casserole. "Maybe it's time we made a point about any future actions like this."

"And how would we do that—convince them that it's a bad idea to interfere in our marriage?" Greta took a bite of the delicious chicken, cheese, corn tortillas, sour cream and green chiles mixture. It melted on her tongue. And even more unhappily, put her own cooking—which she'd yet to share with Shane—to shame.

Shane shrugged his broad shoulders restlessly. Still regarding her intently, he waggled his eyebrows at her in a teasing manner. "By dramatizing our displeasure and staging a giant newlywed spat, of course."

"I DON'T THINK I'm going to be able to do this," Greta said an hour and a half later as they parked in front of Jackson and Lacey McCabe's home in downtown Laramie. After doing the dishes together, both of them had showered and dressed for an evening out. Shane was wearing a clean pair of jeans, dress boots and a nicely pressed fancy blue-and-black Western shirt. Greta was wearing delicate white sandals and a long white-and-yellow floral print sundress that showed off her shoulders and back. They looked like a very respectable young couple. Too respectable, in fact, for what they were planning.

"Sure you can." Never one to dwell on the negatives of any situation, Shane reached over and gave her knee a friendly pat through the smooth cotton fabric of her dress. "Just be your usual sweet, sassy self. And I'll be the bad guy. I've had plenty of experience doing that."

He wasn't giving himself nearly enough credit. "But I'm no good at lying," Greta protested.

"Then you'll just have to trust me to get you genuinely ticked off, won't you?"

Prophetic words, Greta decided short minutes later, as she smiled at her husband like some bright, overeager kindergarten teacher.

No sooner had they walked in the door, than Shane began his merciless assault, swaggering around as if he were heaven's gift to women in general and her in particular and tweaking her about anything and everything that came to mind.

"We all hear you got some help setting up house,"

Jackson said. His arm around his new bride, Lacey, Jackson looked supremely happy.

"Good thing, too," Shane drawled. He smiled at her guilelessly in a way clearly meant to provoke. "'Cause Greta here—good as she is at kicking up her heels on the dance floor—probably never would have gotten around to it."

"Shane McCabe!" Lilah admonished in shock, astonished at the merciless way her youngest son was egging his new bride on.

"It's true," Shane said. "I didn't realize how undomestic Greta was till we got home tonight and had that delicious dinner waiting for us. She didn't even know she had to have a pot holder to get the dish out of the oven. If I hadn't been there to stop her, she would've burned her hand."

Guffaws abounded as Greta gave Shane a look. "So I don't know much about cooking," Greta admitted with an indifferent shrug that had Shane's three brothers chuckling all the more. "I think the man should pitch in around the kitchen, anyway."

"Not in our marriage," Shane said.

Greta gave him a fiesty smile. "Want to bet?"

"Now, now," Tillie said, waving her hands nervously. "Of course Greta will cook, once she gets her business up and running and the two of you get settled in, won't you, dear?"

"Why should I?" Greta returned, still holding Shane's gaze. She let out an aggravated sigh and continued a great deal more petulantly than she felt, "He's likely to make fun of anything I serve him, anyway."

"No, honey, he won't," Lilah McCabe said hastily, attempting to smooth things over.

Shane smirked and made no effort to do anything that

would lessen his bad-boy rep one iota. "Sure I will." Shane reeled her in to his side and imprisoned her in the circle of his arms. "If it deserves to be made fun of. But you've got one thing right, Greta, honey," he drawled, holding her even tighter as he gave her a completely uncalled-for smack on the bottom, "like every other woman on this earth, you were put here to serve your man. And that being the case, I'll expect you to—*ow*!" He looked down at her elbow as he made a big show of rubbing his ribs. "Now, honey, that hurt."

Not half as bad as she wished it had. Sorry she'd ever agreed to come here with him tonight, and even sorrier she'd let him enact his plan to stage a newlywed spat for everyone to see, she loosened her hold on her temper, stepped back and slammed her hands on her hips. "And that's not all that's going to hurt if you don't stop with the male chauvinist behavior."

Shane gave her one of his *Who, me?* looks. "What male chauvinist behavior?" Shane asked innocently.

"Smacking me on the bottom, for one thing!" she retorted, as the gazes of everyone in the room snapped to her, then to Shane and back again. "Pretending I'm ever going to exist only to serve you *just* because you happen to be my husband, for another!"

Shane's brothers were openly nudging each other and guffawing now.

Their mission accomplished, Greta was sure he would privately blame the tension on the familial interference and cease and desist.

She should have known better.

Shane wasn't about to be left looking like an idiot in front of his brothers. Never mind a *hen-pecked* idiot.

"That's not what you said the other night," Shane declared, fabricating merrily as he went along. He wrapped his arms snugly around her waist and tugged her against him once again, so they were touching chests, tummies and thighs. "In fact," he said, his voice becoming a husky murmur as he ran his hands up and down her spine, "you not only said you'd—" he paused to kiss the shell of her ear "—you actually wanted me to…"

Okay, Greta thought, that did it. It was time this cowboy was brought to heel, family audience or no.

"Ouch!" Letting her go, Shane hopped around comically on one foot and rubbed the other where she'd stomped on it. "Now, Greta, honey, you gotta start watching where you're putting your heels and elbows," Shane cautioned loudly enough for everyone to hear.

"Gladly," Greta snapped right back. And knowing exactly where she wanted them to go, she turned on her heel and walked out.

"YOU CAN START SPEAKING TO me anytime now," Shane said as he parked his pickup in front of the ranch house and came around to help her out.

Mindful of the difficulty of getting in and out of the truck gracefully when wearing a dress, Greta gathered the long, swirling skirt of her sundress with one hand and braced her other on the door Shane was holding. "To make that possible, I'd have to *want* to speak to you," she told him haughtily. Ignoring the hand he offered, she jumped down. "I don't."

He caught her around the waist, steadying her, as her delicate sandals hit the ground. "You're not still mad at me for kissing your ear and smacking you on the bottom?"

Greta shrugged off his warmly possessive—even tender—grip. "As a matter of fact," she told him even more haughtily, knowing she still wanted to sock him for his hopelessly outdated, totally chauvinistic, behavior, "I am."

Half of his mouth quirked up in typical insolent fashion. "Never happened before, huh?"

Greta did her best to look down her nose at him—not easy when he was a good four inches taller than she was. "Not without me completely decking the offender," she told him sweetly.

"Now that would have been sexy!"

Greta stormed inside, switching on lights as she went, and headed for the kitchen. "And in front of both sets of parents and all your brothers and their wives, too!"

Shane trailed after her lazily. "I thought we'd agreed we were going to make it look good!"

"We did that, all right." Greta jerked open the refrigerator and pulled out a can of cherry soda.

Shane spread his hands wide. "So?"

Greta rolled her eyes as she slammed the refrigerator with her foot. "So did you have to enjoy it so much? And don't deny it—you loved every second of being the lout!"

Shane helped himself to a soda, too. "Only because it brought so much color to your cheeks." He popped the top and licked the fizz before it bubbled over onto the side. "I haven't had so much fun teasing a girl since recess in third grade."

Greta jerked her glance away from the sensual motions of his tongue. "Well, I hope you enjoyed it because I am not going to give you a chance to do it again!" she said sullenly, pulling out a chair.

Shane sat down across from her. He tossed his hat onto the table and stretched his long legs out in front of him. "Hey, come on. You knew I was just teasing, even if no one else did."

Greta popped the top so quickly it bubbled over in an explosion of fizz. Swearing at the mess she had just made, she got up to get a dishcloth. "Too bad I wasn't teasing," she grumbled bad-temperedly as she dampened the cloth at the sink.

"What do you mean?"

Greta shut off the water with a snap of her wrist, wrung out the cloth, then returned to the table. "I mean I'm not cooking for you—ever."

Shane sipped his cherry soda indolently. "Did I ask you to cook?"

"No—" Greta wiped the table and then her can with quick angry strokes "—but it was very clear we were headed that way."

"And how did you figure that?"

Greta threw down her cloth. "Because I've been here before, that's why!"

SHANE NEARLY CHOKED on his soda. "You've been married?" He did a double take.

"Engaged." Ignoring the ladylike thing—which would have been to get a glass—Greta lifted her can to her lips.

"To whom?" Shane demanded, peculiarly upset by the news. He straightened abruptly, his feet hitting the floor with a thud. "Not Bucklehead Chamberwaist?" he declared.

"No, not to *Beauregard Chamberlain,*" Greta replied in utter exasperation, not sure why she had even started this. "To a guy named Walter."

Her revelation did not soothe Shane in the slightest. "Who's he?"

"A wealthy businessman I got involved with when I was still living in Dallas."

"Let me guess." Shane's lips curled cynically. "He met you when you were a Dallas Cowboys cheerleader."

"Bingo."

Shane thought about that for a second. "Do you always date rich guys?"

"No." Greta sat down across from Shane again. "And for the record I didn't even know Walter had money when we started dating."

Shane's eyes gentled. "How did you meet?"

Greta's glance dropped to Shane's hand and the way he was running his thumb and index finger around the rim of the can in absent, circular motions. "At the children's hospital." With effort, she tore her glance from the soothing ministrations of his hand. "I was doing volunteer work there in my spare time. He was helping with a fund-raiser. Several dates later, I found out his family had just donated a new wing of the hospital, but I didn't know that when I started going out with him. When he said he sold cars for a living, I thought he meant at a car lot, not owned a string of dealerships all through Texas.

"Anyway, it was a whirlwind courtship. I was so busy with the football games and other events, and the rehearsals for them, plus I was teaching dance lessons to children in a studio there in the off season and volunteering every second I could at the children's hospital, I didn't really have time to think. When Walter proposed at Christmas about two months after we started dating, I just said yes." Which had been just about the biggest mistake of her life, as it had turned out, Greta remembered.

"Your parents must have been happy," Shane observed.

"They were thrilled." Greta noticed Shane's nimble fingers had gone completely still. Greta shook her head and sighed. "All my mother could say was 'What a catch!'" Remembering, she felt an arrow of pain lance her heart. "You know how they always wanted me to be competitive." Shane nodded, his expression sympathetic. "Well, finally I'd done something no other young woman my age in Laramie had done—landed herself a multimillionaire for a prospective husband."

Shane took another sip of his soda. He probably would have heard all about this if he'd ever shown any interest in local gossip, but he hadn't. "What happened to break the two of you up?" he asked in a low, curious tone.

"Pretty much what's happening now with us, more or less." Greta made a face. "Everything changed once we were actually going to get married. I'd already spent two years with the Cowboys cheerleaders and I was ready to quit. Walter wanted me to continue with them as long as I possibly could."

Shane's eyes darkened knowingly. "Let me guess. He liked having a beautiful blond-haired trophy on his arm."

Greta confirmed this was so with a nod. She grimaced unhappily. "You know what a big deal the cheerleaders are in Dallas."

"Sex in a uniform," Shane quipped wryly.

Which had been, Greta thought, all too true. "Yeah, and as much as I loved dancing and performing for such enthusiastic crowds, I was a little tired of being an object of lust for so many men."

"And that broke Walter's heart, I bet." Shane

chugged the rest of his drink, then crumpled the can in his hand.

"Still he was game," Greta continued, unable to help the wry edge of bitterness that crept into her voice. "He would've married me if only I'd cooperated a little more."

"Cooperated...how?" Shane frowned, clearly not liking the sound of this, either.

Greta rested her elbow on the table and propped her head on her upturned palm. "Been the perfect little woman. You know, stopped working and made my career being Mrs. Walter Erring. Before I knew it he was telling me how to dress, think, act, walk. Plus, he was very jealous and possessive. I was like this object that he had added to his mass collection of things. So I broke it off." Greta straightened abruptly, recalling that awful scene. "My parents were hysterical. They didn't understand. I knew they wanted me to try to patch things up with Walter. And I just got tired of explaining why I couldn't, or as my mother put it, *wouldn't*. So I headed to California, where my best friend from high school, Dani Lockhart, was already working, moved into her apartment with her, got a job teaching dance lessons in Beverly Hills."

"And didn't become a Raiders cheerleader there."

"Right. I did get some jobs as the dancing raisin or banana in commercials, and danced in the occasional musical-variety show out there, and I met Bucklehead Chamberwaist, as you so quaintly put it."

"But your life out there was empty, wasn't it?"

Greta nodded slowly as their glances collided across the table. "How did you know?" she asked quietly, aware she hadn't told *anyone* that.

Shane shrugged. "It was the same for me, when I was

winning all those rodeos. The excitement, the glamour, is great at first. But after a while you just want some place where you belong and something to call your own.''

Greta smiled, finding it odd but somehow magical they had bonded over this. ''Like your horse ranch and my dance hall,'' she guessed quietly, taking another small sip of soda.

''Right.'' Shane reached across the table and touched her hand lightly.

Feeling suddenly unbearably restless, Greta pushed back her chair and stood. She carried her now-empty can to the recycling container under the kitchen sink. ''Anyway, when Walter and I broke up, I decided never again would I be a trophy babe for some guy or let any man tell me how to think, act or behave by virtue of me being the love interest in his life.'' She rinsed the can, and tossed it in the bin. ''Anyone who loves me has to love me for me—he has to take me just the way I am, no changes.''

Shane studied her as she shut the cabinet door with a snap. Slowly he got to his feet. ''Is that what you think I was doing to you tonight?'' Amusement tugged at the corners of his lips. ''Trying to tease you into being the perfect little McCabe wife?''

The kitchen suddenly seemed awfully small. Greta crossed her arms in front of her. ''Weren't you?''

Shane shook his head slowly. His smile faded. ''Cooking is not what I want from you, Greta, and you know it.''

GRETA'S BREATH CAUGHT at the sensual intent in his eyes. ''Now you really are dreaming.'' Greta stopped him from coming any closer by holding up a palm. ''Because there is no way on this earth we are sharing the same bed tonight,'' she stated bluntly.

Shane raked a hand through his rumpled sun-streaked hair. ''Well, I sure as hell am not sleeping in a chair or on the floor.''

''You're right. You shouldn't sleep in a chair or on the floor. You should sleep in the barn.'' Greta took him by the shoulders and propelled him in that direction.

Strangely enough, though, he didn't resist as she guided him through the kitchen to the back door. In fact as he swung around to face her he seemed to really like the idea. ''You really mean that?'' Shane asked cheerfully.

In for a penny, in for a pound. Besides, after the way he had treated her at the McCabe family get-together, he deserved it. Greta stomped her foot for emphasis. ''Hell, yes, I mean it.''

''Works for me.'' Before she could so much as draw a breath, Shane dropped his shoulder, pushed it gently against her middle, whisked her up off her feet and slung her over his shoulder.

Just that quickly Greta viewed the world upside down, from the vantage point of his waist. ''What are you doing?'' Greta demanded, grabbing frantically onto his belt.

Shane shoved open the door and shouldered his way through it, being very careful not to bump either of them against the frame. ''What does it look like I'm doing, Greta, honey? I'm making your wish my command.'' He started across the moonlit yard to the big building behind them.

Greta decided it was her turn to give his butt a censuring smack. ''I didn't say *I* wanted to sleep in the barn." She wiggled and kicked her legs frantically, to no avail.

SHANE JUST HELD ON TO HER legs and waist all the tighter. "You know what they say about married couples, Greta, darlin'," Shane told her good-humoredly as he reached the stables in no time and flipped on the interior lights. "Whither thou goest, I go. So where I sleep, you sleep." As cheerful as could be, he stalked down the center aisle. Still carting her about as if she weighed no more than a sack of feathers, he grabbed some clean new blankets from the tack room, headed for the first stall and tossed them onto the new straw that had been spread out across the cement floor.

It was amazing, the difference that his new pressure cleaner, a wealth of pleasant-smelling disinfectant and a good mucking and airing out had made. "Put me down," Greta demanded bravely.

"Gladly." Shane set her down—almost too gently— just inside the stall door. The two of them were bathed in warm yellow light.

"Let me go," Greta demanded, feeling a little dizzy and out of breath now that she'd been set upright again.

"Can't do that, sweetheart." Shane shook his head, shut the door and pulled the latch, trapping them inside the varnished wood stall.

Greta didn't for one minute trust the way his gray eyes were twinkling. She swallowed hard around the sudden dryness in her throat and did her best to look as if she had zero interest in his little game. "I mean it, Shane," she instructed him, wishing she had on something a little more substantial than the thin cotton sundress and strappy sandals. "Move aside."

"Not—" he said smugly "—until you kiss me."

Refusing to encourage him in the slightest, Greta frowned. "You're setting conditions for my release?"

He shoved his fingers in the back pockets of his jeans and appeared perfectly content to wait the night away. He gave her lips a long, thorough once-over that swiftly had her body tingling, let his gaze drop to her breasts, hips and thighs for a leisurely survey before returning ever so slowly, ever so deliberately, to her eyes. "Appears that way, yeah," he said very very softly.

She ignored his baiting as her heart began to race. "What if I say no?"

He shifted his weight and, not the least deterred, only appeared to make himself more comfortable. "Guess it'll be a long night."

She drew herself up to her full five foot ten inches and glared at him. "You son of a—"

Shane lounged against the stall door even as she told herself she was not going to sink to his level. "Greta, sweetheart—" he shook his head at her in mocking censure "—I thought you would come up with something more original than that."

Well, she hadn't expected this. "You're saying one kiss?" Greta asked, aware her knees were already trembling at just the thought. This was a bad idea. So why was she getting so excited just thinking about it? "Then I can go?"

Shane shrugged his broad shoulders lazily, looking impossibly handsome and impossibly determined in the soft light. His lips took on a tempting half curve. "Unless you want to make it two."

Her heart pounded and her body pulsed with need. "I'm not afraid of you, Shane McCabe."

Shane pushed himself forward and closed the distance between them, bringing an even higher level of excitement and adventure into her life. "Good," he murmured in a low, sexy voice that stirred her senses. "Because I don't want you to be. Ever."

Anchoring an arm around her waist, he dipped his head and caught her lips between his own. And for the first time all day, Greta realized, she was exactly where she wanted to be, doing exactly what she wanted to do. His arms were strong, insistent, cocooning her in sensual pleasure, his lips firm and warm and smooth. And just like before, he knew with damning accuracy, exactly how to get to her. Her senses spun as he sucked at her bottom lip and touched the tip of her tongue with his own. A melting warmth raced through her.

Unable to help herself, Greta began to return his kiss, reluctantly at first, then with growing pleasure. Clamping an arm possessively about her waist, he dragged her even nearer, so close their bodies were almost one. That, too, felt incredibly good, incredibly right. Greta moaned low in her throat and moved closer yet. Shane murmured his pleasure, then drew back a little, altering the angle, increasing the depth and torridness of their kiss. Her excitement mounted, fueled by the rasp of their breathing and the feel of his hands moving up and down her back. Greta trembled in his arms. Shane lifted his head, regarded her with questioning silver-gray eyes.

Not caring he'd been right, after all—she did want to make it two!—she looked at him playfully. Took his head between her hands and guided his lips slowly, confidently back down to hers. "Let's try that again."

"I was hoping you'd say that," Shane said.

Longing swept through her with disabling force. The next thing Greta knew he'd lifted her off her feet, swung her around. The desire he felt for her clear, he stepped between her spread thighs, and braced her against the side of the varnished wood stall. His lips moved down her neck, eliciting tingles of fire wherever they touched. Greta closed her eyes and arched against him, the gentle eroticism of his touch flowing over her in warm, wonderful waves. Her passion ignited his own. His hands cupped her breasts, and she pressed her body against his, pulling him against her, hard and urgent, instinctively urging him on. And then there was no more holding back.

His mouth slanted across hers in a fierce, burning kiss that propelled her to answer his passion with her own. Their tongues mated in an erotic dance unlike anything she'd ever imagined. Groaning he reached behind her, and undid the straps holding up the bodice of her dress. Peeling it down, he ran his fingers over the swelling tops of her breasts, and the lacy edge of her bra, still kissing her passionately all the while. Then that too was dispensed with. His manhood pressed against her inner thighs, hot and hard through the rough denim fabric of his jeans, as he molded her breasts with his hands, circled the aching crowns, teased the nipples into tight buds of awareness.

The kiss ended, and his lips forged a burning trail down her neck, across her collarbone, the slope of one breast, then the other. Greta cried out as his mouth circled each nipple, bringing them to taut aching peaks. But he didn't stop there. Engaging every sense, he made his way down her body, slowly, lovingly, until he had dropped to his knees in front of her like a knight, pledging himself to his queen. Aware this was the fulfillment of every fantasy she'd ever had, she hitched in a trembling breath. "Shane—"

He looked up at her, his silver-gray eyes dark with a

passion, want and a need that matched her own. "Let me."

His command was low and earnest. She couldn't deny him any more than she could deny herself. The world dwindled to just the two of them as he lifted the long swirling fabric of her dress, pushing it past her knees, then to her waist. He kissed his way up her thigh, past the thin scrap of lace, to her tummy. Up to her navel, down again. Trembling from head to toe at the long, sensual strokes of his lips and tongue, she caught his head in her hands, tangled her fingers in his hair. She moaned soft and low, knowing she wanted him, wanted this, as she had never wanted before and never would again. "Shane," she whispered hoarsely, and this time it was an entreaty, a plea.

Knowing exactly what she needed, he hooked his thumbs in the elastic of her panties, tugged them down as far as her knees. And then his hands swept back up, parting the folds of moist, tender flesh. Cradling her hips and thighs as if she were the most precious thing in the world to him, he found her with his lips. His tongue plunged inside her and her head fell back. Her body shivered with need. New sensations spiraled—and then blossomed—inside her. And then she came apart in his hands, pleasure ricocheting inside her.

Shane held her through the aftershocks, then sank down onto the straw, and in one easy movement, drew her down onto his lap. He cradled her in his arms, kissing her hair, holding her close, tenderly stroking her arms, her back. Waiting for some signal from her. Some deliberate decision. She knew she could still call a halt and he would honor her wishes. Not that it would be easy for either of them. Both her dress and panties were still half-off, and he was rock hard, straining the front of his jeans.

He leaned back to better see her face. Regarding her tenderly, he tucked her hair behind her ear. "What are you thinking?"

Greta moved her legs restlessly, still aching with the need to be filled. Slowly she grinned. "That this is one time you better finish what you've started, Shane McCabe."

SHANE THREW BACK HIS HEAD and gave a full-blooded laugh that filled Greta with feminine confidence. "I think that can be arranged."

"And one more thing," Greta cautioned as they spread the blankets out over the straw, making a nice cozy bed for themselves. He'd given her the confidence to be aggressive, too, and finished, she shimmied out of her panties, kicked them aside. Shane reached behind her, dispensed with the zipper on her dress, then lifted it over her head, tossed it on the floor. His eyes darkened appreciatively as his gaze drifted over her, hotly skimming her breasts, waist, hips, the shadowy vee between her thighs. "You are so beautiful," he whispered hoarsely.

For the first time in her life, Greta felt beautiful, inside as well as out. For the first time, she felt good enough. Able to please. The knowledge worried her as much as it pleased. What if this didn't last? How hard it would be to go back....

As if sensing her sudden uncertainty, Shane lifted his hand to her mouth. His thumb traced the seam of her lips, and she began to tremble. Greta tugged the hem of his shirt from the waistband of his jeans, dispensed with the buttons one at a time. Parting the edges of the fabric, she ran her hands across his chest. Delighting in the swirls of hair covering the sculpted muscles. "Just so you know," she said, standing on tiptoe to kiss her way down his chest, lingering over the hard pectoral muscles and tight abs before finding the flat male nipples with her lips and tongue. "This doesn't change anything." Even though in her heart she knew damn well it did. "We're still not really married," she asserted stubbornly, doing her best to protect them both from any future hurt and disappointment, in case the odds were right and this arrangement of theirs didn't work out.

"Fine with me." Shane sucked in his breath as she stripped off his shirt, letting it fall next to the crumpled circle of her dress, and undid his belt. He regarded her with a mixture of heat and tenderness that set her blood to racing. "I never wanted to be married, anyway."

"Neither did I."

He couldn't hold back a smile as she knelt before him, took off his boots, then tugged off his jeans. Greta paused, her hand sliding beneath the elastic of his low-slung black briefs. He was hard as a rock beneath her palm. "Then we're in agreement?" She ran her lips down his thighs, felt them tremble and tense.

"Absolutely." Shane groaned and caught her head in his hands.

Senses swimming with the musky male scent of him, Greta peeled off his briefs. "This is lovemaking pure and simple." Greta rose on her knees, and found him with her mouth. She traced the hot satiny skin, learning the mysteries of him with lips and teeth and tongue, knowing with Shane it was safe to be as wild and wanton as she had always wanted to be. "We are not—I repeat, *not*—consummating our marriage," she told him, and felt him throb with wanting her just as she had with wanting him.

"Agreed," Shane said hoarsely, dropping down onto the blanket beside her and rolling so she was beneath him.

Greta sighed her relief. Her emotions soaring, she accepted the warm, wonderful weight of him over her. "As long as we've got that straight," she said loving the way he felt as he fit his body's hard planes to the dips and curves of hers.

"Oh, we do," Shane whispered. Parting her knees with his, he settled more deeply between them. Then his lips were on hers, and his hands were beneath her hips, lifting and positioning her. She felt his manhood poised to enter, pulsing against her. The climax she'd felt minutes earlier came roaring back. Neither of them could hold back. Greta moaned and bucked, and he plunged into her, burying himself to the hilt, making it an all or nothing proposition with each slow stroke. There was nothing soft or gentle about the way they came together then. What stunned her was the knowledge she felt the same wild abandon and primitive need as Shane. Then it was all so hot and fast there was no time for thought. No time for anything but hot kisses and hotter mating.

Clinging to him, to the passion and excitement he offered, she dug her fingers into his back and moved her hips to match the commanding rhythm of his. Over and over he loved her, until a cry of exultation rose in her throat. He felt her tremble and clench around him, and then all was lost and all was found in the wild recklessness that defined their marriage.

SHANE WOKE SHORTLY AFTER DAWN. Greta was still sleeping soundly, curled in his arms, and he was in no hurry to wake her. The truth was it felt damn good, sleeping with her this way, even on a makeshift bed of straw. And that surprised him, almost as much as their passion. They'd made love repeatedly throughout the night, each time better and more satisfying than the last. She hadn't trusted their incredible chemistry at first, any more than he had. But when they began to lose count of how many times they'd each climaxed, there was no denying it. The two of them were meant for each other, at least in bed. And maybe out of it, too. Which was, of course, the rub.

He wasn't quite certain what he'd expected when he'd convinced her to join him in this escapade—wallflower or hellion—or something in between. He did know he'd never expected her to be so innocent and eager to be tutored in the ways of love, so unabashedly amorous yet vulnerable, all at once. To the point he didn't know whether he wanted to tame her or take her under his wing. And that confused the hell out of him, too. Before this, he'd never had trouble extricating himself from a woman when the time was right. But this time it wasn't going to be that way. And that had nothing to do with their marriage. It had to do with how she made him feel—as though he wanted to be a part of her life. Not just for now, not for some silly self-serving reason, but for all time. And just how hokey was that? Shane wondered, aggravated with his romantic musings.

He had no more time to contemplate it, though, as Greta groaned and stretched sinuously against him. "What time is it?"

Shane consulted his watch and tried not to think how warm and taut and utterly feminine her body felt. "Almost seven-thirty." It was all he could do not to haul her beneath him and kiss her long and hard and deep.

But if he did that again, they'd never leave here. Not to mention the fact that with daylight—and horses set to be delivered later that morning, plus a whole host of nosy family itching to get involved in his and Greta's marriage on a daily, hourly basis—came the possibility they could be walked in on.

Greta moaned and, still clasping the blanket to the enticing swell of her breasts, pushed to a sitting position "I've got to get up and get going." She pushed the tangle of blond curls from her eyes.

Shane damned the arousal already starting. "Busy day?"

Greta nodded and for the first time since they'd started making love, averted her eyes. As he watched her uncurl herself from the blankets and search for her clothes, he knew she felt as confused by all that had happened the night before as he did, now that morning was upon them. And that being the case, maybe it was best they talked about it.

"Something bothering you?" Shane asked.

"Well, actually—" Greta bit her lip and looked over at him uncertainly "—yes, there is."

Shane shrugged on his shirt, briefs, and jeans. When Greta said nothing more, he urged, "Keep going."

Greta dropped the blanket just long enough to shimmy into her bra, panties and dress. "Does what we did last night mean we can't get an annulment?"

Shane shrugged.

"Well, obviously we can't get one for not consummating the marriage," he told her kindly, understanding her concern, even if he was no longer sure he shared her desire for a speedy end to their marriage, "but we probably could still get one on fraud, seeing as how we didn't really mean our vows when we said them the other night."

Greta turned away and knelt to slip on her sandals. To Shane's chagrin, she still looked confused and upset. Before he could do more to comfort her, though, he heard the sound of a car coming up the lane. He stepped out of the stall and looked around the open stable doors.

"Who is it?" Greta asked, as she hurriedly picked the straw out of her hair and did her best to restore order with her hands.

Shane sighed. "My father." And he didn't look any happier to be there than Shane was to have him. Together, he and Greta walked out of the stables. They met up with John in the courtyard. He greeted them pleasantly, then said, "Greta, if you don't mind, I'd like a word with my son in private."

Shane knew that tone. It had been used a lot in his youth, usually after some escapade or another.

Greta nodded at John in agreement. She looked at Shane, then reached over and squeezed his hand in a way that said whatever happened, or had happened, they were still in this together. She promised softly, "I'll be inside."

GRETA WENT INSIDE, raced to the kitchen and hurriedly put on coffee. Finished, she returned to the front porch, intending to ask them both to come inside where father and son could talk in a more relaxed atmosphere. Unfortunately it was already too late. She couldn't hear what they were saying, but she could see the looks on their faces as they parted company and John left. Whatever they'd talked about had not been pleasant. She waited for Shane to join her on the porch. "Everything okay?"

"Yeah, sure." Lips compressed thinly, Shane turned on his heel and headed for the stables.

Knowing it probably concerned her, too, Greta followed him into the stable. "You don't look okay." Shane was silent as he knelt to pick up one of the blankets they'd wrapped themselves in the night before. "What did your dad say?" Greta persisted, picking up the other end of the blanket.

"The usual," Shane said tensely. They folded the blanket in two, and then again. "That they expected a lot more from me."

Greta's fingers touched his as she transferred the folded blanket over to him. "It's about our staged spat last night, isn't it?"

Shane looped the first blanket over the stall door, then reached for another. He said nothing, and if it hadn't been for the slight tightening at the corners of his mouth, she might have believed he hadn't heard her. "I'm sorry." Greta reached down to help him fold another. "I never meant to cause trouble between you and your folks."

Hurt flared in his eyes, then was gone as quickly as it had appeared. "This isn't anything new, Greta," Shane sighed. "I've been a disappointment to them from the day I was born."

The sadness and discouragement in his eyes cut her to the quick. More so because she knew, even if he didn't, that it wasn't true. "How can you say that?" Greta scolded. She helped him carry the folded blankets back to the tack room. "I know how proud they are of you and all your accomplishments. You were the PCRA's world all-around champion seven years in a row before you stepped down from the pro rodeo circuit." And he'd broken records doing so.

Shane picked up one of the boxes he'd brought home from his shopping expedition the previous day and ripped it open. "How'd you know that?"

Greta flushed, embarrassed to realize her long-running crush on Shane had caught up with her again. "I uh...kept up." Greta forged on determinedly, helping him shelve the equine supplies he'd purchased. Bridles, bits, vitamins, shampoo, first aid kit. "According to my mother, your folks brag about you—about all their sons—all the time, including you, Shane."

"Yeah," Shane frowned as he pulled out jars of liniment and rolls of thick white gauze, "but I'm the one who disappointed them. They put a high price on education and academic achievement. And although I did okay, I was never interested in school. I always wanted to be outside with the horses. When I refused to go to college, and instead went off to try my hand on the professional rodeo circuit, there were a few years where we barely spoke."

Greta'd had disagreements with her parents, plenty of them over the years, but never anything like that. She could only imagine how painful that must have been for all the McCabes. "But eventually..." she protested, wanting somehow to make this better for him.

"Eventually, yes," Shane said impatiently, whirling around to face her, "they forgave me for that, when I became successful and my earnings topped the million-dollar mark, and they discovered I had socked enough money away to buy this ranch and start my own business. But I think deep down they're still disappointed that I haven't gone to college and studied agribusiness— like my brother Travis—or settled down and gotten married." His eyes shimmered with hurt. Greta knew what that felt like, too. And her heart went out to him.

"Except that you are married," Greta interrupted gently, thinking, he had accomplished one thing on the list. Two, if you counted buying the horse ranch and settling down. "At least so far as our parents know."

"You know what I mean," Shane said heavily, grasping her by the shoulders. "Married as in *really* married."

Not just playing at it, Greta thought, as the two of them walked out into the aisle.

"Anyway, my dad just read me the riot act for not taking our relationship seriously enough." Shane shook his head and looked out at the distance, as if he were at the limit of his endurance. He turned to her and pressed a hand tenderly to her lips. Suddenly the merriment was back in his eyes. "If only he knew," Shane said softly.

Yes, Greta thought, not sure whether to be elated or discouraged at the way things were going. *If only they all knew.*

Chapter Eight

"All I'm saying is that he had a right to be miffed,"
Tillie told Greta when she and Bart stopped by the dance
hall Friday morning. Greta guided her parents out of
earshot of the produce people, who were busy delivering
crates of fresh fruit and vegetables directly into the walk-
in refrigerator. "So if he behaved badly last night it was
his way of letting you know you're just not cutting it as
a wife thus far."

Her mother's criticism was so sharp and well aimed
it took Greta's breath away. The fact that her father
seemed to be backing it up 100 percent was even worse.
Greta signaled to the three cooks she'd hired to prepare
the daily dinner specials to carry on without her, and
then she ushered her parents into the next room.

Greta looked out the window as the dairy truck pulled
up and another delivery person stepped out. What had
been a longtime dream of hers was fast becoming a reality. Her parents should have been damn proud of her,
for the way she was pulling everything together, yet all
they could think was how disappointed they were in her
about her personal life! She turned back to her parents.
"You know how busy I've been with the dance hall,

trying to get ready for the grand opening tomorrow night.''

Tillie straightened the hems of her summerweight sweater set and shook her head sadly. ''Honey, I hate to say it, but that's no excuse. Look at all the other McCabe wives. They work and manage to keep their husbands happy. Lilah worked as a nurse at the hospital all these years and ran a household and raised four boys, and John McCabe is still wildly in love with her. Josie is running an oil rig and keeping Wade very satisfied from the looks of things. Lacey's a physician, and she threw a party last night for the family, moved into a new home, married and went on a honeymoon with Jackson all in the past few weeks. They all juggle. And yet their husbands are all happy.''

Greta went back over to the table where she'd been busy working before the deliveries started. Her chin set stubbornly, she reached for another knife, fork and spoon from the bins. ''You think I can't compete with those superwomen?'' she snapped, plucking the silverware down in the center of the freshly laundered and starched cloth napkin. In the background the sound system played the latest Faith Hill-Tim McGraw duet.

Tillie patted her arm gently. ''I think you're not trying.''

''Look, honey,'' Bart said, as he picked up some silverware and a napkin and, following Greta's lead, began to roll up silverware, too. ''You know your mother and I didn't approve of your hasty marriage to Shane. But once you get past all his wildness—which, by the way, we think is all for show—he's a good man, from a good family. He's got money and a future. And he's proven time and time again he can achieve anything he sets his mind to. No one's got a more competitive spirit than

Shane McCabe. And despite your unusual start to this marriage, when he looks at you sometimes..." his eyes softening, Bart struggled to find the right words "—there is something special there...the kind of spark between two people that doesn't happen everyday."

"It's called chemistry," Greta mumbled, hating the worry she saw in both her parents' eyes. And it had led the two of them to throw caution to the wind and consummate their marriage the night before.

"Yes, well, whatever it is, the two of you have that in abundance. We've all seen it. In fact, we discussed that after you left the party last night. Everyone agrees Shane has never been as intrigued with a woman as he appears to be with you."

"So we think you two should make the best of it," Tillie continued.

"After all, not all marriages are built on love," Bart continued in his father-knows-best tone. "Sometimes that comes later."

Tillie nodded her head in earnest agreement. "Romantic love fades, anyway."

"Has it for the two of you?" Greta asked, her hands stilling abruptly.

Tillie and Bart turned to each other and clasped hands, all the love they had always felt for her, and each other, in their eyes. "Well, n-no..." Tillie sputtered, embarrassed, "but we always knew we were destined to be together."

Bart wrapped his arm around Tillie's shoulders and hugged her close. "You know our story, honey," he reminded Greta gently. "We started dating in high school."

And in high school, Greta thought, Shane could barely give her the time of day. She could count the times on one hand when they'd actually talked to each other in anything akin to a conversation.

"Anyway," Tillie continued enthusiastically, lacing an arm affectionately about Bart's waist, "your father and I've talked about it, and we discussed it with John and Lilah and all three of Shane's brothers last night, as well as Wade's wife, Josie, and Jackson's wife, Lacey, and we're all going to work together to make sure your marriage gets off to a proper start."

Bart nodded, his expression as serious and concerned as Tillie's. "We can't exactly undo that elopement you two had. But we can certainly see your marriage gets off to a much more proper—and public—beginning. Starting tonight."

Greta groaned at the enthusiastic new plans that had replaced her parents' earlier concerns. "The wedding reception," she mumbled again, remembering.

"Right," Tillie and Bart replied in unison.

Greta couldn't help it. She moaned, even louder.

"Now, I know you probably don't have anything appropriate to wear," Tillie continued, reading only the first of Greta's many anxieties about the Big Event.

Greta rolled her eyes. "You can say that again." Plus, she was so busy with deliveries and wait-staff meetings and training she didn't know when she would ever have a chance to shop.

"But not to worry," Tillie smiled brightly. As usual, she was several steps ahead of Greta on the domestic front. "I've already arranged for Jenna Lockhart to come over and get your measurements this morning."

No sooner had Greta managed to get rid of her well-meaning but far-too-pushy parents, than Jenna Lockhart breezed in. The owner of the premier women's clothing boutique in the state, and an up-and-coming designer in her own right, she was also an old school chum of Greta's. Growing up, Greta had often thought that the four Lockhart women were, in many respects, the community's answer to the McCabe men in terms of stubbornness, spirit and family pride. And, not surprisingly, the Lockhart women were just as hard to pin down when it came to their love lives. None had married, or at last count, intended to marry anytime soon. They were all too interested in pursuing their careers and maintaining their freedom.

Given the way her life was going, Greta thought, as the two women retired to Greta's private office to take her measurements, that did not seem like such a bad thing.

Jenna whipped out her tape measure, pad and pen. She took one look at Greta's face and grinned. "Let me guess. Tillie strikes again."

Greta nodded. "She's driving me crazy."

"She and Lilah mean well." Jenna stretched her measuring tape across Greta's shoulders. "And look at it this way, you're getting a wedding reception with none of the usual headaches, since you don't have to bother with any of the details."

Greta held her arm above her head as Jenna measured from the underside of her arm to her waist. "The way things have been going, I don't even want to go."

"Ah, but you must." Jenna paused to scribble measurements down on the pad before grinning optimistically. "Besides, you're going to look beautiful."

Greta didn't doubt that for a moment. It was impossible to slip into one of Jenna's designs and not look stunning, no matter what your size or shape. And the woman in her did want to look as good as possible for

Shane. Still, this was awfully last minute. "You really have something for me to wear?" Greta asked.

"Oh, yeah." Jenna nodded contentedly. "That is, if you trust me to take what I already have in the shop and pick the dress that is so dazzling you'll take Shane's breath away."

Trust wasn't the issue. "I don't have time to come over for an actual fitting—" Greta said as Jenna soberly measured Greta from shoulder to ankle. She had the wait staff coming to pick up the red-white-and-blue Lone Star Dance Hall T-shirts and bandannas that would, along with denim skirts and jeans, comprise their uniforms. They also had to fill out the tax forms required by the government that would enable them to get paid.

"It's okay. I'll use the dressmaker's dummy," Jenna told Greta breezily. "And don't worry about the bill. Your folks are taking care of it."

"Thanks." Greta continued to hold up her arms as Jenna measured her bust, hips, and waist. "You know this party's going to be held outdoors—at John and Lilah's ranch?"

Jenna nodded and rocked back on her heels. "I'm thinking ethereal and breezy, if that's okay with you."

Greta nodded enthusiastically. "Sounds good."

Jenna smiled. "Any idea how you're going to be wearing your hair? Up or down?"

"Probably swept up off my neck," Greta decided. It would be cooler.

"Perfect." Jenna collected her belongings. "I've got another two appointments back-to-back late this afternoon, but I'll have someone bring your dress over to you by five. Will that give you enough time? I know the festivities are supposed to start around eight tonight."

"Plenty of time," Greta said. Now all she had to do was gather up her courage, and go.

SHANE HEARD THE SOUND system from the parking lot. Greta had it cranked up full blast. But judging from the absence of other cars and trucks in the parking lot, there did not appear to be anyone else there with her. Not sure what he'd find, he walked into the club. Greta was in leotards, dancing her heart out, looking every bit as incredibly graceful and talented as a pro. He watched entranced as, completely oblivious to him, she spun and shimmied and poured her heart and soul out to the foot-tapping beat. When the song ended—all too soon in his opinion—she went into the splits bending over her outstretched knee in a deep graceful bow.

Shane broke the silence with a long, low wolf whistle of appreciation.

Greta looked up, her face flushed becomingly. "I didn't know you were there."

He noted the perspiration dotting her face and the way her leotard was clinging damply to her lithe, supple body. "Obviously." He helped her up, trying hard not to notice the jutting ends of her nipples and the way her leotard closely molded the soft swell of her breasts. He rocked forward on his heels, hoping to ease the pressure building at the front of his jeans. "Shouldn't you be saving a little something for the reception tonight?"

Greta grabbed a white cotton towel from a nearby table. She wiped the dampness from her face and neck. Studied him wordlessly. "You don't know, do you?" she guessed softly.

"What?" With effort, Shane kept his eyes from dropping to her breasts again.

Greta smiled wryly as she took him by the wrist.

"Your parents sent over something for you to wear." Wordlessly she led him across the dance floor to her private office. Hanging on the door were two garment bags, one bearing the logo of a local men's shop, the other the logo of Jenna Lockhart's boutique.

Shane stared in amazement at the contents of the longer garment bag. "Is that a wedding dress?"

Greta grimaced. "Yes, as a matter of fact, Shane, it is."

He shook his head in silent commiseration.

"And guess what they sent over for you to wear?" Greta continued sweetly.

Shane drew a bolstering breath. "I'm afraid to ask."

"A tuxedo and black dress boots."

Figured. Shane sidestepped several boxes of brand-new dinner, beverage and dessert menus and seated himself on the edge of Greta's desk. He folded his arms in front of him. "Who's idea was this?"

Greta threw up her hands. "Does it even matter?" She turned a thoroughly exasperated glance to him. "I don't even want to go."

He didn't either. But that was neither here nor there, under the circumstances. "Given the fact that the whole damn town has been invited to this shindig out at my parents' ranch," Shane returned dryly, "I don't think we have that option."

"Sure we do." Greta grinned impishly as she looped the ends of her towel playfully around his neck. "We'll just send our regrets."

"And have my three brothers hunt us down and cart us there, regardless of our feelings?" Shane hooked a hand around her waist and tugged her between his spread legs. "No. No way."

Looking completely comfortable in his loose embrace,

Greta situated herself on his lap. She looked up at him questioningly. "So you don't mind they're carrying this to extremes?"

Shane shrugged. "Well. We did agree to a reception." And he couldn't say he minded anything that would give him an excuse to kiss and hold and be close to Greta.

Greta's lower lip slid out petulantly. "We never said we'd go dressed as bride and groom!"

Shane shifted her around so he could see her face and gently sifted a hand through the tousled mane of her long blond hair. "Greta, honey, you're looking at this the wrong way."

Greta smoothed a hand absently across his chest. "And what, pray tell, is the right away?"

Shane reveled in the soft sensuality of her touch. "Our parents are still trying to make us cry uncle."

A troubled light crept into her pretty blue eyes. "It's gone way beyond that, Shane." In a low, sexy tone Greta filled Shane in on the meeting with her parents that morning.

Shane covered her hand with his own. "Did you tell them how you felt?"

"What's the point?" Greta blew out a soft gust of breath. "They don't listen. They've never listened. If I hadn't had my dancing—" Greta paused and shook her head.

Shane let his hand slip beneath her hair. He'd seen how overbearing her well-meaning parents could be whenever they were trying to do what was best for Greta, and his heart went out to her. Tenderly he massaged the tense muscles in the back of her neck. "That's how you vent all your frustration, isn't it? By dancing your heart out."

Her chin came up and she admitted in a soft, sweet

voice, "As well as every other emotion I might have. Works, too." She made a weary face. "Usually."

"But not today," he observed, wishing they were back at the ranch so he could kiss her and just see where things went from there.

"No," Greta said soberly, letting her hand fall like an anchor to her lap, then rest against his thigh. She sighed loudly. "Not today."

If there had been some way to avoid the festivities, Shane would have suggested it. Unfortunately, there wasn't. "Look. It's a party," he said amiably. "We'll go home, get cleaned up and head over. We can even leave early, if you want."

For the first time since he'd arrived, Greta began to look hopeful. "You promise?"

Shane had never wanted to shelter and protect a woman more than he wanted to Greta at that moment. "We're newlyweds." Shane bent, kissed her cheek and winked. "We can do anything we want and still be excused, as long as we use our passion for each other as an excuse."

Greta brightened as she bounced off his lap. "You think so?"

Shane nodded firmly. "I know so."

SHANE HAD JUST TUGGED ON his black trousers and pleated white shirt when Greta dashed in, in a drift of perfume. Her pretty face was flooded with color, and she was wearing a kimono that stopped well above the knee, lacy white stockings and satin high heels. Shane's gaze traveled the length of her curvaceous dancer's legs wistfully before returning to her face. Damn but she was beautiful, with her makeup on and her pale-blond hair pinned up on the back of her head in a sexy swirl of curls. And she wasn't even wearing her wedding dress yet. Clearly, he thought, she was the most stunning bride he'd ever seen.

"I need your help." Greta grabbed his hand and tugged him anxiously toward the master bedroom where she had been dressing. "I don't think I can get into this dress by myself."

To tell the truth Shane was kind of curious as to what she had on beneath that robe. He grinned wickedly, thinking this was certainly one way to find out. He spread his hands wide and fell in behind her, enjoying that view, too. "I'm here to serve," he told her drolly.

Still clasping his hand securely in hers, Greta cast him a harried look over her shoulder. "I also need a little help with a petticoat."

"Okay." Shane paused, then had to ask, "What's that?"

"This." Greta handed him a white cellophane bag about the size of a rolled-up sleeping bag with something gauzy inside. "Open it for me, and shake it out, will you?"

Shane did as ordered, and the stiff under-layers of the petticoat spread out like one of those highway cones, wide at the bottom, narrow at the top. "Hey, I think this thing could stand alone," Shane said. He let go of it and stood back, and sure enough, it did.

"Tell me about it," Greta muttered beneath her breath. Her eyes still firmly fixed on the petticoat, she shrugged out of her kimono and tossed it on the bed. "I don't know if I should step into it or put it over my head." Completely oblivious to how sexy she looked in her white satin bustier, bikini panties, garter belt, and thigh-high stockings, Greta continued frowning at the petticoat.

Shane struggled in vain to keep the blood from pooling in his groin. Tearing his gaze from the soft curves of her breasts, spilling out of the low-cut satin-and-lace cups, he swallowed hard and attempted to moisten his throat. "Over your head." He didn't think he could handle it if she bent over.

Figuring if they were going to get to that reception at all, they needed to get Greta covered as soon as possible, Shane grabbed the petticoat and helped slide it over her head. The opening at the waist was narrow, and momentarily caught around first her shoulders, then her breasts. Glad for the distraction, he had to help her extricate the layers of organza petticoat from the satin bustier, then smooth it down over her rib cage and settle it around her waist.

"Now take the two strings at the waist and tie them together loosely for me." Greta turned away from him and braced her hands against the wall. She turned her head to his, and her face was suddenly, tantalizingly close to his. "Okay. Now pull them tight," she ordered sternly as he breathed in the heavenly floral scent of her perfume. Her foot tapping restlessly, she waited impatiently for him to comply with her wishes.

He struggled with the strings, pretending he didn't want to ravish her then and there. "Tighter. Okay. That's good. Now knot it, just like that. Yeah. Now for the dress."

He was ridiculously happy to be helping her with this. "Over your head, too?"

She nodded.

Shane's eyes widened with surprise as he picked up the delicate-looking satin dress. "Damn, this thing is heavy."

Greta's lower lip took on a soft, kissable curve as she turned to face him. "Most wedding dresses are."

He studied her curiously. "You know this from experience?"

Greta nodded and had no qualms admitting, "I was so excited when I got engaged to Walter, I couldn't wait to go wedding dress shopping. I think every woman feels the same way."

Shane lifted the gown over her head and helped her into it. "Did you find one you liked?"

"No. I tried on dozens," Greta admitted as she shimmied into the bodice, then smoothed it over her bust, ribs and hips. "But I didn't like the way I looked in any of them."

A precursor to the fate of their union? Shane wondered as Greta turned her back to him, skirts rustling softly.

Being careful not to step on the hem of her wedding gown, Shane zipped and buttoned while Greta studied her reflection in the full-length mirror on the back of the bedroom door. He inclined his head at her wedding dress. "What about this one?"

HER PULSE POUNDING, Greta studied her reflection. The white satin dress Jenna had designed was sleeveless, with a jewel-necked, form-fitting bodice and full, poufy skirt. It was simple. Elegant. And paired perfectly with the narrow, satin-covered tiara Jenna had sent for Greta's upswept hair. "I do like it," she murmured happily. It was the embodiment of all her childhood dreams.

"You ought to." Shane grinned and rested his hands on her shoulders. He met her eyes in the mirror. "You're gorgeous," he said softly.

When he looked at her like that, she felt like the only

woman in the world. Greta smoothed her hands across his chest. "You're gorgeous, too."

Shane grinned. "I'm half-dressed."

Freshly shaven. Blond hair damp and rumpled and scented with shampoo. Bootless, his shirt open and untucked, his bow tie hanging loose on either side of his collar, he was so heart-stoppingly sexy he deserved to be featured in a calender of gorgeous men. And if she didn't stop looking at him that way, he was going to guess what she had already begun to suspect—that her childhood crush on him had deepened and grown by leaps and bounds in the time they'd been together. To the degree where she might very well be falling irrevocably, head-over-heels in love with him…and she might not want this make-believe-it's-real marriage of theirs to end when the time came. And that would be a disaster.

Especially with him looking at her as though he wanted to make mad, passionate love all night long for the second night in a row.

Reminding herself that she and Shane had agreed to end this farce when the time was right, she smiled. And told herself the best course of action was to get him all the way dressed, too. "Let me help you." Trying not to feel so much like a schoolgirl on her first date, Greta grabbed the edges of his shirt and began buttoning it. When she'd finished, she fastened the black onyx studs that covered the buttons.

"We keep this up, we'll never get there," Shane teased playfully as he opened his fly and tucked his shirt inside his black trousers. "I'll have you in that bed in no time flat."

Her mouth dry, Greta tore her eyes from his obvious arousal. "I don't doubt it for a minute." Her expression deceptively tranquil, Greta assisted him with the black satin cummerbund and suspenders. Finished, she reached up to tie his bow tie. "And don't think it isn't where I'd like to be, too, rather than some guilt-provoking reception in our honor," she told him honestly.

Shane caught the back of her palm and kissed it. "Then why don't we stay home?"

Greta sighed. "Because, as you said, if we did, they'd send out a search party," she told him wistfully. "And when it comes to being found in compromising positions in bed—" Greta paused and shook her head disparagingly "—been there, done that."

"True. Although—" Shane shook his head at her disparagingly "—the first time, it was entirely innocent."

Greta rolled her eyes as she helped him on with his tuxedo jacket. "Good luck convincing everyone *we* know of that."

Before she could step back to admire her handiwork, Shane took her into his arms, holding her as close as her poufy skirt would allow. Greta tilted her head up to his. The dark tuxedo and starched white shirt made his skin look very tanned, his eyes very gray.

"Maybe they saw what we didn't," he said softly, smoothing a hand down her spine.

"What?" Greta asked softly.

"This." He slanted his mouth over hers, and she lost her breath at the first touch of his lips on hers. Everything around them faded until there was only the hot, silky pressure of his kiss. And once their lips had touched again, there was no stopping with just one kiss. Yearning swept through her in sweet, wild waves. Greta wreathed her arms about his neck and moved as close as her voluminous skirts would allow. Molding herself against him, she kissed him back again and again and again. With a low moan of satisfaction, he urged her closer yet, wrapping her in the warm security of his tall, strong body, wooing and seducing until her whole body seemed to melt and come alive in his arms, and that was, of course, when the doorbell rang.

Swearing at the interruption, Shane lifted his mouth from hers. He rested his forehead against hers as they both caught their breaths. "Who in the heck is that?" he demanded.

Greta shrugged. She wasn't expecting anyone.

Frowning, Shane danced Greta backward over to the window. He continued to hold her close as they looked outside. A white stretch limo, decorated with pastel-colored streamers, was waiting.

Shane rapped on the window. The driver stepped back and looked up. Shane waved to the driver, acknowledging he'd been seen and they'd be down directly. "At least we'll get there in style."

And thanks to their parents, Greta thought, on time.

"I'VE NEVER SEEN THIS many cars in one place in my life," Greta said as the limo approached the lovely Texas ranch where Shane had grown up. She stared in amazement at the vast collection of cars and trucks parked on both sides of the long paved drive leading up to the sprawling ranch house. "Unless you count a Dallas Cowboys football game."

"Or the DFW airport parking lot," Shane agreed.

Greta shook her head in exasperation, recalling what the newspaper article had stated. "Well, they said everyone in town was invited."

"I know." Shane compressed his lips together tightly. "I just didn't think everyone would accept, especially on such short notice."

Greta looked at the tents erected on the lawn, the catering trucks, the lights, the flowers. The videographer and photographer at the ready. She'd seen less production on a Hollywood film set. "Talk about going overboard," she muttered. Clearly this was not going to be the cake-and-punch only event she had been hoping for. Worse, the more involved the festivities, the longer the reception—and deception—would last. "And are those—oh, my heavens—chairs? Shane!" Greta leaned forward urgently and gripped his arm. "Do you see that?"

Shane stared at the five hundred or so white folding chairs. Many of them filled. Even more people standing around. He released a long breath. "Looks like there's more than a reception planned here, doesn't it?"

Greta's heart sank like a stone. "Looks like a ceremony, too." Beginning to panic, Greta gripped his arm even more tightly. "I don't think I can go through with this."

Now that he'd scoped out the situation, Shane didn't seem half as upset as she was by the elaborate goings-on around them. "Sure you can," he told her confidently.

Unable to figure out why he wasn't more upset—after all, Shane liked being backed into a corner even less than she did—Greta protested. "Shane..."

He leaned over, wrapped a comforting arm about her shoulders, and kissed her cheek. "Just trust me, Greta. It'll be fine."

As soon as the vehicle stopped beneath the canopy leading to the front porch, the doors to the limo were yanked open. Shane's three brothers—all wearing tuxes—were ready and waiting. As was Dani Lockhart. And two of Greta's other dear friends, who were all—not surprisingly—carrying bridesmaid bouquets and dressed in very beautiful full-length silk dresses. The photographer and videographer aimed their cameras at them as they emerged from the limo. Greta shook her head at her friends. "I can't believe you didn't clue me in on all this," she scolded.

"Hey, we were sworn to secrecy." Dani spoke for the group.

"Well, you all certainly kept your end of the bargain," Greta said.

"Hey, didn't anyone ever tell you you're not supposed to see the bride before the wedding?" Jackson McCabe demanded.

"I don't think that applies when you're already married," Shane said, as his brothers took him in hand and hustled him away.

Greta stared at Shane's retreating back as she was ushered toward the ranch house. "Where are they taking him?"

"Off to get ready for the ceremony," Dani replied, leading the way. "Which is where you're going, too."

"I am ready," Greta declared over the tumultuous beat of her heart.

"You don't have a veil on."

"That's because I don't have one," Greta replied, unable to think of a single way out of this.

"Yes, you do." Dani patted her arm reassuringly. "Jenna has it upstairs."

Greta was hustled up the stairs, where Lilah McCabe and Tillie were waiting. They both looked stunning in mother-of-the-bride dresses. Lacey and Josie, the other recently wed McCabe brides, were there to offer their best wishes and assistance, and were stunningly attired, too.

"We didn't think you and Shane would ever feel really married unless you had a real wedding,'' Tillie explained patiently.

"So we figured,'' Lilah continued happily, handing Greta a beautiful bouquet of yellow roses, "as long as we were throwing the reception, why not throw the wedding, too.''

"This is your something new.'' A smiling Jenna Lockhart stepped behind Greta and attached the waist-length veil and blusher, via very thin Velcro strips, to the satin tiara Greta had already laced through her upswept hair.

"Your something old.'' Tillie's eyes shimmering with hope and tenderness, she fastened a heart-shaped diamond necklace that had belonged to her grandmother around Greta's neck.

"Your something borrowed.'' Lilah gave Greta a lacy white handkerchief that Shane's mother had carried, tucked into the sleeve of her gown, on her wedding day.

"And something blue.'' Dani waved a frilly blue garter then knelt as she and the other two bridesmaids ever so gently gathered up Greta's voluminous satin skirt and petticoat and helped Greta slip it on. "You're all set.'' And everything was just as it should have been. Except one thing.

He didn't love her.

And she didn't love him.

Or did she?

Down below, the strains of the orchestra on the lawn could be heard, and Greta understood the term *consequences* as never before. She had to call a halt or make this real. And practical or not, she knew what her heart wanted her to do.

Bart Wilson appeared in the doorway. "It's time,

honey," he announced, his demeanor proud and un-flinching, his eyes misty with sentiment.

Feeling as though she'd been hit by a truck, knowing there was no turning back, that the time to stop this train had long passed, Greta clasped her bouquet tightly in her hands. Hoping like heck Shane would know what to do to get them out of this, she headed for her father.

"BLUSHER OVER YOUR FACE or behind your head?" the bridal consultant whom Tillie and Lilah had hired to help throw things together asked Greta as she waited, just inside the house, to take her turn up the aisle.

"Over my face," Greta murmured, knowing if her heart beat any harder it was going to leap right out of her chest.

"You feeling okay, honey?" Bart asked.

Greta nodded, aware her knees were trembling. "Just a little nervous."

"Me, too." Bart patted her arm and smiled before continuing thickly, "It's not every day I give my only daughter away, you know."

Greta knew. Worse, she not only looked like a real bride, she felt like one. And it wasn't just the fact she was actually going through a real wedding ceremony, albeit not of her own choosing or prior knowledge. Thanks to the way he kept kissing her, she was even beginning to feel—in her most unguarded moments—that she and Shane had a chance to make this sham marriage of theirs a real one. But it wasn't going to happen. And she didn't want to delude herself into thinking it would.

Yet, as she walked up the aisle to the hauntingly beautiful and emotional strains of Johann Pachelbel's "Canon in D" and looked first at the faces of their families and friends, and then at Shane, standing so proudly at the other end of the aisle, it was all she could do not to be swept up by the moment…to believe that, if they only tried hard enough, made their vows real enough, they could take the passion they felt for each other and the circumstances that had brought them together and turn it all into a real marriage. And that feeling—that the impossible might just, with a little love and a little luck, be possible—only intensified as her father stood with her before the minister to give his only daughter away at the altar.

SHANE HADN'T EXPECTED any of the hoopla awaiting him and Greta, but he'd thought he could handle it nevertheless. He thought he could get through it without involving his emotions or altering his plans to stay with Greta as long as they both deemed necessary—or even pleasurable—and then go their separate ways, never to be bothered by familial matchmaking again. And he managed just fine until he saw Greta walking down the aisle on her father's arm. Then suddenly this getting-married business became very real.

And to his growing chagrin, it stayed real through their vows, through the exchange of rings, the lighting of the unity candle and the extinguishing of their own individual candles. It stayed real through the kiss and the walk back down the aisle and the sit-down dinner that followed. But never, Shane realized ruefully, did it seem more genuine than during the champagne toasts.

Chapter Nine

John McCabe went first. For the first time all week, he looked proud as could be of his son. Shane wasn't sure if he was happy or aggravated to discover his seemingly solid marriage was the reason. As much as he yearned for his father's approval, the thinking behind it put a pressure on him he didn't need. Things between Greta and him were muddled enough as it was.

"You've pulled off a lot of stunts, son," John raised his glass of champagne to Greta and Shane, "but running off and marrying Greta is one we approve of...."

To Shane's increasing discomfort, Bart Wilson followed, his own mood sunny and optimistic. Whatever reservations he'd had earlier in the week seemed to have faded in light of the "appropriateness" of the match.

"Greta's always been an independent-minded young woman—to the point where her mother and I were both beginning to think she wouldn't ever settle down and get married and have a family. But—" Bart winked at his new son-in-law in man-to-man fashion "—if anyone can tame our Greta and help her settle down, it's you, Shane."

Travis, the best man, lifted his glass next. He was the most cynical of all four McCabe sons. Shane could see that beneath the surface geniality, Travis still had his private doubts about Shane and Greta and the reason for their nuptials. Clearly he didn't think saving Greta's reputation or proving a point about the consequences of matchmaking merited a lasting marriage. And though Shane would have agreed with that sentiment wholeheartedly days before, now he wasn't nearly as sure what should be done. He'd asked Greta for at least a few more weeks together and she'd agreed. Now, after they'd made love, he found himself wanting to continue their marriage. But was it fair to Greta? She deserved a lot more than a temporary thing—they both did.

"Maybe it has something to do with being the baby of the family," Travis quipped with a facetious grin, "but Shane's always hated coming in last at anything." Glass raised, Travis shook his head. "So I should've known when our other two brothers got married to such warm, wonderful, all-fired pretty women that Shane wouldn't be far behind in settling down with his own."

Competition had nothing to do with it, Shane thought, incensed. He'd married Greta to have a little fun and prove a point, that was all. But it was clear not one of all the people there, including Greta, really believed it. They all thought he was competing with his brothers. And they didn't automatically see that as a bad thing. To them, all four of the McCabe brothers should want to get married and settle down, pronto, so John and Lilah could have some grandkids.

Dani Lockhart, the maid of honor, went last. "If there's one thing Greta's always lusted after, besides Shane—" Dani paused as everyone laughed "—it's adventure. And having gone to high school with this handsome fella—" Dani angled her thumb at Shane and gave him an admiring look "—I know that if any man can make things unpredictable and exciting enough to keep Greta thoroughly engaged in this marriage, it'd be Shane McCabe. So, I'd like everyone to lift their glass and wish this most unexpected and handsome and wonderful and fun couple long life and happiness.'' Her eyes brimming with happiness, Dani toasted Shane and Greta, then finished huskily, ''To the bride and groom.''

''To the bride and groom,'' everyone in the room echoed.

Shane and Greta clinked glasses, linked arms and sipped. As their glances meshed and held, Shane found that Greta seemed to be as caught up in the festivities as everyone else. It should have alarmed him to discover that she was beginning to take their impetuous union seriously, too. But it didn't. In fact, it made him feel damn good to know they were really married now. That it was, in fact, so official now in the eyes of the Lord and the community that ''no man might ever put it asunder.'' So official it would be heck to undo. And the more time he had with Greta, the better the chances she would want to just stay married, too.

The cutting of the cake followed. Then, as the strains of ''The Way You Look Tonight'' began, their first dance as husband and wife. Able to see how much the emotional nature of the festivities were getting to her, Shane tugged Greta newlywed close and whispered playfully in her ear, ''Not to worry—we're almost through the part where we make a complete spectacle of ourselves.''

''I know,'' Greta whispered back, cuddling closer.

As they swayed to the romantic music, Shane delighted in the feel of her head on his shoulder, her body so closely entwined with his. Maybe it was the way she had her silky, blond curls twisted up on the back of her head, showing off the slender, graceful neck, or the scent of her perfume, maybe it was the gorgeous, damn-near-ethereal way she looked in her wedding gown and satin tiara, but right now all he wanted to do was pick her up and take her back to his ranch so they could start honeymooning together in earnest. Right now all he wanted was to kiss and hold her and tell her everything that was in his heart and soul, and hear everything that was in hers. And if the way she was suddenly looking up at him was any indication, she wanted it, too. More than anything in the world.

"This is all so real," Greta said as their eyes met and held.

"I know." Shane regarded her soberly as their dance together ended. If ever there was a time to tell her how he was beginning to feel, it was now. "In fact, later, I'd like to talk to you about that."

To Shane's pleasure, Greta looked as if she would like to hear more about his plans to do just that. But too late, the music was already swelling as the orchestra leader announced the father-daughter dance. Loath to let her go, even for a minute, Shane dutifully took Greta by the hand and led her over to Bart. And while the orchestra played an oh-so-romantic version of "It's a Wonderful World" she went into her father's arms for the first and—unless things got revised again between them soon, as he hoped—maybe last time as an officially married woman.

Shane reclaimed her when the orchestra leader invited everyone there to join Greta and Shane on the dance floor that had been erected on the lawn. And it was at that moment Greta spotted them. "I don't believe it," Greta murmured, as she saw Bonnie Sue Baxter, Shane's ex-fiancée and the woman who had cuckolded him, join hands with Beau Chamberlain and tug him onto the dance floor. "Bonnie Sue and Beau are both here!"

Shane lifted a brow. "You didn't know?"

"No." But *he* obviously knew. "When did you find out they were here?"

Shane shrugged, unconcerned. "I noticed them both come in during the prelude, when I was standing up there, waiting for the wedding to get started. They weren't together, though."

"Bonnie Sue probably sought Beau out." Otherwise there was no explanation, because Beau hadn't known about Bonnie Sue Baxter, never mind her history with Shane. Besides, it wasn't the kind of thing he would do. He didn't go in for juvenile tricks. And pairing the two of them together—at her and Shane's wedding celebration—would be a juvenile trick.

"Jealous?" Shane lifted a brow.

Greta shook her head, her unease increasing. "It's not that." But she had no further opportunity to explain because Bonnie Sue and Beau were dancing closer. The next thing she knew, Bonnie Sue was tapping Greta on the shoulder, cutting in.

"Hope you don't mind, honey," Bonnie Sue said. "But I want to dance with your hubby."

Beau tapped Shane. "I want a chance to dance with Greta, too."

Just that quickly she and Shane were separated. Beau danced a stunned Greta off in one direction. Bonnie Sue danced an impassive-faced Shane off in another. Beau's regard was that of a best guy friend and big brother. "Care to bring me up to speed here?" Beau asked.

No, Greta thought, embarrassed, but she'd better before the straight-talking Beau privately recounted what she had said to him earlier. "Our mothers told us they were planning a reception for us to celebrate the nuptials. We didn't know about the wedding ceremony part of it."

"The question is," Beau queried lightly, his concern for her evident, "why did you go through with it?"

Good question. Up to the moment they'd actually said their I dos again, Greta would've said they were bullied and backed into it. Had that been the case, the second recitation of their wedding vows would have felt as scary but meaningless as the first. Except this time their vows weren't meaningless. This time she'd found herself meaning them with all her heart and soul. How crazy was that? Knowing she wasn't ready to voice any of that out loud, Greta merely shrugged and said, "We didn't want to hurt their feelings."

Beau continued to guide her around the dance floor with movie-star smoothness. Quirking a disapproving brow, he predicted, "When they find out the truth about this sham, they're going to be even more hurt and disillusioned."

Maybe they won't ever have to know, Greta thought, then immediately wondered where that thought had come from. "Did you say anything to Bonnie Sue about what I told you?" she demanded uneasily, aware her palm had begun to sweat.

"No. But it was clear that unlike everyone else here tonight she still thinks this is just another one of Shane's legendary escapades. And that's all it'll ever be, to her, despite all this." Beau inclined his head at the festivities around them, then frowned as he looked at Bonnie Sue and Shane, who were every bit as deeply engrossed in intimate conversation as Beau and Greta were.

Beau continued, "She's just waiting for the grand finale that'll bring it all to an end. She'd thought—

hoped—it would be this wingding tonight. That the two of you would refuse to say your vows or stage some big funny scene that would get everyone off the hook, including your folks, and make it look as if it had been planned all along. For some sort of funny, wonderful, ultimately helpful-to-everyone reason. Apparently, all of Shane's previous escapades always ended up bringing about some desperately wanted but previously thought-to-be-impossible change."

"That's true," Greta murmured thoughtfully. "I never thought about it that way, but every time he pulled a prank, it was because of some problem or other that couldn't be solved by way of regular means. There was always some underlying situation that was brought to light. Attention garnered. A solution brought to the fore." The time he'd masqueraded as a state board of education auditor had helped illuminate a situation with a diabolically clever but emotionally abusive teacher whom students had long sensed needed to go, and the teacher had subsequently been removed from the classroom. His pushing the antiquated dress code rules to the limits had resulted in new dress codes being written for the school district. Ditto town curfews for teens. And parking rules and regulations within town limits. His decision to pitch a tent on Main Street had resulted in the permanent placement of two previously homeless families, right there in Laramie. And there had been other whimsical changes, too. Alterations in school district lunch policies and menus, and the way booster club money was distributed.

Beau studied her. "So what's really going on here? Is there some ultimate good that will be done here, that we'll all find out about in the end?"

Like the fact Shane and I really are falling in love

with each other and we want our marriage to continue? Greta thought. Knowing if she could voice her secret hopes to anyone, it was Beau, Greta murmured, "Maybe it's not a sham, after all."

Beau peered at her closely. "How much champagne have you had?" he asked incredulously.

Greta thought back to the way she and Shane had looked at each other during the vows, to the way they had touched and kissed and held each other when they'd made love the night before. Sure, passion had brought them together that way, but tenderness and a kindred spirit had kept them together long after their bodies had been satisfied. "Maybe we're falling in love."

Beau's grip tightened on her in a protective, brotherly way. "Has that rodeo cowboy said as much to you?" he demanded seriously.

"No, but, I feel it," Greta asserted stubbornly. *When he makes love to me,* she finished silently.

Beau studied her. "Are you sure you're not just getting caught up by the atmosphere of it all?"

"What do you mean?" Greta asked as one dance ended and another started and Beau still showed no signs of letting go of her.

In a low, practical voice, Beau explained, "What's happening to you could be the same thing that happens to a lot of inexperienced actors on a movie set. They put so much energy into creating this fictional romance that they get caught up in the chemistry of the moment and start thinking the feelings are real. And then they have a really intense, torrid romance off the set, as well. They just can't help it, the feelings they've created are that powerful. Then, when the movie ends, and the two of them are no longer acting together eighteen or twenty hours a day and the carefully crafted illusion fades, bang! It's over. And they realize there was never anything real or lasting there to begin with, and they're devastated. Worse they feel like complete and utter fools."

Greta felt a sick feeling welling up inside her. "You think that's what's happening to me."

Uncertainty flickered in his eyes. "I know you've developed a real thing for this guy. Anyone can see that. In fact, I think that's why the toasts were so optimistic and why your marriage is now getting the seal of approval from practically everyone. When you walked down the aisle to Shane and you looked at him the way you did, and he looked at you the way he did—if that was acting, kiddo, it was an Academy Award performance."

"Only I can't really act, we both know that," Greta murmured, distressed.

"Right. So…?" Beau let the sentence trail off.

So Shane could. He could carry any prank to the absolute limit. Could and had. Which left her where? As much as Greta hated to admit it, she knew Beau was right. She had been wearing her heart on her sleeve. She wasn't sure she could say the same for Shane.

"I'm not saying that you shouldn't just go for this, if it's right for you," Beau continued seriously, giving her hand a reassuring squeeze. He gave her a sober, heartfelt look. "I just want you to make sure that you protect yourself, that's all."

"LOOKS TO ME AS IF THOSE TWO are pretty darn cozy," Bonnie Sue murmured to Shane from the other side of the dance floor.

Shane refused to get jealous for no reason, even though something about Bucklehead Chamberwaist and his movie-star aura and his protective attitude toward

Greta really irked him to no end. ''They're just friends,'' Shane told Bonnie Sue, wondering why in the world he had ever dated Bonnie Sue for six years, anyway. Had it been habit? Or just the fact he'd been too stubborn and too lazy to correct his mistake? And it had been a mistake. He could see now how self-centered and witchy Bonnie Sue was at heart.

Bonnie Sue batted her eyelashes at him coquettishly as she moved in closer, pressing her slender body against his. ''Is that what she told you?''

Shane pulled his torso away discreetly because he didn't want to cause a scene. Using his grip on her waist and wrist and a judicious angling of his knee, Shane kept Bonnie Sue Baxter at a respectable distance as they continued to dance. He would cut Bonnie Sue loose now, except that he knew if he didn't hear her out, she'd go straight to Greta to finish whatever it was she felt she had to say. He didn't want Greta suffering through that. ''What's your point, Bonnie Sue?'' he asked with thinly veiled impatience.

''You have only to look at the two of them while they're dancing to see Beau's awfully concerned about her.''

As much as he was loath to admit it, Shane knew that was true. And that rankled, too. He was Greta's husband now. He was clearly the only one who should be watching over her.

''Everyone knows Beauregard Chamberlain's first wife put him through hell—to where he said he'd never marry again. Since then he's paid attention to only two women. Our own Laramie native, film critic, Dani Lockhart—whose blood feud with him is fast becoming legendary. And Greta, the only woman he's dated in the two years since he became single again.''

Shane shoved aside the memories of the videotape of Greta and Beau attending all those glamour-filled movie premieres and award shows. "So?"

"So?" Bonnie Sue smiled cattily. "Has it occurred to you that in marrying Greta right beneath Beau's nose, so to speak, that you might have done some damage to Beau's hunky reputation? Damage that a movie star like him can't afford?"

Shane could see how Beau's ego might be hurting. He hadn't thought about the press angle, though. He glanced back at Beau and Greta. Was that what their bent heads were all about? It was apparent they were talking about something intimate. And serious.

Shane paused, irritated to discover how much the idea of Greta with any other guy, other than a friend, of course, rankled. Telling himself the two of them were just friends—he had absolutely nothing to be jealous over—'cause there was nothing going on between Greta and Beau behind Shane's back—Shane shrugged his broad shoulders aimlessly and turned back to Bonnie Sue. "So he's a movie star. That just means he could probably have any woman he wants."

"And the woman he's wanted consistently since his divorce is Greta," Bonnie Sue put in smugly.

Shane knew what Bonnie Sue was trying to imply. That he was being cuckolded again—or was about to be. He was not buying it. He was not putting Greta in the same class with Bonnie Sue Baxter. Sure, he'd been naïve about Bonnie Sue and her "study partner." He wasn't naïve about Greta. "They're not having an affair," Shane told Bonnie Sue firmly.

"Are you sure about that?" Bonnie Sue asked, smiling thoughtfully over at Greta with something akin to awe. "If they're not, if she's been holding out for marriage all this time, then more power to her," Bonnie Sue murmured with respect.

Shane wondered what the two of them could be talking about for so long. "You sound as though you want Greta to be with him again," Shane murmured. Whereas Shane couldn't bear the thought of seeing Greta become Beau's steady date again.

Bonnie Sue gave an indignant sniff. "I don't deny I think they're probably a better match than you and Greta. Just as I don't deny the possibility—much as it pains me to admit it—that Greta might be using you to give Beau Chamberlain a wake-up call, to make him realize he does want to marry her after all."

Bonnie Sue's assertion hit Shane like a right uppercut to the jaw. No way was Greta in love with Beau. No way was she in love with anyone, except maybe him. Otherwise he would have sensed it. Wouldn't he? Aware he'd been blindsided before by what had been staring him in the face, Shane felt himself tense. "Only one problem with that theory," Shane said dryly, calling on his customary self-assurance. He looked down at Bonnie Sue sternly, wordlessly warning her against sharing her theories with anyone else there. "Greta's already married to me."

Bonnie Sue lifted a brow and inclined her head in the direction of Greta and Beau, who were dancing on the other side of the wooden floor that had been erected on the lawn. "But for how long," Bonnie Sue asked smugly, "if Beau comes to his senses and proposes to her?"

"SHE WANTS YOU BACK, doesn't she?"

Shane carried Greta over the threshold, nodded at their limo driver, letting him know it was okay to leave, then shut the door behind him with his foot. Greta still cradled in his arms, he headed up the stairs to the bedroom. "Who?"

"Bonnie Sue."

Shane set Greta down gently on their brand-new king-size bed, which, thanks to the fact they'd spent the previous night making love in the stables, had yet to be used. But it was ready to go. The crisp mint-green sheets and thick and fluffy patchwork quilt had been turned back, the half dozen or so pillows arranged invitingly. "What makes you think that?" Shane asked.

Greta glided over to the table that had been set up next to the window. It was set with a postwedding feast. A magnum of champagne on ice, a platter of fruit, cheese and crackers. Veggies and dip. Tiny quiches. Finger sandwiches. Olives. Nuts. Pretzels. Slices of wedding cake.

"The fact that she showed up at our wedding tonight and then immediately went after my ex-boyfriend." Greta fingered the card from their parents, wishing them a happy "first night" together as man and wife. She handed it to him. Shane glanced at it—made a mental note to thank both sets of parents for all they'd done—then handed it back to Greta.

"I thought he wasn't your boyfriend."

Greta blew out an exasperated breath and dropped the card with a thud. "You know what I mean." Her expression impatient, she turned her face up to his. "So what was she saying to you?"

The jealousy in her low voice pleased Shane. He reached for the bottle of champagne and began working off the cork. "She thinks my marrying you has put a dent in Beau Chamberlain's hunky-movie-star reputation."

Greta shrugged and, petticoats swishing softly, continued to pace. "I'm sure he'd prefer I were still available to attend the award shows with him. There's something to be said for not having to worry about getting a date, you know."

Shane popped the cork. He held the overflowing bottle over the bucket. "Did you tell him we intend to stay married?" Wiping off the excess with a towel, Shane filled two long-stemmed champagne flutes.

"For a couple of weeks," Greta admitted, accepting the drink he gave her. "He thought the whole thing was a bad idea. And I've got to tell you, after seeing our parents' faces tonight, I have to agree with him."

Shane linked arms with Greta. Silently they toasted each other, then sipped the delicious golden liquid. "What do you mean?" Shane's glance narrowed curiously.

Greta swallowed, looking suddenly miserable as they disengaged arms and she took off her veil. "They think we're in love with each other, Shane."

And maybe, just maybe, Shane thought, undoing his bow tie with one hand, they were.

But he could tell that Greta would never believe him if he said it to her now. Not after everything that had happened, and the cockeyed way their romance had begun. The truth was he had gone about this courtship with her all wrong. It would take time—and a lot of effort on his part—to undo all that. But it could be done. Shane was sure of that. All he needed was time and opportunity. Because if there was one thing his conversation with Bonnie Sue tonight had taught him, it was that he didn't want to lose Greta. And if his instincts were right on this, Greta didn't want to lose him, either. He just had to help her realize that. And the best way to do that, was not through talk, but through action.

Not giving her a chance to debate, Shane took her in his arms. He gave her a cocky smile, saw her eyes turn stormy with desire. Lowering his head, he eased her closer and pressed his lips to hers. Aware he'd never wanted a woman the way he wanted Greta, he kissed her the way he had wanted to kiss her from the moment he'd helped her into her wedding dress. Greta moaned, a soft, helpless little sound in the back of her throat that sent his senses swimming. With a surge of desperation, he deepened the kiss even more. Her mouth was pliant beneath his, warm and sexy, her body soft, supple, surrendering. Her arms lifted, wreathed around his neck, pulled him closer yet. Loving the way she responded to him, the way she trembled when she realized they were going to make love, Shane put everything he had into the kiss. He was determined this night would be every bit as memorable as their first time. Even more so. Her mouth opened and his tongue delved deep, tasting, caressing.

"Shane—" Greta whispered.

"Don't say no to me, Greta," Shane whispered, raining kisses down her neck, across her collarbone, and the uppermost swell of her breasts. "Don't say no to us." Because nothing…nothing…had ever seemed as right as this.

Greta hitched in a breath and brought his lips back to hers; it was all the answer he needed. He reached behind her and unbuttoned and unzipped his way down her back, kissing her all the while. Her caution fading as swiftly as it had appeared, she clung to him, kissing him back, plundering his mouth with voracious intensity, in a way that let him know she did want this, too. Had for hours. And yet, Shane realized in frustration, his kiss both sweeter and harder than he'd intended, there was still so much between them—layers and layers of clothing.

His whole body throbbing, Shane broke off the kiss. "Greta, honey," he told her breathlessly, still cupping her face between his hands, "we've got to get you out of this dress."

Greta looked up at him, her eyes a soft, misty blue. Smiling, she stepped back. No longer the shy wallflower he recalled from his youth, but the fearless woman—the sexy, loving, inherently adventurous and inventive wife—she'd become, she parted her soft lips in an inherently mysterious smile. "Okay, cowboy, I'll go first," she quipped, her eyes wide, the irises mischievously bright, as if she had suddenly thought up something deliciously naughty. Lovingly she splayed her hands across his chest. "But just so you know—" she stood on tiptoe and kissed him provocatively, not stopping till he pulsed and groaned "—you're next."

Still smiling like a woman head-over-heels in love with him, she offered him her back. Not caring they hadn't said the words yet. Might never say the words. He slipped the dress down over her shoulders, her arms, past her waist, until it could go no farther without ripping. Scowling in mounting frustration—he wanted her naked, beneath him—Shane paused to size up the situation. With her petticoat still on there was no graceful or easy way to get her wedding gown past it. Who would have thought getting her out of the dress would be a lot harder than getting her in it? "Wrong way, huh?" Shane asked.

Greta turned to face him, perversely pleased to see she was getting to him the same way he was getting to her. "Appears so," she drawled. "What do you say, shall we try again?"

"Gonna have to," Shane answered, aware he was already hard as a rock, and all they'd done was kiss.

Suddenly looking as impatient as he was to get her out of the beautiful gown, Greta lifted her arms above her head. The action inadvertently pushed her breasts together and Shane groaned at the sight of the plump mounds spilling out of the cups. Inhaling deeply of the rich floral scent of her perfume, he gathered her long, voluminous skirt, crushing it in his hands. "Hold still now," he warned, his desire to make love to her deepening with every second that passed.

"As if I could safely do anything else," Greta quipped, her low sexy voice muffled by the layers of satin. She paused as Shane continued to struggle with the voluminous bell-shaped skirt of the dress. "How's it coming?"

Not soon enough. "Almost there." Past her breasts, over her head, arms. He whisked the length of it over her head. He laid it over a chair, aware that even winning the national rodeo hadn't left him with the same sense of accomplishment as this had. He waggled his eyebrows at her in giddy anticipation. "Free at last."

Greta laughed softly, swished her swirling organza petticoat, before turning back around with a seductive sway of her slender hips. "Not yet, cowboy, but we're working on it."

"Ah, but this is easy." Shane stepped behind her, untied the petticoat and slipped that, too, over her head. Glad to be rid of it, he tossed it aside, turned back to her and lost his breath. He'd seen her clad thus before. Then, knowing the reception was ahead of them, he hadn't dared take more than a quick look, for fear they'd never get there. Now that he had an entire wedding night of lovemaking ahead of him, he indulged till his heart was content. Her white satin-and-lace bustier cupped her waist, ribs and breasts like a second skin, clearly delineating the soft, milky white globes and dusky centers. The top of her lacy garter belt covered her delectably from navel to hipbone. Beneath that were several inches of silky bare skin and the flare of her hips. Bikini panties, transparent, lacy and deliciously brief, shadowed a nest of golden curls and cupped the most feminine part of her. Four garters stretched leisurely across her hip bones, down her bare, lusciously smooth thighs. Midway between her hips and knees, the stockings started, cloaking her slim, sexy legs before disappearing into delicate white satin high heels.

"You like?" she queried sexily as the blood rushed to his groin.

Shane nodded, a pulse throbbing visibly in his throat. If this wasn't heaven, he didn't know what was. He bent and touched his lips to the diamond necklace around her neck. "You bet I like," he said hoarsely, his palms ghosting playfully down her spine, up again, across her shoulders, down her arms.

"I'm glad," Greta whispered as he grinned down at her with a thoroughly male satisfaction. "Because now it's my turn to undress you."

The mesmerizing look of a temptress in her soft-blue eyes, Greta stepped behind him and brought his tuxedo jacket slowly down his arms. Dropped it next to her petticoat. Finished, she stood on tiptoe, pressed herself against him and touched her lips to his, until another surge of heat fired into his groin. She kissed him again, a kiss that was shattering in its possessive sensuality.

Shane groaned, his control fading as surely—and irrevocably—as hers remained. "Greta—"

"Too slow?" Greta teased.

Shane wanted a lifetime with her, but for now—for tonight—he would take each moment as it came. "Way too slow," he confirmed. Intending to remedy that, he reached for his bow tie, only to have her hand cover his. No way was she letting him call the shots when it was her turn to have fun. Recalling his decision to let her take over, at least for a while, Shane merged their lips in a long steamy kiss as she fumbled with his tie. It took some time, but finally Greta dropped the tie next to his jacket. His cummerbund and suspenders soon followed. And then it was her turn to initiate a kiss. Sifting her hands through his hair, she kissed him again. Slowly, lingeringly. Lovingly. She unbuttoned his shirt, helped him out of it.

He grinned at her, intrigued by her boldness and growing more aroused by the moment. "You're enjoying this, aren't you?" Too much, maybe.

"You bet! I never had the chance to be a bad girl growing up." And she was relishing every instant of it now, Shane noted, pleased, as Greta swiftly helped undo his belt, unzip his fly. "Oops," she said when she lowered his trousers past his knees. She knelt next to his dressy black boots, her breasts spilling out of her lacy, translucent bustier. "Guess I better do these first."

Shane reveled in the view. "Depends on how tangled up you like me and my clothes," Shane said hoarsely, rocking forward slightly as he attempted to ease the pressure in his groin. He was beginning to wonder how he had ever managed without her. She brought so much joy to him, so much fire. With Greta in his life, everything and anything seemed possible. Even marriage...the kind that lasted for life.

Still grinning impishly, Greta eased off one boot, then, the other. "Truth to tell," Greta said, her tongue darting out to moisten her lower lip in a way that aroused Shane all the more. She winked at him as she worked the trousers the rest of the way down his legs. "I like you best in nothing at all."

Shane chuckled. His hands itched to caress her. "Keep going and you'll have your wish."

Finished, Greta tossed his pants aside. "Then again," she said, and, still kneeling in front of him, traced her palms over the clinging bikini briefs that hid nothing of his anatomy, "I like you like this, too."

"Sure about that?" Shane taunted playfully. Deciding she'd been in the driver's seat long enough, he caught her by the hand, tugged her up and brought her flush against him.

Greta stared up into his ruggedly handsome face, aware her heart was beating double time. Lower, where their two bodies touched, there was an altogether too-familiar warmth pooling in her middle. "What'd you have in mind?"

"This," Shane said. He bent her backward from the waist, leaning the weight of her against one braced leg. His mouth came down on hers, touched briefly. He watched the shock and the delight in her eyes, then moved to the nape of her neck, where he traced lazy sensual patterns of his own design. "And this—" Knowing he had another surprise left, Shane righted her slowly, released her. An enigmatic smile tugging at his lips, he went to the closet, rummaged around for a moment, then returned promptly, the sought-after object in hand.

"THE HONEYMOON KIT!" Greta exclaimed, a riot of color creeping into her pretty cheeks. Every time she thought she had him pegged, he turned around and surprised her.

A roguish smile tugging at his sensually chiseled lips, Shane shrugged. "J.P. and his missus wanted us to use it." Apparently ready and willing to comply, Shane emptied the contents out on the bed.

Shocked, and trying not to be, Greta looked at the array of lotions, lubricants, textured condoms, all of which promised to be—if used imaginatively—very naughty. "I've never done anything like this," she said.

The hint of evening beard on his face making him look all the more delectable, dangerous and alluring, Shane drew her down to lie beside him on the bed. Her heart raced as he captured her hands with his, and then held her arms pinned loosely on either side of her. "To tell you the truth…neither have I," he whispered wickedly.

"But your rep—" Greta protested as yet another thrill swept through her.

"More fiction than fact." Shane confirmed as he slipped over her, settled between her thighs. "But that can all change," he promised, a playful light in his gray eyes, "if you're game."

Why not? Greta thought. Hadn't she stood on the sidelines watching long enough? Wasn't this her wildest, hottest, most unabashedly erotic fantasy come true? "Okay," Greta said softly. "I'll play. But only if I get to go first."

THAT, SHANE HADN'T RECKONED ON. But then, there was a lot about Greta he hadn't reckoned on. "Since it's our wedding night, I'll be a true gentleman and let your wish be my command.'' He released her and rolled onto his back, and with a look of smug male satisfaction, propped his hands behind his head. Clearly, he was ready to make their lovemaking last the whole night through. ''Play away, Greta, honey.''

''I was hoping you'd say that.'' Beneath her bustier, Greta's nipples had tightened into hard buds of arousal. She studied the flavors, her whole body tingling with need as she recalled just how insatiable and determined a lover Shane could be. But she could be bold and exciting, too, and she'd prove it to him. ''Which flavor lotion do you want me to use?'' Though she meant her voice to sound commanding, it came out breathless.

Shane glanced at the array of choices. ''Pineapple,'' he decided finally, his voice so low and sexy and ready for action it held her mesmerized.

Greta'd read somewhere that for men the more visual the lovemaking experience, the better. She'd never tried out the theory, of course, but she'd always wanted to. She also had an idea what Shane was expecting from her. She was determined to surprise him with something different. Something they hadn't done the previous night. Kneeling astride his thighs, she uncapped the pineapple-flavored lotion, poured a dollop in the palm of one hand. Ignoring the quivering in her middle, she dipped the ends of her fingers into the lemon-yellow cream and then spread it ever so slowly across the uppermost curves of her breasts, down the exposed tops of her thighs, across her belly, everywhere she found bare skin. Shane watched, an ardent light coming into his eyes, the ridge of his arousal growing ever harder, larger.

''Keep going,'' Shane instructed hoarsely. He nodded, letting Greta know what he meant.

Tingling everywhere his heated glance had touched, Greta gulped, ''You want me to—''

''Yes. Take it off,'' he whispered huskily. ''Panties. Bra. But leave the garter and stockings on.''

Wanting to please him, wanting to arouse him as much as he aroused her, Greta reached behind her, and with hands that trembled, undid the back of her bustier. As the edges came undone, she slowly peeled it away. It was a little trickier, but her panties went next.

Determined to prove to him once and for all that she was every bit as wild at heart as he was, Greta swallowed the rest of her inhibitions. She painted the rest of her breasts—nipples, undersides, crests, worked her way down her ribs. Her eyes still holding his, she let her hands drop lower still. Shane groaned. The next thing she knew she was on her back. Shane was astride her, ready to teach her every subtlety, every nuance of desire.

''I wasn't finished yet,'' Greta protested breathlessly. She had only to look in his eyes to see how much she'd aroused him. The reckless side of her—the hellion only he'd brought out—wanted to take it further still.

Shane grinned as Greta anchored her fingers in the elastic edges of his briefs. ''We've got all night to play with our toys. But this—'' Shane winked as he poured lotion in the palm of his hand and stretched out next to her. His glance skimmed her near-naked form hotly as he shifted her onto her side ''—is a man's job.''

Desire flowed through her, in hot mesmerizing waves, even before his lips touched hers. Feelings swelled in her heart, followed swiftly by a need that encompassed her very soul. Greta trembled and clung to him. His arousal nudged her through his briefs. His tongue teased her lips apart and then plunged into her mouth, again and again and again, tantalizing and compelling. Lower still, one of his lotion-slick hands caressed her golden nest of curls. The other flattened against the small of her spine. Tenderly, he stroked the dewy softness, moving up, in, then touched and caressed her breasts, rubbing his thumbs over the tender crests. "You are so beautiful, Greta," he murmured, his eyes dark with wanting her, as he ended their slow, sexy kiss. "Now let's find out how you taste."

She caught her breath as his eyes held hers with the promise of the limitless lovemaking to come. Greta tried to control her need, to draw their lovemaking out as long as possible, but it was an impossible task when his rapacious gaze drifted down her body, his hands skimming over her sides, over her ribs. He shifted her onto her back, gently, cupping the weight of both her breasts in his hands. Aware she'd never felt sexier or more voluptuous in her life, Greta watched as his head lowered. His lips moved over her skin, tantalizing and exploring, over and over, until she shut her eyes and surrendered helplessly against him.

"Pineapple," Shane murmured in a way that had them both chuckling softly. "Definitely pineapple."

Discovery made, he shifted upward. Soon they were kissing again, hotly, until she no longer knew where her mouth ended and his began. Desperate for more, even if he was willing to wait past the spontaneous combustion stage, Greta shifted so she was on top once again. Slowly she lowered herself. She took the hot, hard length of him and drew him inside, then drew herself up, so she was once again on her knees. Over and over, she loved him that way, until he shuddered uncontrollably, the gliding sensation more than he could bear.

"Greta," Shane murmured, as she slipped free.

She replaced her body with the softness of her lips,

the light butterfly tease of her tongue. He'd driven her mad with desire. Now she took him to the brink. Hands on her waist, he caught her, brought her up and over him, then rolled so she was once again on her side.

"Definitely pineapple," Greta said.

Shane laughed softly at their private joke. And then she was surging forward, brushing his chest with her breasts, linking her arms around his neck, and he was finding her with his hands, plunging inside her, commanding everything she had to give. Their mouths mated just as their bodies did, in one long, hot, deliciously passionate, incredibly endless kiss. Then Shane shifted again, so she was beneath him. Wanting everything he had to give, Greta arched and bucked and tightened around him. Wanting to give her everything she needed, everything she had ever wanted, Shane plunged and withdrew and plunged again. Timelessly, seamlessly, until for the first time, Greta knew what it was like to be free, to love someone—really love someone—without restraint.

And for the first time Shane discovered what it was like to love a woman, heart and soul. He hadn't known he could want a woman like this. Hadn't known he could need a woman the way he needed Greta. But he did, he thought, as her climax came, swiftly followed by his.

GRETA WOKE TO FIND the bedroom littered with clothes, the sunshine streaming in. The remnants of their post wedding feast and what was left of their "honeymoon kit" were spilled across the table. She had a champagne headache big enough to kill a wild boar. Worse, she'd forgotten to set her alarm, and today was Saturday. Saturday! Which meant the grand opening of her dance hall was less than ten hours away. She couldn't believe she had been so irresponsible, unexpected wedding or no!

Doing her best to contain a moan of dismay, Greta slipped from a sleeping Shane's arms and headed straight for the shower. Doing her best to save time, Greta filled her toothbrush with toothpaste and stepped under the hot steamy spray. If not for the dime-store wedding ring still on her finger—the one and only accoutrement of a real marriage their mothers had forgotten—Greta might think this whole crazy week was all a dream. But it wasn't a dream. She had only to look down and see her finger was still turning green to know that.

Hastily, Greta finished brushing her teeth, rinsed her mouth, washed and conditioned her hair and soaped her body. The entire process took less than five minutes, and she had just stepped out of the shower and wrapped two thick towels around her—one on her body, one around her hair, when the bathroom door opened. Shane stepped in, clad in nothing but his sexy briefs. Even with very little sleep the previous two nights, he looked wonderful. His tall body was firm and fit. His dark-blond hair was rumpled, his gray eyes sleepy. He was definitely in need of a shave. Then a shower. So why did her pulse pick up and her heart turn cartwheels in her chest just looking at him? Why did, even now, she want nothing more than to make love with him?

To her dismay he took one look at her face and knew she was upset. "Worried about the grand opening of your club tonight?"

More like my heart and my emotional well-being, Greta thought. But she was not about to tell him she'd been so foolish as to fall head over heels in love with him—when she'd known all along what the deal was, that this was but another one of Shane's legendary escapades with a dash of unexpected but much-appreciated friendship and some passionate lovemaking thrown in.

She did her best to hide her feelings, watched him fill his own toothbrush and begin to brush his teeth. "That and about a million other things," she said.

Shane finished brushing his teeth, rinsed and spit. "Such as?" Shane filled his palm with shaving cream. With slow, leisurely strokes, he spread it across his upper lip, face and jaw.

Greta watched Shane begin to shave. She didn't want to discuss any of this, but given how wildly exciting and romantic things had become between them, maybe they'd better. "I was just thinking that I need to find a place for me to live when I leave here in a few weeks," she replied.

They also needed to fashion a graceful end to their marriage that everyone in the community and their families could accept. Determined to take charge of the situation and her feelings, she looked at him sternly.

"We need a definite end date for this, Shane." Before she made even more of a fool of herself than she had last night. Dear heaven, when she thought of the wanton way she'd behaved... She would like to blame it all on an excess of champagne or the romantic aura the evening had created, even her long-held fantasy of for one day being a bad girl just to see what it was like. But she couldn't.

She had acted the way she had because she was falling in love with Shane.

What did she mean *falling?* Greta corrected ill-temperedly. She was in love with Shane. Head over heels in love with Shane.

"Actually, Greta," Shane shaved his jaw with long, clean strokes. He met her eyes in the mirror. "I'm wondering why we should end it at all."

Chapter Ten

"What are you talking about?" Greta asked, her heart leaping into her throat. "Surely you're not considering continuing this sham!"

"You can't deny we're getting to be very good friends. And the sex between us has been great," Shane pointed out practically as he continued to shave.

It had been more than great, Greta thought wistfully, wrapping the bath towel more snugly around her—as if that would protect her from getting hurt. And if Shane'd said he loved her, or even hinted he might be falling in love with her as madly as she already was with him, then she would have jumped at the opportunity to take their relationship to the absolute limit—to make this marriage of theirs a real one in every sense—in a heartbeat. But the sad truth was, Greta reminded herself firmly, Shane hadn't said any of that, not even when they were making love again and again and again. And she wanted so much more from a mate than passionate sex and blossoming friendship.

Knowing it was time to give herself a much-needed reality check, Greta swallowed hard. "We had a deal, Shane. We were going to stay married approximately one week or until our parents cried uncle and stopped trying to get us hooked up with someone.''

"And then we extended it for a couple of weeks,'' Shane reminded.

"For practical reasons,'' Greta pointed out. "So I'd have time to look for a place of my own and wouldn't have to move back in with my folks!''

Shane shrugged, still calm, cool and collected as his gray eyes lasered in on hers. "Now that we've proven we're pretty good house mates, why not just extend it indefinitely?''

He was making this all so logical. She hated it. She wanted tears and laughter and exuberance. She wanted him to shout it to the world and throw his damn hat in the air he was so happy to be in love with her. So happy they'd made love. But that wasn't happening, either. Here he was, turning what had started as one of his escapades into a business deal.

"And why would we want to do that?'' Greta said coolly.

Shane finished shaving and rinsed his face with handfuls of water. "Because neither of us is getting any younger.'' Shane blotted his face dry with a towel and rinsed his razor with water. He shut off the spigot, then turned to face her. "And neither of us has found his or her soul mate.''

But I have, Greta thought, *and it's you, Shane.*

Knowing she really would cry if they continued this much longer, she brushed by him and went into the bedroom to dress.

He followed her and took both her hands in his, as if possessing them would settle the matter without further dissension. "Because we've discovered that having a spouse who isn't really a spouse in the traditional sense of the word is our best insurance against any future matchmaking.''

He had her there, Greta thought, as the dagger he'd just stuck in her heart went in a little farther still.

Shane used his grip on her hands to propel her over to sit with him on the edge of the bed. ''Because we're both making our home in Laramie, and our marriage makes everyone happy—especially our families,'' he continued gently, getting down on one knee in front of her. ''Because we like being together.'' He ran the tips of his fingers across her bare knee. ''And it'll be cheaper to live together than to live apart.'' He shrugged and smiled soothingly at her. '' The list why you should stay is endless.''

And the list why she shouldn't was even longer, Greta thought.

''So you're suggesting we go on pretending to be married even though in our hearts we're really not?'' Greta asked emotionally.

''I'm suggesting that we follow the advice we've been given about making the best of this situation we've gotten ourselves into,'' Shane said firmly.

Greta bolted past him and went to find her clothes. Shane followed and leaned against the wall as Greta rummaged through the bureau, emerging with the most austere cotton panties and bra set she owned, then went to the closet and removed a short denim skirt, white T-shirt and embroidered vest.

''And how do we go about making the best of things?'' Greta snapped, dropping her towel and beginning to dress.

''Easy.'' Shane stepped behind Greta to help her fasten her bra. ''We continue to have a hot, lusty love affair with each other, as well as stay married in the legal sense. Granted, ours wouldn't be the usual marriage,'' he continued as she stepped into her panties and then her skirt, "but there is nothing usual about either of us. We've both always marched to the beat of our own drummers. Why change now? Especially if we stay together, because then we won't have to change.''

Greta lifted a gaze to Shane. Even if *he* didn't, she knew they both deserved better. And because they did, because he hadn't said he loved her, or even might be falling in love with her, Greta knew what she had to do. "This is ridiculous, Shane." She tugged her T-shirt over her head, straightened the hem and neck, slipped on her vest. "We are not staying married.''

Shane gave her a slow, sexy smile, the kind that never failed to make her weak in the knees. "Sure?" He laced his arms around her waist.

Telling herself no way was she falling back into bed with him now, Greta planted a hand across his bare chest and pushed him away. "I insist we stick with our original, amended plan and find a way to give everyone a reason to want our marriage annulled because we clearly are so mismatched." Squaring her shoulders, she marched into the bathroom, picked up a comb and ran it through the damp strands of her hair.

Shane leaned against the bathroom counter. Greta knew if he came even one step closer, her restraint would vanish. "You can do whatever you want," he told her in the softest, most seductive voice she'd ever heard. "But as far as I'm concerned, our marriage is a keeper." He gave her his trademark bad-boy smile. "I see no reason to end what has become a very good thing."

Greta swallowed, aware her heart was pounding so hard it was ready to leap out of her chest. "So what are you saying—that you won't give me an annulment?'' she asked, amazed.

Shane's face changed abruptly. He regarded her with a mixture of wariness and concern. ''Why? So you can go off and be with Beau?''

''You're jealous.'' And worse, in some sort of man-to-man competition with Beau.

Shane's jaw clenched. ''Let's just say I'm protecting my turf,'' he announced flatly.

''I want an annulment!'' Greta said emotionally, knowing she had never been closer to having her heart tromped to bits than she was at that very moment.

SINCE THE FIRST TIME they'd made love, Shane hadn't considered the possibility he would ever have to let her go. He didn't want to consider it now. Drawing on all the scrappiness that had seen him through as the ''runt'' of the McCabe litter, he braced a hand on either side of her, trapping her against the bathroom counter. ''Get this through your head, Greta,'' he told her implacably. ''That's not gonna happen.'' *Not now that I've made you my woman and my wife in every way that counts.* He would use whatever he needed to buy whatever time she needed to make him her man and her husband.

Greta regarded him mutinously. ''And why not?''

The one thing Shane had never been comfortable with was his own vulnerability. And he was damn vulnerable when it came to Greta. She had his heart in her fist and didn't even know it. Shane survived the uncomfortable sensation the way he always had, by hiding his true feelings under the guise of something else—something easily disdained—like ego. ''Because Bucklehead Chamberwaist isn't the only one with the hunky reputation to lose in this,'' he retorted gruffly.

Greta's eyes sparked blue fire. Her lower lip slid out in a most-kissable fashion. "I know how you like to win, Shane, how you like to come out on top," she told him hotly. She shoved past him and stormed out of the bathroom. Hands balled into fists at her sides, she whirled to face him "But this is about more than your ego, Shane. A lot more."

Shane nodded, aware he'd never been more afraid of losing someone in his life. "You're damn right it is," he said, feeling both hurt and furious she could act this way—like she was just itching to be free of him—after the two nights they'd spent together. And the very real vows they'd taken the night before. She might not have taken them seriously, but he sure as heck had. And he wasn't giving up on them now. Not yet.

"You're my wife now, Greta," Shane told her sternly, wishing they could just go back to bed, spend the entire day there and forget all this. "And you're staying my wife!"

"Oh, really?" Greta shook her head, damp silky strands flying in every direction.

"Really," Shane said.

"Well, we'll just see about that," Greta murmured hotly and stormed out.

"ARE YOU TRYING TO HANG those streamers or strangle them?" Beau asked, a scant hour later. Greta looked through the open front doors of the Lone Star Dance Hall, at the wait staff busily setting up the tables for the opening that evening, as per her direction. All were out of earshot. Deciding she needed more tape to do this right, she climbed halfway back down the ladder, so she and was nearly at Beau's eye level. "You were right," Greta sighed, glad he'd stopped by to check on her once again. "It's all been an illusion. What Shane and I have, well—" Greta bit her lip uncertainly "—I don't know what it is, but it's no marriage." They'd been as foolish as actors in a movie, who confused what they were pretending to feel for their romantic lead with what they really did feel in real life.

Beau tore off two pieces of tape, then handed them to her. "Did you tell him?" Beau watched as Greta carefully folded, then applied, the tape to the back of the streamers.

"I tried. He won't listen." Feeling more dejected than ever, Greta climbed back up the ladder.

"He doesn't want to believe that he too, could have been mistaken about what he was feeling?" Beau asked gently as he continued to lend a hand with the red, white and blue streamers.

Worse. Greta stuck the streamers where she wanted them, then pressed hard to make sure the tape stuck to the wall just above the front door. "He doesn't want to let me go," she announced grimly. "Male pride. He thinks if he does he'll be bowing to you, and he's not about to hand me over to you."

When she was halfway back down the ladder, Beau grasped her waist and swung her back down to the ground. "Did you tell him how it was with us?"

"Yes." Greta frowned, thinking back to the emotional scene that morning in their bedroom, even as she studied the Grand Opening sign she and Beau had tacked up above the double front doors. "But he's been hurt that way before." She sighed, feeling even more discouraged and disgruntled.

Beau's brow furrowed as Greta picked up the big red satin ribbon with the bow in the center and prepared to string it across the front door in preparation for the ribbon-cutting ceremony later that evening. A ceremony she wasn't even sure Beau would attend.

Beau helped her unfurl the ribbon carefully. "What do you mean? Left by a woman for some other guy?"

Cuckolded was how Shane'd put it. Cheated on. Betrayed in the worst possible way. Greta nodded, feeling weary from the top of her head to the soles of her feet in a way that had nothing to do with her lack of sleep. "So he doesn't believe me when I tell him I'm not going straight back to you."

"There must be something you can do to convince him not to want to be married to you," Beau said matter-of-factly.

It might have been easier if she weren't so foolishly head over heels in love with him and he so in lust with her, Greta thought cynically. Didn't Shane understand that passion alone would fade? That nothing was as simple as it seemed on the surface, especially marriage? Didn't he understand that the longer this went on—without them *both* being in love with each other—the stronger the likelihood they'd *both* be hurt before it was all over?

"Some way you can turn him off permanently," Beau said.

"Yes," Greta said slowly, as inspiration hit her with all the force of a Mack truck. "There is." She turned her bright eyes to Beau, suddenly seeing a fast way out. "But I'm going to need your help," she told him determinedly.

Beau put his arm around her shoulders. "Anything."

Relief poured through Greta as she realized her time in this marriage—with her loving fiercely and not being loved in return—was about to come to an end. She wrapped her arm about Beau's waist and looked up at him. "When you show up at the grand opening tonight," she whispered in strictest confidence, "here's what I want you to do...."

SEVERAL BLOCKS AWAY Shane sat on an examining table in the emergency room.

"Backing into a barbed wire fence is not exactly how I would've expected you to spend your honeymoon," his brother Jackson McCabe drawled, as he cleaned the jagged cut across Shane's left arm with hydrogen peroxide. "What's going on?"

Shane grimaced. He couldn't believe he'd been so clumsy and inattentive himself. "I don't know what you mean."

Jackson numbed the area with a topical anesthetic. "Last night at your wedding you looked on top of the world." With a surgeon's skill, Jackson began to stitch the edges of the jagged cut together. "Less than twelve hours later, you drag your sorry self in here looking as though you've lost your best friend."

Shane grimaced and stared at the walls of Laramie Community Hospital. "Maybe I have."

"Want to tell me about it?" Jackson continued stitching with the patience of a saint. He paused to give his younger brother a compassionate look. "I may not have all the answers, but I'm usually a pretty good listener."

Shane knew that was true, and it had been that way long before Jackson had become a doctor. When they were kids, Jackson had been the one Shane turned to with problems, when he turned to anyone. Shane usually hadn't listened to the advice Jackson gave him—he preferred to go his own way, in his own time—but he'd always felt better after they talked. More understood. And still more important, Jackson had never betrayed any confidences. Given the torn-up way he was feeling inside, Shane knew he had to confide in someone before he backed into more than a strand of barbed wire. He sighed. Clenched his hands around his torn, bloodied shirt. "I think I blew it with Greta."

Jackson shook his head in silent dissent. Finished stitching, he applied an antibiotic ointment over the wound to help prevent infection. "Impossible. Counting the elopement, you haven't even been married to the woman a week."

"Yeah, but that was plenty long enough for me to act like a complete Neanderthal." Shane sighed and briefly explained about the deal he and Greta'd had and the conversation they'd had that morning before he left the ranch house.

To Shane's increasing displeasure, Jackson did not look at all surprised.

Jackson ripped open a package of sterile gauze. "We all thought it might be something like that. Until we started seeing you and Greta together." Jackson fit it over the cut, then taped it in place. "Are you sure you're not in love with her?"

Shane's fists clenched. His gut churned. His whole body was tense, his emotions in turmoil. "That's just it. I think—hell, I know I am." There. He'd said it out loud.

"But you couldn't tell her," Jackson surmised, preparing a tetanus shot.

"No." Shane grimaced as Jackson swabbed his other arm with alcohol. "Instead I acted as if it was all about sex."

Jackson primed the needle. "When you know it's a helluva lot more."

"Right." Shane was so upset he barely felt the injection his brother gave him. He sighed and shook his head as, finished, Jackson swabbed the injection site with alcohol. Shane watched Jackson tear the wrapper off a Scooby-Doo Band-Aid. "I don't know why I couldn't have just been honest with her, told her what was in my heart," Shane muttered. After all, two of his brothers and his father had been able to do so.

"I do." Jackson grinned as he ripped off the plastic strips and stuck the Band-Aid over the pinprick of blood that had appeared on Shane's arm. "You already had everything planned out just perfectly and you didn't want your world rocked on its axis. Which is what admitting that you loved her and wanted to turn what started out as just another one of your damn fool escapades into a real marriage, would do."

For the first time all day Shane relaxed. Jackson did understand. The bond between him and his brother had never been stronger. Shane shrugged on his shirt. "What should I do?"

Jackson deposited all the used swabs and syringes in a covered waste can, stripped off his surgical gloves and dropped them in, too. Finished, he turned back to Shane. "Level with her."

Shane buttoned his shirt. "I'll talk to her tomorrow."

Jackson shook his head, disabusing Shane of that notion in an instant. "You don't want to wait even that long."

Good idea but impractical as hell, given the circumstances, Shane thought. "The grand opening of her dance hall is tonight. Everyone we know is going to be there." Not exactly the surroundings he'd choose to make the single most romantic declaration of his entire life.

"Even more of a reason for you to set things straight right this instant," Jackson advised soberly.

IT WAS ALMOST TWO O'CLOCK in the afternoon when Shane appeared in the service entrance of the dance hall kitchen. He nodded at Greta. "I need to talk to you."

Greta wondered at the plain blue chambray shirt he had on. It was store bought, not custom-made, and so new it still had the boxlike creases in it across the middle. Wondering what had gotten into him, she nodded at the three chefs busily preparing that evening's dinner specials and went back to writing on the chalk-board that would sit just inside the entrance. "It'll have to wait."

Shane strode past the pots of bubbling potatoes and cooling fruit pies. "It can't wait."

"Well, it will have to," Greta said as she continued neatly printing out the day's menu.

The head chef turned to Greta. "It's about time for you to go home and get ready, anyway."

"My thoughts exactly," Shane said, happy to find he had an ally at her place of business. He swept Greta into his arms honeymoon style and, ignoring the stiff, uncompromising set of her limbs, carried her out to his pickup truck.

"Must you always make such a show?" Greta demanded as he set her down on the ground next to the passenger side.

Shane opened the door and helped her in. "I'll do whatever I have to do to get your attention."

She regarded him grimly, looking anything but rested and relaxed. She stubbornly folded her arms in front of her. "I have to be back in two hours."

Shane noticed she was no longer resisting. "I'll get you back here in plenty of time, I promise," he said gently. He had no choice. She'd never forgive him if he didn't.

The ride out to the ranch was swift and silent.

"So what couldn't wait?" Greta asked as soon as they arrived.

Eager to prove himself every bit the gentleman she deserved in a marriage partner, Shane rushed around to get her door. Although she didn't look as if she wanted his help with much of anything, she let him open it for her, anyway.

"I want to apologize for this morning." Hands around her waist, Shane swung her down from the pickup truck.

"Why?" Greta curled her fingers around his bicep as her feet hit the ground. Steadied, she dropped her hand and stepped back. "You said exactly what you feel." Hurt glimmered in her pretty blue eyes.

"That's just it," Shane said earnestly. Taking her hand in his, he led her toward the porch. "I didn't." He ushered her into the coolness of the ranch house. "I said I wanted to stay married to you because it was convenient."

"Don't remind me," she muttered cantankerously.

"That's not it."

She regarded him warily. "Then what is?"

Shane sank into one of the easy chairs and pulled her down onto his lap. He wrapped his arms around her and held her close, shoring up his courage to try again. "I want you to stay my wife because I love you. The way I've never loved anyone else. The way I am always going to love you."

Greta turned to him, her eyes shimmering moistly. Not sure she'd understood him, he repeated it all, verbatim, again. Greta gulped. And this time, tears spilled over her lashes and flowed down her face. "Oh, Shane," she whispered, looking happier than he'd ever seen her.

Shane rushed on, fighting panic, not about to leave anything unsaid this time. "I don't care if you don't love me, too," he told her earnestly, stroking her hair, her face, her neck, her trembling lower lip. "I'm willing to give it time," he told her hoarsely. "I want you to give us time. Because I feel sure, with enough time, with enough love—you—we—"

"Shane?"

"Hmm?" What had he said wrong this time?

"Hush," Greta whispered. And then she gave him a look. That look. The one that said all his worrying had been for nothing. She wasn't going anywhere.

She wreathed her arms around his neck. Tears still streaming down her face, she pressed her lips to his. "I love you, too, Shane," she whispered thickly. Trembling now, all over. "Do you hear me? I love you, too." He would have kissed her then but she shook her head, caught her breath and held him at bay with one hand pressed against his chest. "That's why I was so upset this morning when you said what you said, because I thought I was the only one feeling this way."

How could he have hurt her that way? When hurting her was the last thing he'd ever wanted to do. Shane held her even closer. "You're not alone in this," he whispered, kissing her then—her eyes, her lips, her hair. "If I have my way, you'll never be alone again."

He lifted her off his lap, carried her upstairs, to the bed. And there, in the sunny bedroom, on the rumpled sheets of their bed, he made love to her as if they had all the time in the world. He caressed her feet, stroked her ankles, the backs of her knees, her inner thighs. He kissed breasts, belly, thighs, held her bottom in his hands. Brought her closer still and watched her body respond, savoring the sweetness of her, the fire, the way she looked at him, in wonder and yearning, as if she couldn't help but feel that way.

And she kissed him and loved him, too, her actions unspeakably tender, gentle, passionate. She stroked him with her hands, loved him with her lips and tongue, until he couldn't stand it anymore, until he had to have her, had to claim her and make her his. He rolled, so she was beneath him, her hot body pressed up against him. He slid his hand down her tummy, to the sleek nest of curls and the dampness beneath. She lifted her hips to him, arched against his hand as he stroked and kissed and touched. And then he was easing into her; there was no more waiting, only the two of them soaring, flying free.

After, he held her close and savored the feel of her in his arms. He pressed a kiss into the fragrant softness of her hair, wishing they didn't have to go, knowing they did.

"What are you thinking?" Shane murmured, keeping his arms wrapped around her as their heartbeats slowed.

"That I've never been happier," Greta murmured, reluctantly rising and leading him from the bed, "than I am right now."

"Me, too," Shane said, kissing her again. "Me, too."

To save time, they climbed into the shower together. Shane stepped beneath the spray and shook his head ruefully. "I should have known better than to listen to anything Bonnie Sue had to say."

Greta froze in the act of putting shampoo into her hair. "Why? What did she say?"

Shane turned her away from him and began to work the shampoo into a lather. "It's too ridiculous," he said with obvious chagrin.

I knew she was going to cause trouble. And gut instinct told Greta that trouble was not over yet, no matter what Shane thought. Greta closed her eyes and braced herself against the wall. "Humor me and tell me, anyway, so we'll never fight over this issue again." *So I'll know what to do.*

Shane massaged her scalp with firm, sensual strokes and slow, lazy circles. "She had some idea that you were using me to get to Beau—"

"Why would I want to do that?" Greta asked in stunned amazement as rich bubbles of shampoo spilled across her shoulders onto her back.

Shane turned her around to face him, so the water from the showerhead spilled directly over her hair. "To make him marry you."

At the mention of Beau and the memory of her most recent conversation with him, Greta felt the color leave her face. Aware Shane was studying her intently, Greta sputtered, "Beau and I—we were never—I mean, I told you, marriage was never even on the horizon—"

"I know," Shane said. He looked at her expectantly. "That's what I told Bonnie Sue."

Swearing inwardly at the second predicament she'd foolishly gotten herself into, in the space of a week, Greta turned away from Shane's calmly assessing gaze and plucked the conditioner from the shelf. "But she didn't believe it," she guessed grimly.

Shane took the bottle from her, put a dollop on his palm, rubbed his hands together, then spread the silky lotion through her hair. "She thinks every woman thinks the way she does." Shane shook his head, continuing, as inwardly Greta's guilt built and built. "But I should have known better. I should have trusted you. I should have known you'd never use me to get to Beau, or make a fool of me by deceiving me. Or cheat on me the way Bonnie Sue cheated on me.''

Oh, no, Greta thought as she felt all the blood drain from her face. How was she going to tell Shane she had planned to do just that, this very morning, with no less than the man he, and every one else in town, erroneously considered to be Shane's arch rival for her affections?

''What's the matter?'' Shane filled his hands with soap, then handed the bar to her.

Tell him, Greta urged silently.

And have him turn his back on you now? And have Bonnie Sue Baxter be right about you after all?

Her reckless plan to give Shane damn good reason to leave her had never seemed more treacherous than it did at that very second. But it wasn't too late, Greta schooled herself firmly. She'd made a huge mistake, but it could still be rectified. All she had to do was act fast and Shane would never know about the break-up-provoking humiliation that she had planned for him that very morning.

''Nothing. I'm just—I've really got to get back to the dance hall,'' Greta said hurriedly as she washed Shane's back and he returned the favor.

''Grand opening jitters?'' Shane guessed, his touch more gentle and comforting than ever.

More like marriage-about-to-be-on-the-rocks-again jitters. Not to worry, Greta assured herself firmly. She could fix this. All she had to do was get a hold of Beau in advance of his arrival at the dance hall, tell him everything was fine, the plan was off, and she'd never have to worry again.

THERE WAS ONLY ONE PROBLEM with plan B, Greta thought two hours later, as people began queuing up outside, waiting for the doors to open promptly at five-thirty. She couldn't get ahold of Beau to cancel Plan A.

"That's the sixth time I've seen you with the phone in your hand," Shane teased, as Greta frowned and hung up again. "Who are you calling?"

Tell him.

And have him get really mad? And feel even more hurt and betrayed?

"Just a friend," Greta said, fervently wishing her ocean of regret—and the reason for it—away. She looked past Shane. "There's Dani now!"

Greta rushed to greet Dani Lockhart who, as a special favor to Greta, had agreed to act as a hostess that night. Dani hugged Greta, then stepped back to survey her denim dress, hammered silver belt, and boots. "You look great."

Greta admired Dani's fire-engine-red dress and matching boots. "So do you." Knowing if anyone could help her out of this jam she'd gotten herself in it was Dani, Greta turned to Shane. "If you wouldn't mind, um, could you step out front and tell everyone it will just be five more minutes, then we'll have the ribbon-cutting ceremonies, open the doors and begin seating."

Shane chuckled as he turned to Dani. "This is the tenth fool's errand she's sent me on since we got back here." He looked at Greta, his eyes so warm and silvery a woman could drown in them. "If I didn't know better," Shane drawled sexily, leaning in close, "I'd think you were trying to get rid of me."

Greta breathed in the tantalizing fragrance of his aftershave. "I'm just—"

"Nervous. I know." He leaned in even closer and squeezed her hand. Then looked over at Dani. "Maybe you can calm her down."

With another sexy smile, Shane left to carry out Greta's orders. Greta grabbed Dani's hand, threaded her way through the bustle of activity and tantalizing aroma of chicken-fried steak, and dragged her to a stool close to the service door of the kitchen. "You've got to stay here and watch for Beau. He's due here any minute."

Dani looked at her as if she'd grown two heads. "Are you okay?" she asked bluntly.

"No, and I don't have time to explain why I'm not, right now," Greta said sharply, aware time was dwindling to a precarious degree. "Just keep Beau from getting anywhere close to me tonight. And I mean anywhere close to me."

Dani held up one hand, requesting permission to interrupt. "Are you forgetting that Beau and I have a blood feud going, and that's putting it nicely? He is not going to want to talk to me. So, short of having him bounced out of here, I don't see how I can possibly—"

"Dani, please!" Greta said. The way things were going, she would never get herself out of this mess, let alone with her marriage to Shane in one piece! "Just for one night forget all that and do this for me. Please."

Dani's expression changed at the urgency in Greta's low voice.

She was confused, but understood the solemnness of the situation nevertheless. She abruptly stopped arguing. "Sure."

"Good." Greta breathed a sigh of relief. She cast a glance over her shoulder and saw her husband winding his way toward her. "And don't mention this to Shane, either," Greta hissed.

Dani's eyes narrowed contemplatively. "Whatever you say."

Shane took her hand in his. "The wait staff says

they're all ready. The mayor's here to cut the ribbon. And so are the film crews from local TV stations and the newspaper photographers. So anytime you want to head out there to open the front doors…''

Greta pasted on her most-brilliant smile. She took the arm Shane offered her. The sooner they got this over with, the better. ''Let's go.''

To Greta's relief, the ribbon cutting went without a hitch. By five forty-five, every table was full, and there was a waiting list for the next hour. The DJ she'd hired to run the sound system was doing a fine job of starting the music. Shane's entire family was there, as was hers. And there were people already out on the dance floor kicking up their heels. She had just headed back to the kitchen to oversee the meal service when Beau ducked in the back door. Dani stood, as planned, and planted herself directly in Beau's path. Words were exchanged. Then Beau tried to charge past Dani. Dani stepped in front of him. Greta—seeing Shane was nowhere in sight—was relieved to discover she had the time and opportunity to call the whole thing off.

Color flowing into her cheeks, she rushed toward Beau.

Beau pushed past Dani at the same moment Shane stepped in the service door behind Beau. Greta stopped dead in her tracks, knowing anything she said or did would be observed by Shane.

That was all the opening Beau needed. Right on cue he swept her into his arms and bent her backward from the waist.

''Darling,'' Beau said loudly enough for everyone in the kitchen to hear as he gathered her close for a staged romantic kiss. ''I am so sorry. Please. You've got to forgive me and give me a second chance!''

Chapter Eleven

"Not now!" Greta mouthed.

Before she could explain there had been a big change of plans, Shane was already striding forward, looking very much as though he wanted to punch someone, no questions asked. "What's going on?" he demanded of Beau and Greta.

"It's not what it looks like," Greta told Shane hastily as she grabbed ahold of Beau's shirtfront and hauled herself upright.

"Sure it is," Beau said, giving Greta a deeply romantic look that she knew darn well he didn't begin to feel.

Shane studied them silently for a moment. "Then what is it?" He demanded in a voice far too casual to be believed.

To Greta's dismay, Beau made no move to let her go. Rather, he kept his arms wrapped protectively around her like a vise. "Exactly what it looks like," Beau told Shane heavily, using every ounce of leading-man charisma he had. "Greta's finally come to her senses." Beau poured it on thick. "She knows she should never have walked away from me and married you on the rebound."

Shane turned to Greta with a quiet smile. "Is that true?" he demanded, hurt turning his eyes a deep, smoky gray.

Playing to the script they had previously agreed upon, Beau confirmed, "She told me so this morning."

"This morning," Shane repeated, evidently recalling how rancorously he and Greta had parted.

"But that was before you and I talked this afternoon, Shane," Greta amended hastily. Giving up on doing any of this gracefully—never mind without an audience— Greta wiggled and shoved her way out of Beau's arms.

"Meaning what?" Shane advanced on Greta incredulously, not stopping until they stood toe-to-toe. He hooked his hands in the back pockets of his jeans. "If we hadn't 'talked' this afternoon, you'd be with him now?"

Greta tilted her chin up defiantly. Their eyes met, held. She knew she dared not be anything less than honest. "The way things were at that point," she explained, sorry now she'd ever tried to embark on an escapade of her very own, "I didn't think I could continue with the marriage. But now that I know that you really do love me, Shane," Greta gripped Shane's arms and finished desperately, "I don't have to do this thing with Beau."

"What thing?" Shane demanded as Greta blushed from the tips of her toes to the roots of her hair.

She didn't know quite how to answer, especially in front of an audience.

Still waiting for his answer, Shane looked at Beau.

Beau lifted his hands. They'd deviated so far from their script, he clearly had no idea what Greta wanted him to say. "Don't ask me. I'm just here to claim her," Beau said dryly.

"As what?" Shane demanded. "Your mistress? Your wife?"

"Whatever she wants," Beau said, looking at Greta steadily, with a meaning only she could read. "And she knows that."

Aware Shane didn't seem to want to be touched at all—especially by her—Greta released her grip on his forearms. "Let's go somewhere private," Greta urged Shane, "and I can explain."

"That doesn't work, either, honey," Bonnie Sue drawled. "I've tried it. This is one arena where Shane doesn't like any competition."

Where had she come from? Greta wondered, whirling around to glare at her. And how long had she been listening? And were those customers in the kitchen area now, too? Plus her parents? And Shane's!

Bonnie Sue Baxter made a face of mock indignation. "Looks like I hit a nerve, doesn't it?"

"I don't know about that, but Greta couldn't have gotten better publicity if she'd tried," the photographer from the *Laramie News* quipped as he lifted his camera and began snapping away. "This is definitely a page-one story."

Ignoring everyone else, Shane continued to stare at Greta. He was a force not to be denied. "Tell me the truth, Greta," he ordered. Her hot-blooded lover vanished and in his place appeared a cowboy who always rode away alone. "Did you ask this guy to come here tonight and make a move on you and help break us up?"

Greta didn't know what to say to that without making things worse. Certainly not the truth. She stared at Shane, tongue-tied, miserable, hideously embarrassed.

Shane shook his head grimly. "Well, there's my answer."

Desperate to salvage something of the evening, and her marriage, Greta turned to Beau and said heavily, "Look, I know what we agreed to earlier, and I appreciate all your help, but I've changed my mind." She gave him a look that said this, at least, was on the level. "I want to stay married to Shane." She spoke as if underlining every word.

Beau studied her, his concern for her evident to everyone in the room as all activity ceased. The music coming from the dance hall seemed a million miles a way.

A muscle worked in Shane's jaw. He was watching her and Beau with a look fiery enough to scorch them both. "Let me get this straight. You told *him*—" Shane jerked his head at Beau "—you wanted out before you told *me?*" Incensed, Shane angled his thumbs at his chest.

Greta swallowed as her knees began to shake. "He's my friend."

"Looks as if he's more than a friend, to me," Bonnie Sue Baxter remarked snidely.

Having had more than enough help from Shane's ex-fiancée, Greta whirled, finding she was quickly becoming of a mind to deck someone, too. "You stay out of this!"

"Someone has to look out for Shane's interests," Bonnie Sue said smugly, delighting in the chaos Beau's sudden declaration had created. "Clearly, you're not. But then, maybe you just enjoy being fought over. Too bad for you Shane is the type of man who doesn't play those kinds of games."

As Bonnie Sue had found out herself, Greta thought. Deciding there was only one way to shut her up, Greta snapped, "Guess you discovered that the hard way, didn't you, Bonnie Sue?"

Bonnie Sue gasped. More than a few eyebrows rose. And Bonnie Sue retorted, "It's just too bad for you that Beau, here, is so quick to give up on you," Bonnie Sue continued. The implication being that Greta wasn't worth fighting for and hence would now end up alone, too.

"I'm not afraid to fight for Greta, if that is what it takes," Beau said, jumping to Greta's defense.

Greta groaned. Of all the lame-brained things to say!

Shane growled, "Neither am I." Then paused to give Beau a grim look. "That being the case," Shane said. "Want to take it outside?"

Beau looked back at Shane. Although nothing was said, some understanding—that seemed to exclude everyone else in the room—seemed to pass between the two men.

No, Greta thought.

"Sure." Beau shrugged finally, still holding Shane's gaze, more confidently now. Beau smiled, a slow, thoughtful movie-star grin. "Why not?"

All of a sudden Greta felt that things—though outwardly calm—had just taken a turn for the worse. "Now hold on a minute, guys. This really isn't necessary," Greta said hastily, recalling all too well how much Shane liked living life to the limit and Beau liked mixing it up in his action-adventure films. Clearly, the two men thought they had just found a new level of excitement. But this would be no fun-filled battle with another stunt-trained actor. Before all was said and done, blood could actually be shed! And Shane had already had stitches once today! "The last thing we need here on opening night is a fistfight in the parking lot," Greta continued lightly.

Shane looked at Greta. He shook his head at her naïveté. "Who said anything about using our fists?"

THEY WERE PULLING HER LEG, Greta thought. *They had to be.* "What's it going to be then, a kick-boxing duel?" she asked both Shane and Beau, sure they'd back down now they'd made their point, which was that she never should have started this little escapade that had swiftly landed her in way over her head. She should never have tried to put something over on Shane, even if they *hadn't* kissed, made up, made love and declared their love for each other.

Shane rubbed his jaw smugly. "Pistols."

Greta wrung her hands. Every bona fide Texan she knew liked to live in a way that was larger than life. Here, in one of the biggest states of the nation, bold brash behavior was considered a virtue. But to even talk about a duel was downright ridiculous. And furthermore Shane McCabe knew it!

"You can't be serious," she said, chastising both men in a low, derisive voice.

"Why not?" Shane's change of tactic was as smooth and seamless as his smile. "You've been needing publicity for your dance hall, haven't you?" Giving her no chance to answer, Shane looked at Beau. "And don't you have a movie opening soon?"

Greta groaned. Beau always had a movie opening soon.

Dani Lockhart, the film critic in the group, was quick to volunteer. "It's about a love triangle, between a married woman, her husband and the glamorous interloper. Not so coincidentally—in life as in fiction," Dani continued, illuminating their gathering audience, "Beau here plays the smarmy interloper."

"Watch who you're calling smarmy," Beau said, glaring at Dani, their ongoing feud never more apparent than at that moment.

"I just call 'em as I see 'em," Dani snapped back.

Shane gestured at Beau and nodded at the service door and the alley beyond. "Let's you and I discuss this outside, man-to-man."

"Sure."

The two men exited the building and stood talking a short distance away. The show clearly over, for the moment anyway, everyone began going back to work. Dani walked over to stand by Greta.

"They aren't really going to do this," Greta fumed as the two women watched from outside the double doors. "Shane is just angry with me, so he's yanking my chain." The same way they had yanked their parents' by running off and getting married. This was just another of Shane's escapades. Only this time she was going to be the brunt of the joke, rather than taking part in it.

Dani sighed thoughtfully, her eyes still on Shane. "He does have a flair for the dramatic." She laughed softly. "Maybe he should have been the one in films."

Shane's three brothers joined the two men at the other end of the alley. The talking continued. Soon there were smothered grins all around. "Now I know they're up to something," Dani declared.

"Don't I know it," Greta muttered, her low voice getting testier by the second. "The question is what."

After a moment Jackson McCabe returned to join them. "They're going to do it," he announced to one and all, looking remarking calm and okay with everything, despite the fact he was a surgeon who spent time patching up people who ended up on the wrong side of a bullet. "Travis went to get the guns."

So where's the hitch? What am I not seeing? Greta wondered frantically. "They're going to kill each other over me?" Greta exclaimed dryly.

Wade McCabe joined them, too. The multimillionaire oilman also looked awfully calm. "No. They promised no one would get hurt."

TRY AS SHE MIGHT, Greta could get no further information out of any of the McCabes. To her astonishment, the four McCabe brothers even enlisted the help of the local police and the DJ hosting her opening-night festivities. Twenty minutes later the street in front of the dance hall was roped off. The crowd was gathered out front, buzzing with excitement.

Shane and Beau did not disappoint.

They came swaggering back, old-fashioned gun holsters—the kind the cowboys wore in the days of the gunslingers—hugging their hips. Big pearl-handled pistols reminiscent of the Old West were tucked into each holster. Greta didn't know what the two were planning. The best she could hope for were gag pistols that shot out flags that said *Bang!* But she didn't like it one bit. She was fuming. Her patience with their male shenanigans at an end, she stormed over to head them off at the pass. "I demand you two stop this right now!" she said.

"Too late for that, Greta, honey," Shane said. He looked at her with eyes so cool it was a miracle she didn't freeze right there in the street.

"He's right." Having taken Shane's side in whatever it was that was going on, Beau nodded at the crowd that had gathered. "The people here are expecting a show,"

Beau said, with a movie star's penchant for attention and adulation, "and we can't disappoint."

Before Greta could say another word, the DJ took over, explaining via the microphone that it was a battle of hearts and Greta was the prize. He guided Greta safely out of harm's way, stationed the men fifty paces apart in the center of the street and explained the rules. Both men had to wait for his signal, then the quickest draw and or best shot would emerge the victor. "May the best man win."

The crowd grew hushed.

The DJ gave the signal and stepped out of the way.

Both men stood facing each other, hands on their hips.

Five heartrending seconds passed. Ten. Fifteen. Later, Greta could never say who drew first. She only knew in a flash both pistols were whipped from their holsters. Aimed. Fired.

The sounds of the guns going off were simultaneous, drowned out only by the screams of the bystanders as both men reeled backward, not just playacting but visibly hit—Shane in the shoulder, Beau in the chest. And then the screams of horror and excitement turned to astonished laughter as vibrant pink and purple splotches appeared on the men's fancy Western shirts.

"PAINTBALL!" Greta fumed as Travis McCabe chuckled beside her, amused.

"Shane picked them up during his rodeo days from one of the clowns." Travis, the oldest of the four McCabe brothers, turned to her. "I figured you knew."

Greta's jaw clamped shut. Vaguely aware she'd never felt more like decking someone in her life—those two someones being Shane McCabe and his newfound partner in crime, Beau Chamberlain—Greta folded her arms in front of her and continued to stare at the street. "I never go to the rodeo."

"A shame," Travis said, his low voice full of brotherly admiration. "Watching Shane compete is something else."

"He does like to capture the attention of the crowd, doesn't he?" The way Greta said it, the way she was feeling, it wasn't a compliment. Damn him anyway, for topping her called-off escapade with one of his own. Damn him for involving Beau in it, too! How could they?

Travis nodded, still thinking of his brother and crowds. "He does indeed."

Greta marched toward the center of the street, as both men met in the center and shook hands. Shane swaggered over, grabbed Greta around the waist, and kissed her cheek. Before she could respond, Beau walked over, too, grabbed Greta by the waist, and kissed her, too. The crowd roared with delight. Then both men swept off their hats and bowed, letting the crowd know it was the end of the show in the street. More hoots, hollars, whistles and applause followed. The music started once again. Greta suppressed an ironic grin at the selection: Garth Brooks's "Friends In Low Places." How appropriate.

"Looks like you won," Beau told Shane, indicating where he had been hit—in the heart, as opposed to where Shane had been hit—in the shoulder.

Who cared who won? Greta thought, when she'd just been made the biggest fool ever. Even though she'd been at the center of the dispute, she felt the way she'd felt back in high school—excluded, watching from a distance, while all the popular kids raised heck and had a blast.

Shane shrugged his broad shoulders. "I'd call it a draw," Shane said.

"And I'd call it a real crowd pleaser," Dani Lockhart said, joining them, too. Dani sized Beau up with a cynical look, then continued in a voice dripping with sarcasm, "This ought to bring in buckets of attention for your new movie." She spoke as if his behavior were loathsome.

"Whatever." Beau shrugged. He paused in the act of blotting the vivid pink paint from his shirt long enough to look at Dani and quip, "In any case, it's bound to be more worthwhile than one of your reviews."

Dani's eyes glimmered with a flash of temper. "At least I can write," she retorted silkily. "Now if you could just act."

Beau rolled his eyes. "Says the lady with the poison pen." He handed the paint-smeared handkerchief back to Greta, stabbed a finger at Dani and said, "You know what I think? I think you're just a failed actor, masquerading as a critic!"

"Oh, don't you wish!" Dani fumed right back, bright pink color flooding into her cheeks.

Dani and Beau headed off, still quarreling and tossing insults at each other, right and left.

The local television reporter, there to film the opening of Greta's dance hall for a thirty-second time spot at the end of the newscast, rushed up and stuck a microphone in Shane's face. "Tell us the truth, Shane. Was this one giant publicity stunt on behalf of Greta's dance hall, your new horse ranch and Beau's new movie?"

Shane looked at him. He pretended to be dumbstruck by the astuteness of the question. "No use hiding anything from you, is there?" he drawled.

The reporter beamed and cast a look behind him at

Bonnie Sue Baxter, who'd clearly been giving him an earful. Thusly prodded, the TV reporter continued, "Does it mean then you'll be getting your marriage to Miss Wilson annulled?"

Shane looked at Greta.

Greta held her breath. *No,* she thought. *Please, Shane, say no.*

Shane nodded. "You bet."

Chapter Twelve

"Nice," Travis said early the following morning, as Shane led a cutting horse from the stables to the pasture.

"Thanks." Shane turned the beautiful bay out into grass, then shut the gate behind it.

Travis, who was clearly in big brother mode, accompanied Shane back to the stables. "I'm surprised you're working today," Travis continued.

Shane went back to get the chestnut quarter horse and turn him out, too. He worked quickly, slipping on a lead, heading right back out, the beautiful animal in tow. He wished Travis would just go away and mind his own business. "What else would I be doing?"

"I don't know," Travis said sarcastically. "Maybe trying to save your marriage."

Shane gave his new horse an affectionate pat, then shut the pasture gate. "Why would I want to do that?"

Travis leaned against the pasture fence. He looked as though he'd slept a heck of a lot better than Shane. Travis angled his head at Shane. "Maybe because you've fallen head over heels in love with the woman?"

Beginning to feel increasingly annoyed—why wouldn't his family mind their own darn business?—Shane did what he was sure would tick off his older brother in much the same way. He turned the conversation back to Travis and Travis's love life. ''Just 'cause you're still upset over losing Rayanne the way you did, don't give me any lip,'' Shane said. She'd died years ago, before the two of them could make it to the altar, but for Travis the tragedy might as well have been yesterday, his grief over what might have been, if only the wedding-day accident hadn't occurred, was that deep and that profound.

A shadow passed over Travis's eyes. ''I'd give anything to be able to live that day over,'' he said.

''I know you would, big brother,'' Shane said gently, glad he didn't have a burden like that to carry around himself. ''But my situation isn't the same.'' He hadn't wronged his woman, Greta had wronged him.

Travis pushed the brim of his hat back and slanted him a look. ''Isn't it?''

''You and Rayanne were getting married for all the right reasons.''

They'd loved each other from the time they were kids and had always known they would marry someday. ''That's not the case with Greta and me.'' Briefly Shane explained how and why he and Greta had gone to J. P. Randall's Bait and Tackle Shop in the first place.

''I figured it was something like that in the beginning,'' Travis said with an exasperated sigh.

''And the end, too,'' Shane grumbled, wondering when he would ever stop feeling so betrayed.

''Now who's still not being honest?'' Travis ribbed.

''What do you mean?'' Shane headed back to the stables. ''I told her I loved her. And she still betrayed me.''

''But that was before you told her you loved her.'' Travis watched Shane pick up a pitchfork and begin to muck out the stables.

"Doesn't matter," Shane said grimly, having never imagined he could feel such gut-wrenching pain over a woman. When things had ended with Bonnie Sue, he'd felt only relief. "Greta still betrayed me." Seeing her in Beau's arms, for whatever stupidly concocted reason, had made him feel cuckolded all over again. It wasn't a humiliation he suffered lightly.

"So Greta made a mistake." Travis stood clear of him. "In the end she was trying to set things right before you went off half-cocked and dumped her in front of everyone."

Shane hadn't meant to say he intended to end the marriage. He hadn't meant to do anything except get the heck out of there after the mock gun battle. He'd figured the dumping of each other could come later. When his temper had cooled and he'd stopped wanting to kiss her and claim her as his all over again. But when the reporter had asked him, calling it quits had just seemed like the thing to do, for all of them.

Able to see how conflicted he was, Travis clamped a comforting hand on his shoulder. "Just remember this. The kind of passion you and Greta shared this week comes along once in a lifetime—*if* you're lucky." The depth of Travis's own regrets shimmered in his eyes. "Right now you still have time to try to fix things. You wait much longer, little brother," Travis frowned a warning, "that may not be the case."

"Honey, you look terrible," Tillie said fretfully as she set a plate of bacon and eggs in front of Greta. "Did you get any sleep at all?"

Greta took a deep breath, and through sheer force of will, pushed back the tears she could feel gathering behind her eyes. "Not much."

Bart put his newspaper aside. "It looks as if you cried all night," he said.

"That, too." Greta hadn't known she could hurt this much. She hadn't known she could love so much, and she would love Shane, forever and always, even if he didn't really love her back. She knew that now. Silence rebounded at the breakfast table.

"I'd like to wring that Shane McCabe's neck," Bart grumbled.

"What happened last night is not Shane's fault," Greta told her parents wearily, knowing it was past time to put everything—and she did mean everything—on the table. "At least not entirely. I'm to blame, too."

Bart and Tillie exchanged confused looks. "What do you mean?" they asked in unison.

Briefly, Greta explained how and why she and Shane had really decided to elope.

"You know, in the beginning, we all thought the two of you might just be playing a prank on us to teach us a lesson about interfering in your love lives," Tillie mused. "But then when we saw you two together—the way you looked at each other—when we saw those sparks, we thought you really were in love with each other." She clasped her hands in front of her. "And we were so happy for you, darling."

"Which is why we gave you the real wedding of your dreams," Bart continued, nodding, "because we wanted you and Shane to get your marriage off on the right foot."

"And it almost worked," Greta admitted wistfully. "Maybe it would have, if Shane had just told me he loved me a little bit sooner. But he didn't, and I thought he wanted to stay married because it was convenient, and I got upset, took a page from Shane's book and decided to use clowning around instead of straight talk to solve my problems. So I concocted a compromising situation with Beau, so that Shane would think I was using him and had been all along and would want to let me go. But before that could happen,'' Greta admitted wistfully as all the feelings she'd had in that wonderful tumultuous moment came pouring back, ''Shane confessed his real feelings.'' In what had undeniably been the happiest moment in her entire life. ''And I told him I loved him, too.''

Bart poured more coffee for all of them. ''But you didn't tell him about your plan with Beau.''

Greta shook her head sadly, her regret about that boundless as the universe. ''No,'' she said as tears filled her eyes again. Her hand trembled as she lifted her coffee cup and took a sip. ''And I couldn't get to Beau in time to cancel the ruse.'' Shame and frustration warred within her. ''Shane saw us together. Jumped to all sorts of conclusions. Lost his temper. Challenged Beau to that silly duel, and well—'' Greta sighed again, heavily this time ''—you know the rest.''

To Greta's surprise Tillie looked more thoughtful than upset. ''Maybe he's cooled off by now, too,'' she suggested gently.

Greta recalled the look on his face when Shane had told the TV reporter their marriage was going to be annulled. ''I rather doubt it.'' There was only so much damage any man's pride could take. Greta pushed her bacon and eggs around her plate, sure she couldn't eat a single bite.

Tillie reached across the table and patted Greta's hand. ''Honey, if you love him, don't let your pride stand in the way,'' she counseled softly.

Bart nodded. ''It's possible, you know, that Shane

may have no greater clue about what's in your heart than we did.''

GRETA STAYED THROUGH breakfast with her folks and continued her heart-to-heart talk with them. She told them how pressured she felt to be the very best at everything, the entire time she'd been growing up. They were stunned, but willing to talk about it, as openly and honestly and calmly as she was. "We only wanted the best for you," Tillie told her, when Greta had finished. Greta looked into their eyes and knew it was true. Relief, that she had been good enough for them, after all, and that they hadn't been as constantly disappointed in her as she'd always thought, filled her soul and left her with a blessed feeling of peace.

"We just wish you'd leveled with us much sooner," Bart said gently as tears of reconciliation spilled down all their faces.

"In any case," Tillie said firmly, "we promise not to push or pressure you again."

Bart nodded affirmatively. "But you have to promise to level with us, too, about everything," he cautioned. "Because we do want to understand. And we can't read your mind, much as we often try." He grinned.

"I will," Greta promised emotionally as Tillie passed the tissue box around. "This keeping everything to yourself is for the birds." Feeling so much better, at least as far as her parents were concerned, Greta glanced at her watch, noted it was already mid-morning. "I've got to get going."

"Is there anything we can do for you?" Tillie rose and began to clear the table.

Greta shook her head as she and her father pitched in to help. "No."

"If there is, you let us know," Bart said sternly.

Greta promised she would, then, having been assured they did not need her help with the dishes, she gathered her things up and headed for the dance hall. There, at least, Greta was relieved to discover everything was in perfect order. The night janitorial firm she had hired had already been in and left everything sparkling clean, and ready to go for the second evening's festivities. All she had to do was tally the previous night's receipts and check the messages on her machine.

She had just gotten started doing both when Beau Chamberlain came in, bouquet of pink and white carnations in hand. "I thought I might find you here."

Greta looked up from the old-fashioned adding machine and ledger on her desk. She still had a bone to pick with her old friend. She sat back in her desk chair. "If those are by way of apology to me—"

Beau attempted to hand them over. "They are."

Greta refused to take them. "I'm not sure I accept." She regarded Beau sternly. "You about gave me a heart attack last night, when you agreed to that shoot-out with Shane."

Beau shrugged, sat down on the edge of Greta's desk and dropped the flowers—which still held a grocery store sticker on them—to her lap. "What can I say...I felt for the guy? His pride was at stake. To him he'd been publically humiliated and, being the ultimate competitor he is, figured he had to do something just as public to end up on top again. Besides, how was I to know he wouldn't carry you off in the end? I figured after the shoot-out, he'd either pretend to die in your arms or emerge the victor and claim you as his woman all over again. You know—make a huge deal about kissing you and letting everyone know the romance was still on, hot and heavy as ever. I had no idea he was going to win the shoot-out and then dump you.''

Greta grimaced as she fingered the cellophane enclosing the flowers. ''Nicely put.''

Beau looked at her over the rim of the sunglasses he hadn't yet bothered to take off. ''That is what happened, isn't it?'' Beau demanded, sliding the glasses even farther down his nose.

''Unfortunately, yes.'' Greta sulked, wondering why she had ever considered this nosy parker a friend. Unlike her parents, he wasn't making things better, he was making them worse.

''So what are you going to do about it?'' Beau asked.

''I don't know,'' Greta said. She frowned at Beau in annoyance. She'd been thinking about her options.

Without warning, another set of footsteps sounded in the hall. Shane stepped into Greta's small cubicle of an office. Tense seconds passed as the three of them regarded each other. Although Greta was tempted to jump up and frantically explain once more that this was not what it seemed, she stayed put.

Shane noted the flowers in Greta's lap. ''Those from Beau?''

Greta nodded, aware her heart was beating triple time, even though, to her relief, she saw no jealousy or resentment on Shane's face.

Beau rose. ''Well, I know when I'm no longer needed,'' he stated meaningfully. ''I'm headed back to Los Angeles. I've got preproduction meetings on my next movie to attend.'' Beau leaned over, kissed Greta's cheek, then walked over to shake hands with Shane. ''You be good to her, you hear? Or you'll be dealing with me.'' The door slammed after him.

Tears glistening in her eyes, Greta picked up the flowers and dropped them onto her desk.

Shane sauntered closer. He stopped just in front of her, put his hands flat on her desk, leaned across it and studied her face. "You look terrible," Shane said, as if the fact of that made him very happy indeed.

Greta knew her eyes were swollen and her nose was all red—she'd be lucky if both returned to normal by the next century, at the rate she'd been crying. She sent him a withering look. "If one more person tells me that, I'll deck them," Greta declared. She stood and walked around her desk to poke him in the chest. "And for the record, you don't look so hot yourself, cowboy."

His lazy grin widening, Shane ambled closer yet. He placed both his hands on her shoulders, cupping them with a gentle possessiveness that robbed her of her breath. "That's 'cause I didn't sleep a wink last night," he said softly.

Refusing to give in, Greta regarded him stubbornly. "Neither did I."

Shane's tender glance continued to rove her upturned face. "Nor did we get much sleep the night before that," he reminded softly as a sexy sparkle crept into his gray eyes, "though for a very different reason."

Greta drew a deep breath. If he was going to try to make love to her here and now— "So what are you prescribing?" she demanded hotly. "A day in bed...together?"

Shane laughed at her audacity and waggled his eyebrows at her. "Or two or three," he quipped mischievously.

Reminding herself he had dumped her the night before, and in a thirty-second TV clip no less, Greta glared at him. "If you're here to break my heart again, you better do it fast. I can't take much more of this torture."

Shane sat down on the edge of her desk and hauled her onto his lap. "I'm not here to break your heart, Greta," he told her with a soberness that gladdened her heart and soothed her soul. "I'm here to mend it. And our marriage. And everything and anything else in our lives that need it. Because I realized something today, Greta." Shane pulled two solid-gold wedding bands from his pocket. He took off the cheap ones that had been turning their fingers green—the ones both just happened to still be wearing despite everything—and replaced them with the solid gold bands, filling her in on the specifics behind his actions all the while. "The love I feel for you is not going to go away," he told her huskily. "Not today or tomorrow or the next day. What I feel for you, I feel for life. And I think—" Shane murmured, searching her eyes with all the love and caring he'd just expressed "—you feel the same way about me."

Tears of joy spilled down Greta's cheeks. "I do," she whispered earnestly, wrapping her arms about him and holding him so close she could feel their hearts beating as one. She kissed him then, before he had a chance to change his mind and take it all back. "Oh, Shane, I'm so sorry." Happiness—to have him in her life again—trembled in her voice and filled her soul. "I should have told you what I'd planned with Beau last night before it ever happened," Greta declared, willing to take her share of the responsibility.

Shane smoothed her hair with the flat of his hand with long gentle strokes. "It wouldn't have changed anything if you had," he admitted ruefully. Apology radiated from his gray eyes. "I would have been just as hurt and ticked off and liable to go off half-cocked and do something reckless and irresponsible, because I hadn't yet owned up to some very simple truths about this whole love-and-marriage thing.''

''Which are...?''

Shane kissed the back of her hand. ''First of all, honesty is always the best policy, and that goes double when it comes to the ones you love. It's time I grew up and told people exactly what I think and feel instead of responding with the troublemaking behavior of my youth.''

''I'll agree with you there.'' Briefly she told him about her talk with her folks. ''I made the same pledge—I have to start saying what's in my heart, too, instead of just acting as if it doesn't matter and walking away.''

''Good.'' Shane drew her close for a long, leisurely kiss that filled her with warmth.

''What other truths did you learn from all this?'' Greta asked. More than anything she wanted them to start off correctly this time.

''We can't live our marriage with one foot out the door.'' His low, husky voice was filled with emotion. ''We have to stick with it and each other through thick and thin if we want to live happily ever after the way our folks have—and I do want that.''

Contentment unlike anything Greta had ever known swept through her. ''I do, too,'' she confessed as they paused for another slow, sexy kiss. Knowing they had all the time in the world together, Greta leaned back and looked into his face. She was wearing her heart on her sleeve again. But it was okay. ''You know, I've learned a couple of things from all this, too,'' she admitted happily.

''Such as?'' Interest flared in his eyes.

Greta flattened her hand across his chest, loving the warmth and strength of him every bit as much as the unpredictability and wildness. She swallowed hard, for the first time in her life determined to say and do and live it all. ''There's no place for fear or cowardice in a good marriage. I can't be afraid to tell you what's in my heart. I have to have faith that we'll be able to work things out, no matter how difficult.''

Shane nodded. ''And I promise,'' he said hoarsely, ''I'll do the same.'' He paused to kiss her again.

Greta kissed him back, then waited till he looked at her before she continued again. ''And last but not least it's never a good idea to wait for a more-convenient time to tell someone you love them. Because when it comes to the people you love—'' Her voice caught at the thought of all she had nearly lost. She drew a deep breath and forced herself to continue again. ''You can never let them know that often enough. So every day, from now on, Shane McCabe,'' she vowed, the look of love in his eyes giving her more courage than she'd known it was possible for any one person to possess, ''I promise to let you know that I love you in a hundred different ways.''

Shane grinned as he got up to lock the office door. ''I like the sound of that.''

Greta smiled, knowing this was her place of business and that no one else was due for several hours. That—plus her abiding love for Shane—gave her the freedom to do anything she wanted right here and right now. ''I thought you would.''

Shane settled back on the desk, tugged her back onto his lap and began to unbutton her blouse. ''I suppose this could happen in the bedroom?'' he asked with mock seriousness.

Greta sucked in a breath as his hand bypassed the lace of her bra and cupped her breast. "Oh, yes."

"And in the kitchen?" With customary thoroughness Shane kissed his way down her neck.

Her nipple pearled in his palm. Lower still, there was a spreading heat. "Most likely," Greta said breathlessly.

Shane's hand moved to her other breast, giving it the same warm and tender attention with his hand before following that with his lips. "You know, I used to think being married was the most restrictive covenant a man could endure," he confessed, pausing to kiss her lips softly, evocatively, "but now I'm thinking it doesn't sound bad at all," he told her, all the love he felt for her in his eyes. "In fact, it sounds like the best thing going."

"I'm glad you feel that way." Greta grinned and, more than ready for some of their wild, unrestrained loving, began unbuttoning his shirt, too. "And speaking of marriage…when are your folks renewing their wedding vows, by the way?" He'd told her; several people had; she just couldn't remember.

"Both the rehearsal dinner and the marriage ceremony are being held next week." Taking her by the hand, Shane led her over to the sofa against the wall. "Which in turn presents another problem." He kicked off his boots. She kicked off hers.

"What?" At his behest, Greta followed that with her skirt, blouse, bra and panties.

Shane unzipped his jeans. "My parents had their heart set on all of their sons being married before they celebrated their anniversary and re-tied the knot, so to speak."

"And you all are now—" Greta murmured thoughtfully as she and Shane finished getting him really, really comfortable.

"Except Travis," Shane finished for her.

Greta thought about that for a moment as the two of them lay down on their bed of discarded clothing and stretched out side by side. As far as she knew, Travis McCabe wasn't even dating anyone. He hadn't, since his fiancée had died in a tragic accident just minutes before they could make it to the altar. Greta looked at Shane. "What's his opinion of all this?"

Shane shrugged. He wrapped his arms around her, and brought her close, fitting her softness to his hardness, infusing them both with sizzling warmth. "Like me, he doesn't think there's a chance on this green earth that it's gonna happen."

Greta smiled as Shane found the sensitive spot behind her ear with the tip of his tongue. She arched against him, wanting so much more, knowing the waiting, the long, slow, luxuriant love play would make it all the better when they did finally join together. "Does Travis want it to happen?"

"Not really." Shane winked, as he settled his lips over hers and prepared to get down to business. "But that," Shane said optimistically, tilting Greta's lips up to his, "doesn't mean it won't."

LOOK OUT FOR SOME FAST AND LOOSE MATCHMAKING FROM

Cathy Gillen Thacker once again brings her special brand of down-home romance to a *new* four-book miniseries

John and Lilah McCabe have four of the sexiest sons Laramie, Texas, has ever seen—but no grandbabies! Now they're fixin' to get a whole passel of 'em.

September 1999—#789 **DR. COWBOY**
Cathy's 50th Harlequin book!

October 1999—#793 **WILDCAT COWBOY**

November 1999—#797 **A COWBOY'S WOMAN**

December 1999—#801 **A COWBOY KIND OF DADDY**

Round 'em up at a store near you!

Every Man Has His Price!
HEART OF THE WEST

At the heart of the West there are a dozen rugged bachelors—up for auction!

This December 1999, look for
Hitched by Christmas
by Jule McBride

Luke Lydell was supposed to be Claire Buchanan's last fling before her Christmas wedding—a gift from her bridesmaids. But Claire told herself she didn't want him...not in that way. She didn't need his hard body, she didn't need the passion that sizzled between them. She needed him to find her missing fiancé.

Each book features a sexy new bachelor up for grabs—and a woman determined to rope him in!

Available at your favorite retail outlet.

HARLEQUIN®
Makes any time special ™

Visit us at www.romance.net

PHHOW6

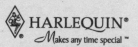